Ella Beaufort knew better than to rely on a sexy stranger. But with two sisters to support on the modest earnings of the family sheep station, she accepts shearer Cal Lynton's help—along with his intoxicating kiss. The most Ella can hope for is an affair. Something a woman in her situation wouldn't dare—or would she?

Heir to his family fortune, Charlton Alfred Landon Lynton abandoned his privileged life to prove his independence. He doesn't have time for a woman, but once he woos the lovely Ella into his bed, he is ready to make her his wife...until she shocks him with her refusal, claiming she can only marry a rich man! Angry and brokenhearted, the heir in disguise leaves the beautiful golddigger behind...

But amid the breathtaking landscape of South Australian, Ella and Cal are destined to meet again. Will their heated reunion lead to cruel confrontation—or the kind of passion that lasts a lifetime?

Visit us at www.kensingtonbooks.com

I0666511

Books by Virginia Taylor

South Landers
Starling

Published by Kensington Publishing Corporation

Ella

A South Landers Novel

Virginia Taylor

LYRICAL PRESS
Kensington Publishing Corp.
www.kensingtonbooks.com

Lyrical Press books are published by
Kensington Publishing Corp. 119 West 40th Street New York, NY 10018

First Electronic Edition: October 2015
eISBN-13: 978-1-61650-925-5
eISBN-10: 1-61650-925-2

First Print Edition: October 2015
ISBN-13: 978-1-61650-926-2
ISBN-10: 1-61650-926-0

Printed in the United States of America

To RJT, all my love forever

Author's Foreword

I set out to tell the story of my grandmother, Daisy Elsie Aslin, who was one of the first women in South Australia to attend the university. After I'd looked up various dates and women's rights, I wrote a story that had nothing to do with cities and education but a whole lot to do with how hard women worked during the settlement of our colony. I'll leave education and rights for another story. Thanks, Grandma

Acknowledgements

To best selling author Debra Holland, who judged Ella in a competition and liked the story so much that she gave me enough heart to keep sending my 'unsaleable' setting to publishers.

To my sheep farmer cousin, Robert Hodges, who told me about dipping and shearing sheep.

To Dr. GregLewis, maths PhD, who researched sheepish numbers for me.

Prologue

The best part of the house faced north where the sun shone all day in summer. Edward Lynton stood staring through the French doors of his library, across his close-clipped lawns, past the tall cast-iron fountain ringed with his rose beds, and toward the rolling hills in the distance.

Stained by the red clay soil, sheep dotted the gentle rise beyond his boundary fence. His shepherds rode his fine strong horses around his flock, bringing in the dusty strays for shearing.

"Good view," said a deep voice behind him.

He turned. "The view would be better if you were outside supervising the men. Look at those two slackers on the right." His head indicated, and his grandson stared, his hands deep in the pockets of his fine, English-made woollen trousers.

"I wouldn't say they're slacking." Charles, as if idly, flicked the pages of a leather-bound notebook on the library table. "I don't doubt they're discussing tactics. They have a mob in front and a mob behind, and the dogs are trying to join the groups."

"If you'd been there, two groups wouldn't have formed," Edward said, his jaw stiff.

"Ah, so you do have faith in me." Charles gave a lazy grin.

"You've been here long enough to know the workings. How many have been brought in now?"

"I couldn't say off hand."

"It's your job to say—off hand."

"If it matters to you, I can ask." Charles raised his gaze from the book, his expression guarded. "But first I want you to look over my figures, if you would. I've been working on this for months and I—"

"I'm not interested. I've spent enough money on you as it is. Look at you," Edward said, loading his tone with contempt. "Dressed by London tailors, shoed as well as the princes of England, clad in silk and linen shirts and damn me if I didn't even import the finest mahogany furniture for your bedroom. Do you think those men outside who are doing your work for you will ever sleep in sheets as soft as you have?"

"I believe that they have the potential to be any—"

"Balderdash. None had the start you had. And they're outside earning their wages while you stand here trying to inveigle me to spend even more money on your toys."

"I'm inviting you to invest—"

"Just like your father. Money, money, money—that's all you want of me. Be damned to you. If you want money, you can work for it the way I do." Edward snatched the notebook out of Charles's hands and threw the thing at the carved red cedar fireplace. He watched the pages flutter in the updraft from the empty grate.

Charles stood staring at him for a moment, then he nodded. "I see. I'll get the sheep yarded and counted, and I'll report to you." He squared his wide shoulders, ignored his notebook, and left the room.

Edward ripped up each page separately and put the scraps into his wastebasket. The matter had now been dealt with.

Chapter 1

Thick stone walls protected the woolshed from the afternoon heat, but an odor of rancid sheep oils and stale feces scoured the air. Cal Langdon ignored the calls of "tar boy!" that sent short, good-natured Joe scuttling to any of the ten shearers with his wound sealer. He ignored the sweat dripping into his eyes. Mentally, he totaled his wages as he sent another shorn sheep down the ramp.

This two-week job of shearing on the Beaufort Station finished off his three-month stint. In that time, he had earned enough money to buy the fittings for his warehouse, enough to pay the carpenter, and almost enough to match that of his business partner. He glanced at his tally on the chalkboard, noting he had finished seventy-three animals. At fifteen shillings a hundred, he was doing well. Before the day's end, he expected to make at least one pound.

Preparing to collect his next sheep from the holding pen, he straightened. The most visible of the three sisters who owned this property, Miss Dorella, stood just inside the open loading doors, her sun-streaked hair outlined by the view of the sparkling sea. She turned her large hazel eyes from the chalkboard and smiled at him.

He acknowledged her presence with a nod.

Using a single hand, she smoothed her halo of hair. Her time-honored female gesture told him she was conscious of his scrutiny. The ill-fitting, black mourning gown she wore was the same garment she had worn last night when she had helped her more confident sister serve the shearers' supper. A woman with a figure as fine as hers ought to be flaunting her attributes rather than concealing them.

Her focus shifted to Girl, then back to him. "Is that your dog?"

His black and white border collie sat not a yard away, watching his every move. As soon as he started one sheep, Girl moved his next to the pen gate. "She is."

"In that case, you'll need to yard her with our dogs. We don't let dogs roam free." After a pause, possibly waiting to see him tug his forelock, Miss Dorella turned to Alf, the balding, mid-thirties team boss. She raised her voice over the click of the shears, the baaing, and the shouts. "How is the wool quality this year?"

"Average."

"Better than last year?"

"The same."

Cal opened the gate and pulled out his next sheep.

Miss Dorella followed Alf, who sent his sheep down the ramp. "How much do you think we will we make from this year's fleeces?"

Alf stopped working to scratch his pink pate. "Prices are the same as last year."

"Not higher?"

"Only for merino."

She massaged the side of her neck. "How long do they take to pay?"

"Depends on how long it takes to get the wool to the buyers. What do you reckon, Cal?"

Cal dragged his sheep to his shearing space, wondering why Alf had given him this opportunity. He had assumed, although Alf hadn't stopped him speaking to the other woolgrowers along the way, that he hadn't approved of Cal's idea. "That would depend on how you plan to transport your wool."

"Via paddle steamer to Victoria—the same way Papa would if he were alive."

Cal might have suggested another mode, but because her defensive tone told him she had decided to cling to her father's ideas, he left the subject. "We had good rains upriver this year," he said, making his first clip of the hogget's head. "As soon as the flow reaches us, the paddle steamers will load up the bales."

Her big-eyed gaze held his. "How long will it take for the flow to reach us?"

"A month, maybe two."

Her eyes clouded and her full bottom lip worried her top one. She averted her head and moved to the sorting table, where frizzy-haired Benji picked twigs and short ends off the fleeces. Cal finished the hogget's head and began on one leg. Within minutes, he sent the sheep between his legs down the outside ramp. When he straightened, he noticed Miss Dorella standing in the area separating him from the wool classing, her attention concentrated on Girl. "When do you plan to pen this creature?"

"Not while she's helping."

She raised her eyebrows. "Helping? I call that sitting."

"She's a well-trained dog," Alf said, adding to the tally board. "She don't cause no trouble."

Frank, a fresh-faced lad of twenty-one and the youngest member of the team, laughed. "And she don't make no noise."

"He's trying to tell you she was born deaf." Cal dragged his next sheep to his clipping space.

Cheeks slightly pink, Miss Dorella lifted her chin. "If she can't hear, she won't obey the rest of us, and so she certainly ought to be penned... while she is not *helping*."

Cal grinned, surprised by the comeback. Usually, good-looking women relied more on their appeal than their logic.

"What do *you* think of the wool?" She eyed him sideways as she leaned back, her elbows on the rail behind. This position emphasized her womanly curves. A flare of desire shortened his breath, but he had no time for distractions.

He dragged the next sheep to his clipping space. "It's coarse. You get a better quality when you breed to merino."

"Papa wanted good eating sheep, as well."

He faced her, wishing she would go away. "You make more money from exporting wool."

"We can't change the breed now."

He ignored her, but she didn't leave. When he glanced up, he saw Alf watching the byplay with narrowed eyes. With reluctance, Cal answered. "You can change within two generations of breeding."

"We need ready money."

He racked back the sheep's head and began clipping the belly, wondering why she had chosen a shearer to be her financial adviser. "The bank will lend you money on the property."

She made a dissatisfied face. "The property already has a, um, mortgage."

"How many acres do you own?"

"Five thousand."

"Fix a few fences and stop your policy of overgrazing, and the bank will extend the loan. The way this place looks, you're not running more than one sheep per acre." He turned his sheep to the side.

She straightened, at last silenced.

"You want five per acre to make a good profit," he said, greasing her departure.

She raised her chin. "I don't know why such a clever man as you puts up with these conditions. The smell is simply dreadful."

"The floorboards are slatted. The sheep's crutchings fall through. Half the stink would be eliminated if someone got under the shed and raked out the dags."

Her crinoline began to swing and, as her skirts twirled, she said, "Someone? Who?"

He shrugged.

Her skirts found an abrupt balance. "*I* certainly won't be crawling under a floor and raking out...smelly things."

He was pleased to see he had annoyed her. Perhaps she now might stop bothering him. To make sure he had the last word, he slid the scrambling sheep between his legs down the ramp and extended to his full height of six feet and two inches. "Leave the raking to your stockman."

She inclined her head. "Which will, fortunately, give me time to re-breed the sheep to merino." A nail on the post behind her halted her dignified exit. With gritted teeth, she freed the fabric of her skirts.

Giving a perfect example of deportment and slightly flushed, she left the woolshed.

* * * *

The hinges protested loudly as Dorella, squirming internally, opened the kitchen door. A blast of heat from the wood oven greeted her.

Rose, her flawless complexion undisturbed by the temperature, stood kneading dough on the central table. She glanced up. "Ella, dear. At last. We're very much behind with the cooking. Put the mutton on to roast would you, please?"

Ella took the meat from the safe. Wondering how to explain about the wool money, she began rubbing the legs with lard and salt. "I just took a moment to talk to Alf." She tensed, awaiting criticism. Rose would never have considered setting foot in a shearing shed and she expected Ella to recognize the same social boundaries.

Her elder sister lifted her head. In the color of mourning, the twenty-three year old looked serenely beautiful. "You needn't have. I planned to talk to him tonight before supper."

"He didn't have a lot to say." Ella placed the roasting dish into the oven. "He thought the new shearer would be more help, and the man did seem to know everything about the sale of wool." Her lips tightened.

She'd had to prize out each reluctant fact from the newest member of the team *and* hear criticism of her gentle Papa.

Rose heaved a sigh. "Didn't you ever wonder why Papa didn't pay his debts with last year's clip money?" She cut her dough into squares, placed the scones in the oven above the roast, and stood staring at Ella, checking the elegant, figure eight knot of hair on the back of her collar.

"He must have had reason not to."

"But you did the accounts. Surely you saw the amounts he owed?"

"He only gave me the accounts he wanted balanced."

Rose sat at the table, cupping her chin in her palm. "And since he couldn't balance his gambling debts, he hid them."

"He didn't always lose," Ella said in defense of Papa. "And we'd had a drought."

"The rain was steady this past winter."

"That was the first we have seen for years. You must remember how dry the land was before you left."

"I'm starving," a voice interrupted from the hall. Vianna, the youngest Beaufort at eleven years old, stood framed in the doorway, hands behind her back and a hopeful smile on her face. A miniature version of Rose, she had the same pure blue eyes and soft pale hair. She wore a starched white smock covering her black cotton dress.

"The shearers' afternoon tea is almost ready." Rose indicated the oven. "You can have a scone as soon as they're cooked. Fill up the jam pot while you're waiting."

Vianna gave Rose a glance of resentment. "I don't know how. Ella usually does that."

"Ella has potatoes to peel."

Reminded, Ella pulled the sack out of the larder and began loading the potatoes onto the table. "Use a plain white bowl, Vi. I don't think the shearers will appreciate a rose-patterned jam pot." She watched her little sister inexpertly scrape the newly made plum conserve into a thick white soup dish and smiled encouragingly. Vianna had never been asked to help in the kitchen before.

Rose picked up a knife and began on the first potato. "One more meal, only one, and we've completed our first day as shearers' cooks. These past six months have been the longest of my life."

"I expect time will pass faster now that the sheep are being clipped." Ella pulled out another ladder-backed chair and sat beside Rose with her knife, her smile wry. She would have liked to discuss the sale of the wool, but facing Rose with reality right now would serve no purpose.

"The happiest day of my life will be the day we leave."

"Mine will be when we can afford new dresses." Vianna glanced at Rose's stylish black silk gown. "Though you have them, already."

"My godmother is very generous."

"And so are you." Ella lifted her head to stare into her older sister's eyes. "You could have stayed with her, and yet you came back to help us."

"My first duty is to my younger sisters," Rose said in her annoyingly placid way.

Ella didn't want to be anyone's *duty*. She lifted her chin. "We could never have managed without you."

"Not if we wanted nice scones." Smiling wickedly, Vianna pushed a monogrammed spoon into her jam dish.

"You little baggage." Ella gave a rueful laugh. "I'm no cook, that's certain. I've never had the same proficiency as Rose in any of the feminine arts."

Dimples formed in Vianna's cheeks. "That's why Papa sent her instead of you to the city to find a husband. Poor Rose."

"He sent me because I'm the oldest. The oldest should be married first." Rose frowned at her potato.

"And when she is, Vi, I'll learn a few airs and graces. You'll need some, too, if we're going to live in the city."

"You'll like being away from the smell of sheep and the flies. I didn't miss that for one minute. I think I've always been a city girl at heart." Rose sighed. "But, since we're in mourning, even if I were still there, I wouldn't have been able to attend any social functions. Fill the big bowl with water for the potatoes, Vianna."

Vianna filled the bowl from the sink and plopped it on the center of the table. The three sat together companionably. Vianna helped by dropping the peeled potatoes into the bowl while mulling about the finer points of her pony, Miffy.

Finally, Rose rolled down her pin-tucked sleeves and took the scones out of the oven. "I don't miss the parties and balls as much as I miss the social interaction," she said as Vianna tucked in.

Vianna licked the jam from her upper lip. "We don't often do social interaction here."

Ella forced a smile, recalling her gauche interchange with the handsome shearer. "Now, off you go. You need to finish the lessons I set for you."

Vianna folded her arms across her flat chest. "I finished the arithmetic, and I'll do the grammar later. I really ought to exercise Miffy. I haven't taken her over the jumps since last week and it's only a month till the town picnic."

"A month?" Turning her back, Rose took a starched white cloth from the dresser drawer. "We'll be gone by then. And before you dash off to see your pony, you can set the outside table for the shearer's afternoon tea."

"Me?"

Ella sighed. "Let her go." A month seemed far too soon to leave the only place she'd ever lived. "I can do the table. It will only take me a minute." She opened the oak dresser. Her reflection in the glass of the door didn't surprise her: untidy hair, damp curls around her sweaty face, and big rosy cheeks. Resignedly, she piled up the nine thick white plates needed for the outdoor table where the shearers ate their meals and shifted the weight of the plates onto her left hip.

"Well, perhaps Vi should set our table in the dining room for tonight. Three places, the knives on the right and the forks on the left."

"I know where knives and forks go," Vianna said with a tilt of her pert nose. "But I'm sorry. I don't have time to help, not with all the grammar lessons I need to finish." Grabbing another scone, she swung on her heel and, head high, she left.

"Am I too hard on her?" Rose asked Ella.

Ella shook her head. "Being brought up by her sisters is hard on her. We had a mother." With her right hip, she nudged the back door open.

Like Vianna, she'd led a pampered life until six months ago, having been responsible only for the housekeeper who'd run the homestead after Mama died. Mama had drowned while crossing the river with a flock of sheep, for which Papa blamed himself. From then on, he kept a strict eye on his daughters, stressing time and again each danger on the land. Ella knew the dangers on the land far better than she knew how to run the property.

How embarrassing that an itinerant shearer knew more about Papa's land and sheep than she did. She could walk through the flocks and had often helped with rounding up, but sales and numbers and routine maintenance had never been discussed with her. Only by reading the account books had she learned about the regular outputs of money and the far fewer inputs. However, she could learn. Anyone could.

To learn how to do a task, a person needed no more than a good set of eyes and ears. Learning courage was another matter. She had never been intrepid, and Papa's fears had become hers. She screwed up her face as she carefully placed the plates on the long outdoor table. A woman brought up on a sheep station ought to be able to swim or at least be willing to wet her feet. Surely being brave was only a matter of trying?

Sighing, she strode to the woodpile, where she chopped the kindling, which she then delivered to the washhouse. After clearing the ashes from beneath the copper and resetting the fire for the next day, she folded the clean laundry, sorted the dirty, and hurried to the stable paddock to fill the trough. When she found the task already done, she raced into the stables and doled out the chaff. Leaving a measure in three stalls, she refilled the water buckets, ran to the kitchen for scraps for the flustering hens, and flustered a little herself.

A quick glance at the sun, already on the downward dive into the glistening sea on the horizon, told her she just had time to prepare the table in the dining room for the evening meal. Rose was nowhere to be seen, possibly napping. Ella's courage stiffened by the clench of her jaw, she dashed through the courtyard and past the woolshed. Not once in her twenty-one years had she stepped into the sea, a river, or a creek. Not once. Today she would conquer her fear.

A short time later, she reached her destination, the dappled billabong that fed from the river bordering the property. Her feet slowed. The sweat on her face cooled as she contemplated the water, the gracious red gums, and the delicate undergrowth surrounding the area. Despite the heat of the late afternoon sun, she shivered. Drawing a deep breath, she lowered herself onto the withered grass to remove her shoes and stockings.

She stayed, staring at her toes, knowing Mama's drowning had been an accident and not a foregone conclusion. Before she could convince herself she had no need to prove herself to herself, she rose to her feet, scooped her crinoline to hip height, and stepped in. Yellow mud oozed between her toes. Within the next few moments, the woman who didn't know her paddocks had been overgrazed and her sheep didn't produce the finest quality wool would overcome an even greater obstacle. Abject cowardice. Holding her breath, she studied the pale ocher gleam of the water. Her feet hesitant on the slimy pebbles, she waded two paces, reaching ankle height. Her breath ached in her throat.

From behind, she heard a crackling of leaves. A small branch split and dropped. Two white cockatoos flew overhead, screeching, and a dark shape launched at her. She screamed, flailed, and fell backward.

The water dragged at her heavy skirts. She skidded straight into the deep center of the pool. Bubbles burst around her face and into her nose and mouth. Her inverted crinoline floated over her head, caging her.

Water rushed past her ears and she saw nothing but the blurred white of her arms. Time stood still. She would drown, just like Mama.

A sudden shadow, a clamp on her wrist, and her arm was caught.

The fabled bunyip did exist. She would die, torn and bloody.

Terror galvanized her. She thrashed out, gouging at the slimy black shape. With inexorable strength, the bunyip forced her upward. She gulped in fresh air, spluttering, fighting to evade its flesh-tearing teeth.

"Keep still!"

She blinked the gritty water from her eyes, gasping, swiping at the new shearer, unable to believe she didn't see a bunyip.

"Stop hitting me, and I'll get you to the bank." He scooped one iron-hard arm around her shoulders.

She clenched her elbows around his neck, and he hauled her until he found a footing. Then, with her pasted to him like a sodden leaf, he staggered to the sandy edge. "The bunyip," she said, her throat constricted. "The bunyip tried to drown me."

"You fell." His lashes were thick, wet, and dark.

Latched to him, afraid to let him go, she glanced into his grayish-green eyes, the same color as the hills in the distance, her mind a blank. Water streamed off his dark hair and a trickle ran from his cheekbone to his set jaw, sliding onto a firm, tanned neck.

"Girl only wanted to play with you."

"Girl?"

His strong hands held her at the waist, and his large frame supported her. The thud of his heart beat against her chest. With his head, he indicated his drenched and chastened dog sitting on the bank. "Girl."

"Your dog." Numbly, she eased her stranglehold of his neck. Stepping back, she huddled in her own arms. She couldn't cling to a man she didn't know, a man who stood tall, wide-shouldered, and sternly handsome, gazing at her with concern. "What are you doing here?"

He flicked back his soaked hair. "This is the direct path to the homestead. I took a swim in the river to freshen up before supper."

"You can swim?"

His wet blue shirt clung to his manly chest. She quickly averted her gaze.

"I would have been a very brave man to pull you out of the billabong if I couldn't."

Hearing the lightness of his tone, she set her quivering jaw. "Your stupid dog almost drowned me. That wretched animal shouldn't be roaming free, as I..." Suddenly aware of her skirts hitched over her crinoline, she shook the drenched black fabric to her ankles, shamed by the display of the cage and most of her wet underwear. Mortified that more than her fear showed, she hauled in a shuddering breath. "I'm sure I can have you arrested for trespass and willful destruction," she muttered, wanting to weep.

He stepped back, his expression amused. "Destruction? I don't suppose you noticed I saved your life."

"After your dog attacked me." Pushing back the curtain of hair dripping over her nose, she began to shiver, a reaction she couldn't control. "I thought she was a bunyip."

"A bunyip?" He raised his eyebrows at Girl, who shook off a halo of water droplets, stretched full length, and grinned at him. "A mythical monster?"

She glanced at the hills, backlit by the endless blue sky. "If a jet-black, hairy creature attacked you in a billabong, you might believe in mythical monsters, too." She swiped her wet sleeve under her nose.

"You weren't expecting Girl. So you have an excuse."

Her mind clutching at this justification for her craven behavior, she stared at her lily-white toes. "Nevertheless, please make sure you pen that dog this time." She kept her tone firm, hoping to reclaim a modicum of dignity.

With his long fingers, he lifted the front of his shirt, finally masking his chest. "She never leaves my side."

"However, she *did* leave your side, moments ago, to spring at me." Ella made contact with his eyes and lost her breath again.

"You gave her such a fright that she won't again."

"I gave *her* a fright?"

"She has expectations of being caught when she leaps. She didn't expect to sink her ship. Now, since you have fully regained your feet, I will take my leave." He turned and collected his leather hat from the grass.

Glancing quickly at her bodice, she breathed with relief when she saw the black fabric had remained rigid and opaque. If not her dignity or her feet, at least she had maintained the upper part of her wardrobe.

He jammed his hat on his head, gave a courteous nod, and walked away. Bedraggled and humiliated, she watched him stride off, square-shouldered and lean-hipped, with his jaunty dog trotting at his heel.

Chapter 2

Just after dawn, Ella lit the fire beneath the copper and rammed in the dirty laundry. With Rose, she cooked the shearers' breakfast of mutton chops, bread, and gravy.

Ever since she had dripped back to the homestead before supper last night, her thoughts had rarely strayed from the shearer, Cal. But for him she might have drowned. However, if he hadn't ignored her orders about the dog, *she* might have waded up to her knees in the water and gone back today to sit in the shallows. Within weeks, she might have been swimming in the river, like him. But, why? Soon she would live in the city and have no rivers to cross.

An hour of laundering refocused her mind, and she finally poled out a single load, glad she didn't need to cope with the shearers' clothing yet. The men could reek to the high heavens for all she cared as long as she could have respite from endless boiling, stirring, wringing, and transporting to and from the line and the ironing pile. She stood back, her reddened hands on her hips, waiting for the load to cool enough to put through the wringer.

"Where on earth did you find that dreadful gown you're wearing?" Rose said behind her.

Ella spun around, her body concealing the drying frame. "In the bottom of my tallboy." She glanced down at the tight, faded floral she wore. "I had it set aside for a patchwork quilt but I decided to give it a second life as my gardening gown first."

"You should be wearing mourning. What would people say?"

She swallowed. "I don't have another mourning gown, Rose. That's why I wore the gray skirt last night. The last black garment I owned has been ruined." Shifting aside, she indicated the gown that had been drenched in the billabong, hanging rusty and wrinkled over the frame.

Rose put her fingers to her forehead. "Not again. I thought you would have learned from last time that you can't boil cheap black cotton."

"I forgot." Not for the world would she tell Rose she had almost drowned. Rose would not understand her sister's need to prove herself. Nothing fazed Rose.

Rose gave a sympathetic nod. "I've made the bread. And the shearers will want their luncheon any minute. Alf said 'twelve on the dot.' If I'm to be ready on time, I'll need help with the serving." She had already changed into a looped black silk morning gown, another of those given to her by her doting godmother. "I told Vi she could ride until luncheon, and then she would have to study. I thought that's what you would have wanted." She gave a wry lift of her shoulders.

"If you could help me with the mangle, I can be with you sooner."

Rose eyed the steaming snarls. "Leave your wash to cool." She left.

Ella followed, hoping Rose meant that when the load cooled she would help.

"Yesterday, when I was talking to Cal"—Ella hesitated while Rose opened the kitchen door—"the new shearer, he said—"

"Nothing that would interest me at this moment, dear. Could you slice the mutton, please? I'll get the cheese and pickles."

"He said—"

"You know better than to engage in idle conversation with shearers." Rose inclined her head, a faint smile on her lips.

"I do know, but I was speaking to him about the wool." Ella rubbed her forehead.

"You shouldn't speak to him at all." Rose calmly emptied a jar of pickled onions into a blue bowl. "You know what shearers are. You'll only encourage him."

"There would be no point in me encouraging him," Ella said, her voice thin with frustration. "He's a shearer, a seasonal worker who wouldn't have two pennies to rub together for three quarters of the year. He's no use to me, and aside from that I could be plastered to him and he would lift me aside. You're the one men admire."

"So Papa thought, which is why he expected me to marry well enough to restore his fortune."

"You can't believe Papa expected that."

"His intention was clear." Rose raised her eyebrows. "He also expected you to take care of Vianna."

"Of course he did, and of course I would." Ella's path had always been set. She had a younger sister to rear and an older sister who needed her support until she married. She sat at the table, absorbing Rose's perfect features. "But we have to change our plans. We can't leave in a month as we thought. We can't get the money for the wool-clip for ages. The drought has virtually stopped the paddle steamers."

Rose rested her forefinger on her lips. "We'll put the property on the market, then."

"But when we sell, we have to pay off the mortgage and settle Papa's debts. We need the money from the fleeces to live on."

"Did you tell me this before?"

Ella's head ached. "You know we won't have any other income."

"What if we don't settle Papa's debts?"

"We have to. He owed money to people who need it as much as we do," Ella said, hearing the plea in her tone. "Shopkeepers and the neighbors."

Rose looked perturbed. "How long do we have to wait for our wool payment?"

"Up to three months."

"We'll miss the entire ball season. Not that I mind. But if we only have the money from the fleeces, we'll soon run out, and then where will we be?"

"We won't run out if we invest the money and live on the interest." Ella cleared her throat. The bank had promised ten percent as long as the capital remained undivided. "We sold the fleeces for seven hundred pounds last year, so we won't have the lifestyle we once had, but if our inheritance stays intact everything will turn out well."

Rose frowned. "But when we marry we will split our inheritance, of course." She began to take more food from the larder.

"Of course," Ella said, her cheeks stiff. She couldn't insist on Rose aiding her sisters after marriage. If need be, Ella could support Vianna alone. For all she knew the skills of an educated lady would be in great demand in the city. Concentrating, she marked out the bone in the lamb leg. "We should be able to buy a house for less than two hundred pounds, which won't set us back too much."

"After we've sold the fleeces." Rose used an insistent voice.

Ella nodded, although she wanted to say they could hardly do so before, given that the only money they had was set aside to pay the shearers.

She had thought when Rose returned she would take over Papa's affairs, but Rose had no goal other than to return to her former life. Ella would rather stay on the property but she saw no point when she had neither the skills nor the means to run the place.

Dispirited, she did her best to slice the meat evenly, then she loaded the serves onto a big blue and white dish. During the past few months, she had been running on the spot. At least now she knew she only had to keep doing so for another three months. With unlimited supplies of meat, an orchard full of ripening fruit, and a vegetable garden that could be called adequate to their needs, she could manage.

"Just pray we have no rain during the shearing and a dousing afterward." The kitchen door had already closed behind Rose.

* * * *

After the midday meal, while the team relaxed with a cup of tea, Cal strolled over to the stable paddock with Girl to check that Alf's Clydesdales had plenty of water. A single stock horse grazed in the area, as well. He grabbed the bucket from the pump and heard snorting and fidgeting inside the stables. Out of pure curiosity, he opened the main door.

He breathed in the tang of horse and hay and leather. The cobbled floor had been neatly swept and a bale of clean straw lay in a corner. Shiny tack dangled from hooks and polished saddles sat across a wooden rail. In the first stall, he saw a neat little Welsh pony. In the adjacent stall stood a lanky, elegant mare with a chestnut coat, and in the next, another of the same. Money had been spent here once and a considerable amount, but now only a one-horse trap idled on the property. He saw no need for a carriage pair.

He checked the animals' water but each had been adequately supplied and each had a scattering of chaff in a bucket. The Aboriginal stockman took good care of the horses—astonishing, for the man had to see to the whole station alone. No wonder so much of the fence maintenance had been ignored.

He strolled back to the woolshed, wondering why Miss Dorella hadn't sold the chestnuts if she needed ready money. His financially canny mother, Irene, would pay upward of one hundred pounds for the pair.

* * * *

Ella lay on her belly under the shed raking the crutchings into a pile and praying not to be seen. A lady wouldn't do this, and for good reason she didn't want anyone to know that Papa had left his daughters in a fix. She threw the rake onto the wispy grass outside.

"Missus?" She turned and saw the aboriginal stockman's shiny black face peering at her under the slats.

"Shh! If you want me, I'll see you at the house," she whispered to him.

"Help Missus?"

"Have you moved yesterday's sheep back to the paddocks?" she murmured, crawling backward. She came to her feet outside the woolshed, gazing at Jed, who grinned good-naturedly at her.

The stockman nodded. "Get more?"

Pushing her hair out of her face she glanced at the sheep the shearers had finished and had no idea how to estimate if they needed more before tomorrow. "Bring them all in, Jed. Tomorrow. Not here. Elsewhere." She gave an indiscriminate wave of her hand, hoping that because he did this job yearly he would simply continue as he had.

He smiled, nodded, and reversed.

She stared at the wool-matted sheep's droppings by her foot. "But first get the barrow and take these droppings..."

Cal sauntered out of the woolshed. His thick dark hair softened the outlines of his strong face. Her insides flipped but miraculously she kept breathing.

"...as far away as you can."

Without a blush, Cal said, "Take the dags to the corner of that paddock." He indicated the weed-filled area adjacent to the woolshed. "Spread them tomorrow with the droppings from the woolshed paddock."

Jed smiled, nodded, and disappeared.

"Spread them?" Ella said, with a surreptitious brush of her skirts. "Let alone he's my stockman, not yours."

"The droppings recondition the soil after overgrazing. Whatever comes from the land should be returned to the land." He ignored the second part of her statement.

"Whatever comes from the kitchen should return to the kitchen, and that's me."

"Before you leave—perhaps you don't know that the horses in the stables need to graze in the paddock during the day?"

And perhaps she deserved being patronized because she didn't know how to take care of her sheep. She widened her eyes. "Leave the poor dears to stand in the sun and ignore the fact that they might get dirty? Surely not." She waited.

"Doubtless, they have pretty blankets to wear that would stave off that possibility," he said, his voice smooth. "Apologies if I stole your next line."

She laughed. The man was quick witted. The kitchen door squeaked. Vianna dashed outside and made a beeline for Girl, who sat by Cal's booted foot, staring up at him as if the sun shone from his face.

Virginia Taylor

"Your dog is just too, too sweet." Vi dropped to her knees and stroked Girl's white ruff and in return had her face licked by the dog. "She was so good when she sat under your table last night."

"She what?" Ella asked, nudging her sister with her toe.

"I took my roast mutton out to her after dinner," Vianna said, her tone overly innocent. "It was too tough for me."

"You're a fussy little miss." Cal tapped his hand on the side of his leg and his dog stood.

Vianna stared in amazement. "How did you make her do that?"

"Border collies are easy to train. They're highly intelligent."

"Ours certainly are. They know enough not to obey us." Vi's mouth tilted at the corners. "That's why we keep them penned. They like to round up the hens and race down the road yapping at leaves."

"Your dogs are the same breed as Girl. They're workers. When they're not kept busy they're bored. You need to give them a job."

Ella's jaw loosened. He could explain to either of her sisters, but he could only throw orders at her. "They won't obey us."

"Does your stockman work the dogs?"

"They won't obey him either."

"Why would you keep dogs that don't earn their way?"

"They used to work for Papa. I have a great plan, though. Before I plow the fields, I'll retrain them." She glanced at him.

He pushed his hands into his pockets. "They won't need retraining."

"That's wonderful news, isn't it, Ella?" Vianna wrapped her arms around Girl's neck. "Why won't they need retraining, Cal?"

Moving only his eyes, he glanced from Vianna to Ella. "Dogs have fairly good memories."

"If you could tell Ella what they know, she would have them rounding up the sheep in a trice. You must excuse me now." Vianna gave him a winning smile. "But I have to finish an arithmetic test. I just wanted to tell you how much I like your dog." The kitchen door banged behind her.

"You make a formidable team." Cal's lips relaxed. He had the sort of rugged face an artist might use to depict a leader of men, with his straight nose and his defined jawline. His thick eyelashes softened the effect slightly, but he would never be seen as anything other than good looking. "I'm guessing that if your older sister joined in, you would have every man in a ten-mile radius fighting to do your bidding."

"No one asked for your help." Ella reached behind her for the door handle, her heart doing a silly pitter-patter.

He examined her expression for so long that her cheeks warmed. "Tomorrow morning, I'll put your dogs through their paces."

"No."

"If you're sure." He inclined his head "But if you're worried you might have to thank me, you can put your mind at ease. I like dogs."

"I'm not worried I might have to thank you." She tried a tilt of her nose. "I'm worried I'll have to pay you."

"That's right. It was my duty to pull you out of the billabong after I had let you be shoved in." His eyes focused on her lips and stayed. "You don't have to pay me. Perhaps we could make this a favor for a favor."

For one particularly stupid moment, she thought he wanted a kiss. Her face re-warmed. She stood, holding her breath. As he opened his mouth to speak, the kitchen door swung open again. "Ella, dear. Could you help me move the flour bag?"

She glanced at Rose blankly.

Cal cleared his throat, compelling her to look at him. "My dog is used to uncooked bones," he said, his tone bland. She thought he was the most unreadable male she had ever met—and easily the most compelling.

With a helpless nod, she said, "I'll find some for her—and she'll find them in the *dog's yard*."

His mouth relaxing, he headed toward the men's quarters. His dog, naturally, followed.

After staring for some seconds at his impressive back view, she entered the kitchen.

"You're letting that shearer distract you, Ella, dear. I hope you're not distracting him, too," Rose said, opening the larder door. "We want the wool shorn as quickly as possible."

Ella drew a deep breath but ended up not answering because she wished she could distract him.

She'd never interested a man and likely wouldn't ever have the opportunity.

* * * *

Edward Lynton stared at the leather traveling trunk ranged at the foot of his ornately carved tester bed. With a hollow laugh, he swung open the lid, tramped over to his tallboy, and dragged open the top drawer. "Sam!" He grabbed a handful of ironed shirts and threw them at the trunk, where they landed. The sleeves twined like arms on men during a night of raucous drinking. "Sam! Get in here right now!"

"He's coming," called his housekeeper, Mrs. Collins.

Edward piled clean nightshirts on his other linen. "And has decided to take his own good time," he muttered. He straightened and scratched his head. "Cravats, cravats, how many will I need?"

"A clean one for every day," Sam, former stable master, former sheepherder, and erstwhile traveling companion, answered from where he stood in the open doorway. A short, stocky man, he had grizzled hair; a weathered face; and large red, sun-spotted hands. Pushing seventy, he was more or less the same age as Edward. "How long do you reckon on being away?"

"As long as I want to," Edward replied impatiently. "Get the carriage to the door. We're leaving as soon as I have packed."

"Yes, m'lud," Sam said, pulling at his forelock. "We won't worry about food. You and me is camels. We can travel for days without nothing to eat nor drink."

Edward ignored the humbug. His older brother had been an earl in the Old Country, and Edward was a sixth son. He was, strictly speaking, an "Honorable." He had no use for a written address in this damned heat-begotten, fly-ridden hellhole. Unlike his brothers and their sons and grandsons, who shivered in their draughty English manors scratching for their next penny, he had earned himself a fortune. In this colony, no man was richer. No man was more self-sufficient. "Tell that interfering woman to get a move on. She's known for the past ten minutes I mean to go, and she should have packed plenty of food by now."

"Yes, y'grace." Sam made a move to leave.

"Shut this trunk and get it out to the coach."

"You might be wantin' to pack a change of trousers and your shaving gear."

"Don't tell me how to pack my trunk. If I wanted shaving gear, I would have put it in." Edward used a dangerous tone.

Sam moved over to the trunk and flipped the lid shut. "Enough room in there for a couple of changes of boots as well, I'd say."

Edward ground his teeth. "Get them from the lobby and wrap them in newspaper. Leave that, leave that," he said, referring to the strap around the trunk. "I'll want to put in my shaving gear, too."

"Mornings is better for traveling. Don't know why we can't leave tomorrow. Don't know why you didn't get Mrs. Collins to pack for you." Sam reopened the lid.

"If I want anything around here done properly, I have to do it myself. And we leave when I say we leave. Where has that blasted woman put my trousers?"

Sam ambled into the dressing room and came out with an evening suit, two spare jackets, and a jumble of trousers. Only his stumpy legs could be seen under the load. "You're acting like a dotard, no lie," he said in a muffled voice. He dropped the clothes onto the bed. "We should have left a couple of months back, if you ask me."

"I didn't ask you."

"More's the pity. No man's an island."

"I'm bored here, that's all. Here, give me that." Edward took a pair of folded trousers from Sam and dropped them into the trunk. "It's bound to be quieter in Adelaide at this time of the year. Everyone will be in the hills or on the coast."

"Quieter? Nowhere could be quieter than here. You mean if you might be looking for someone, you might find him."

Edward heightened his chin. "Irene extended a very gracious invitation to stay with her, and I've decided to take it. I need a rest. I can't spend my life watching each thing every person here does and fixing their mistakes."

"Ha!" Sam folded a tweed jacket. "Pity you didn't think that way years back and p'rhaps he wouldn't've gone."

Edward crossed his arms, frowning. "I won't have his name mentioned."

"Whose?" Sam asked, a triumphant grin on his face.

"Shouldn't you be outside harnessing horses?"

"I left the lad at it. Thought he might have the idea of it after ten years training," Sam said in a sarcastic voice. "Times, I can leave him to scratch his own arse."

"Yours is not such a complicated job that youngsters can't do it." Edward clamped his lips. He wouldn't be criticized by an employee, even though the former hostler had arrived on the same ship with him from England some thirty-one years ago and helped Edward and his sixteen-year-old son stock parcels of land. Back then, they hadn't decided on sheep, but his son, Henry, had a good eye for business. He also had a good eye for women, hence Irene, Edward's widowed daughter-in-law. She, of the sharp tongue and even sharper wit, lived in Edward's town house.

"You wasted a good man," Sam said in an accusatory tone. "Not only did he learn to be the best shearer you would ever meet, he can manage the men better'n you ever did. And do the books, too. You deserve to stew in your own juice, and I don't know why I'm helping you even now."

"Because you're a nosey-parker. You don't want to miss your chance of saying 'told you so.' You won't be getting it, I can tell you. I was right not to extend him money, and I'm right to leave him to fall to his knees.

And so you shall see. Within another month, he'll be begging to return."

Sam shook his head, sadly. "You don't know him. You never did."

Chapter 3

That night, Ella dreamed of a bubbling, boiling cauldron. She dreamed of hauling herself out of deep pools of suds, surrounded by sheep droppings. She dreamed of sheep circling her and laughing...baaing...

With a bump, she awoke. She sat up, noting the moonlight reflected on her silver hairbrush and the close bleating of a sheep...more than one, directly under her window. Pushing her hair out of her eyes, she peered through the muslin and saw a few white, newly shorn wraiths wandering between the henhouse and the laundry. Somehow the creatures must have escaped from their enclosure behind the woolshed. She immediately slid out of bed and into her dress shoes and raced through the kitchen to the yard. The moon lit her way. Trees rustled urgently, and the wind whispered low.

The track from the main road came straight between the orchard in front of the house and a wooded area, running parallel to the river and leading to the loading bay of the woolshed. Ella headed toward this track. "Shoo, shoo," she said in a tight murmur to an old ewe she passed near the back corner of the house.

She reached the track and peered toward the main road. Four sheep trotted through the trees in the orchard, glancing at their green haven. More sheep plodded through the wooded area, grazing at will. She turned around the front of the house, taking the long way to her vegetable garden and ending almost where she started, on the kitchen side of the house, hoping to find her vegetables as yet undisturbed.

She groaned as she watched five sheep pick their way through her turnips and the last of her carrots, and she ran forward, freezing when she spotted Cal and his dog.

He put up his hand in a gesture of recognition while his dog kept the sheep in a huddled group. "There may be more out on the road," he said in a deep undertone, "but I'll go after them later." With effortless ease, he lifted the rear end of a sheep to set its course in the direction of the path between the rose garden and the front part of the veranda. "I think it's more important to return this lot and secure the fence. You go back to bed. Girl and I can handle this." He tucked his shirt into his trousers. Apparently, he'd left his bed in a hurry, too, but he hadn't been as careless as she.

Caught in her nightwear, she almost did as he asked but, however justly served by embarrassment, she couldn't let a virtual stranger assume her responsibilities. Awkwardly clutching the embroidered linen to her neck, she said, "Thank you for your kind offer, but these are my sheep and my problem." She spotted the herb garden. "Oh, no! They've munched their way through the last of the plantings."

With waving arms, she herded the scattered sheep into Cal's group. His dog kept them moving along. She and Cal barely spoke. The mob had to be rounded up before they did any further damage. Aside from that, she didn't want to wake anyone else to see her acting like a demented windmill.

When the last visible sheep had been put behind the broken fence, Cal retrieved a rope from the stables. He tied the length from post to post and leaned back. "I'll rebuild this part tomorrow. The rope is only good enough short term."

"You can't. You have to shear. Jed will do it."

He shook his head with reproof. "Jed will need to take this mob out to pasture. Before he can bring in the next flock, the fence needs to be able to hold them." He tapped his leg and his dog came to heel.

"Was this my fault? Should I have told him to take the last lot to pasture before he went back to his camp?"

He sighed. "He needs someone to tell him where you want the sheep to graze."

"I don't think Papa minded. The sheep move onto fresh grass when they need to."

"That's one theory."

"If there's another...?"

He shot a cynical glance at her. "Your sister knows nothing, either?"

"Oh, less than me. She also cares less than me, but she has so much else to do that she doesn't have time to worry about the little things."

"On a sheep station, the most important job is the sheep."

Tired and feeling more than useless, she said, "I suspect Girl woke you when the sheep began to escape. And since she never barks, I have to assume she wasn't penned. I can only be grateful, and I won't say another word on the subject of unconfined dogs."

Reaching out, he tugged Ella's braid. "What? No more little lectures, Miss Dorella?"

She couldn't remember the last time she'd been teased or offered a gesture of warmth. "Ella." She cleared her throat. "*Miss* Ella."

"Cinderella." He stared at her from beneath hooded lids.

"So the local children used to call me when I was a youngster. That's why I use the shortening. I should also thank you for pulling me out of the billabong." She pushed the loosened curls from her face. "But, I didn't throw myself into the billabong, as you know."

"Are you insisting I apologize for Girl's mistake? I do."

She drew a deep breath. "You've made up for that by being amazingly generous with your help. I've been ungracious. Thank you for hauling me out of the water."

"My pleasure." He lowered his lids and stared at her. His mouth thinned. "As for rounding up your sheep, it's apparent you can't run a sheep station. You should move to the city as soon as you can."

"Or marry a landed gentleman who will take on this property and my sisters." Contrarily, she objected to being told to do what she meant to do.

"I don't doubt you'll find one if you try."

"Really?" she said with goaded inflection.

"You're comparatively attractive." Without meeting her gaze, he checked the knot on his rope fence.

Her jaw clamped. She crossed her arms over her chest. "Rose is amazingly beautiful, but during her two years in the city, she didn't find *any* husband, let alone a rich one."

"Perhaps she had another plan."

"What do you mean?"

"Perhaps she wanted to marry for love. People do, you know."

"Papa wouldn't have prevented her marrying anyone she chose, though, like any parent, he would have preferred her to choose wisely. No, I just don't think there are as many available men in the city as we suppose." She glanced at him sideways. "Then again, we need quality rather than quantity."

"I agree. Too many men would be hard to bear."

She propped her fists on her hips. "So, you think this is amusing?"

"I'm agreeing with you." He held her gaze.

"Why start now?"

"Cowardice."

She laughed. "I don't suppose there's any point in bemoaning my fate to you."

He glanced away. "We discover our strengths during trying situations."

"You would have left me to drown if you believed I would discover my strength."

"There is a difference between what can and can't be changed."

She sighed and turned toward the house. "A woman's place is in the home. I know. Jed is managing the sheep, and he is a godsend. If we had to pay him..."

"You don't pay him?"

"Not with money. He has no use for it. We pay him with flour and sugar, meat when he wants it, and the skins of the slaughtered sheep." She glanced back at his chiseled, moonlit face. "Good night and thank you. If you want sugar and flour, or a sheep...?"

He shook his head. "Make me a hearty breakfast in the morning and that will be payment enough for my services. Now, off to bed with you."

She skittered off, now shown beyond doubt that the fences had been in a bad way for some years. Instead of noticing, she had congratulated herself for managing without servants, and she had patted herself on the back because she maintained a vegetable garden and a grove of fruit trees. Assuming the sheep only needed to eat and drink until she and her sisters left had been as easy as closing her eyes.

Sometime in the next few months, she had to put the property on the market. A run-down holding would not sell for the price needed to meet their obligations. As she climbed into bed for the second time that night, she mentally rearranged her daily tasks.

She was certain Cal wouldn't doubt that a fit, twenty-one-year-old woman could mend fences.

* * * *

Cal slept until dawn. As the sun yawned behind the hills, he rose out of bed, washed, and shaved. Unfortunately, he didn't have time to teach Miss Ella how to run her station. He had his own way to make, but at least he could give her a helping hand. With this in mind, he freed the station's dogs. Girl stood close to heel while the others sniffed his shoes and bounced happily.

They sat and stayed on instruction, giving him enough confidence to lead them to the pump by the stables. He filled a bucket, from which they lapped with enthusiasm. After letting the dogs settle for some minutes, he took them to the holding yard, which contained the escapees from the night before, and he tried a few commands.

Distant choral bleating warned of the arrival of the next mob of sheep. "Heel," he said, and the dogs followed. Girl didn't let him out of her sight. The mounted Aboriginal stockman herded the sheep toward the woolshed paddock. Cal sauntered around to the gate and opened the latch for the native, commanding the dogs to guide the sheep through the space. They managed, but if they hadn't, Girl would have. She, however, stayed with Cal.

As the last sheep leaped frantically through the opening, the stockman gave Cal a wide grin, showing a set of strong white teeth in his shining black face. He wore old canvas trousers belted with a frayed piece of rope and a sweat-stained calico shirt. "Boss's dogs," he said, looking pleased. Leaning down, he closed the gate.

"Have you worked with them?"

The stockman shook his head. "Boss's dogs," he repeated, smacking his dusty hat against his thigh. "Belonga 'im."

From that, Cal assumed that Mr. Beaufort had not let the stockman use the dogs. The aborigine seemed competent. He'd certainly started rounding up at first light. If he'd not been allowed to work with the dogs, this rather pointed to Mr. Beaufort being one of those people who disliked delegating responsibility. Cal had spent his life with an old man who had the same inability to ease his grasp.

Knowing the shorn sheep needed to be returned to their pastures today, he indicated the flock in the woolshed paddock. "I'll take these fellas to the river with the boss's dogs. When they've had a drink, you can move them back to the hills."

After Cal had let the dogs work the sheep to the river and back and had retrieved a sturdy log from the water's edge, he walked them to their yard, the log on one shoulder. Since someone had left a pile of meat and cooked bones for them, they seemed overjoyed to be penned.

Next, he cut and shaped the log, depositing what was now a strong post by the roped fence. A quick glance at the homestead's chimney showed that the ladies had started their cooking. He strode to the house and knocked on the door. By his calculations, he had barely an hour until breakfast.

Miss Ella came to the door, dressed in a green riding skirt. Apparently tailored for her in more affluent times, her outfit clung to every curvaceous, gorgeous handful of her. A slow ache curled in his belly.

"Good morning," she said, smothering a yawn.

Normally, carnal thoughts didn't disturb him, but normally he managed six hours of unbroken sleep. He jammed his hat on his head and concentrated on the task at hand. "I worked the dogs. You shouldn't have any trouble with them. They know their job."

"I don't know their job." She drifted outside.

"They respond to the regular commands. Heel. Sit. Stay. Down. You only need point them in the right direction and they'll follow your lead."

"I can't have a lead until I know what they're supposed to do."

Amused, he scratched his chin. "In that case, I'll show you tonight after the shearing is done." He moved off toward the lean-to near the stable, where he had found the ax.

"Why not now?" She trailed behind Girl.

After shoving a pair of pliers and the cutters in his pocket, he retrieved a roll of fencing wire. Her persistence made him smile inside. "I'm going to fix the fence."

"How did you know the wire was there? I meant to buy some."

"It's the logical place to keep fencing wire—sheltered and handy." He collected a mallet and a shovel and walked toward the woolshed, practically grinning.

She followed beside Girl. She cleared her throat. "You mentioned the dreadful state of the fencing on the property... Although the sheep aren't worth much after shearing, every shilling counts. Do you mind if I watch you? Knowing how to fix a fence might come in handy."

He nodded although he doubted she would do more with the information than check on the aborigine's skill. Cal would have been ready to swear Jed could do any task on the farm. He also would have been ready to swear that the man had Miss Ella bluffed. "I'll dig this old post out. Your job is to pass me the tools I require."

She stood, glancing warily at the collection of tools he had placed on the ground.

Highly entertained, Cal untied the rope from the rotted center post and kicked the wood out of the way. A few shovel loads of soil revealed the base, which he lifted out. She passed him the mallet, with which he hammered in the new post, and then the roll of wire. He threaded the fallen end around the notches he'd cut and pulled. With the pliers, he made a neat twist.

"This wire doesn't need replacing. We only needed a new post here. When the wire is broken, you need to rejoin it thus and thus." He demonstrated with the lower strand. "I had a word with your stockman this morning. I told him to take the shorn sheep to the eastern pastures. He seems to think the feed out there is adequate."

She nodded and took a breath. "I was wondering if, when I am out riding, I see a sheep with a broken leg or one badly injured, what should I do?"

"You would have to kill it."

"That's what I suspected." She took the pliers from him.

He checked the other strands of wire, standing in view of the stable area where Miss Vi had mounted her Welsh pony and had begun pulling on her gloves. In the paddock adjacent, the two stock horses and the two chestnuts grazed companionably with the Clydesdales. The morning sky above glowed pink and orange.

He saw two riders leave the main road and canter in a dusty cloud along the track past the homestead. He moved back so they couldn't see him but he could see them. He kept an eye on the men. One dismounted and beckoned to Miss Vi. Miss Vi turned in her saddle and indicated the right of the main road. The first man spoke again, keeping his hand on her skittish Welsh pony.

"Do you know those men?" Cal pointed in their direction. Road travelers rarely looked savory, but these two had an anxious-to-please attitude that seemed out of place.

Miss Ella walked to the corner of the woolshed and glanced where he indicated. "They're just leaving. I think they may have been asking for directions." She turned back to Cal. "What else am I neglecting on the station? When we talk about what can be changed and what can't, what are my priorities, other than the fences?"

The men, one tall and thin and the other short and fat, rode off at a canter.

"If you get your fences fixed and your feed paddocks plowed and fertilized, you'll be on the right track."

Miss Ella said, "Then, when we sell, will we be offered a good price?"

He shrugged, sympathetic but determined not to appear so. "The country has been in drought, but you have a good flow in your river. If the inside of the homestead is as well cared for as the stables, you have a fair chance."

As if on cue, the meals' triangle rang out. "Oh, no," she said, clapping her hands to her cheeks. "I haven't set the table yet." She ran off.

Smiling lightly, he stared after her for a moment, then he left to wash his hands under the pump. If she wanted to sell for a good price, with just a few small improvements she might. If she thought she could manage more than maintenance, she would be wasting her time. Clearly, she'd not been trained to run a station.

He, however, had been trained from birth and he had worked hard, taking on untold responsibilities, hoping to earn respect. Where he had come from, a rich old man doled out his money to relatives who obeyed him to the letter. He didn't require input from a grandson who had spent years formulating ideas only to have them grounded. Cal liked nothing more than planning improvements, but he couldn't train Miss Ella.

To learn only a fraction of the skills she needed to run her property would take time. For him, time was money. The best shearers earned close to five pounds per week, but only for three months of a year, at most. Wanting big money fast meant he had to shear as quickly as possible.

Regrettably, he agreed. She needed to find a rich husband.

* * * *

Ella filled the buckets. Her first task after washing the breakfast dishes was normally the daily watering of the vegetables, but this morning she'd had to replant and stake the sheep-ravaged garden, which delayed the watering until mid-morning. As the pump stood alongside the stable wall, she worked in clear sight of the log seats the shearers claimed for their morning smoke-oh.

Not until her fifth trip from the pump to the gardens did she see Cal emerge from the woolshed. The sight of him now, as this morning, set her insides leaping with excitement, yet last night he'd done no more than tug on her braid. Apparently, she needed more from the man than advice, a painful thought she couldn't repress.

"Ella," Rose called from the kitchen window. "Can you help with lunch?"

Ella took a deep breath. "Not for a while. After this, I have to attend to the laundry. If you would put out the fire beneath the copper, you'll save me some time."

"I'll do that for you," Rose said. "I wish you knew a way to save *me* time."

Not until the linen bleached in the sunshine did Ella wearily enter the kitchen. "I do know a way to save time," she said to Rose, watching Vianna take the white plates for the shearer's lunch from the dresser. "If we ate our meals with the shearers, we would have only one lot of serving and no dining room to prepare."

Rose rubbed the back of her neck. "But could we bear to eat every meal with rough, sweaty males?"

"I could." Vianna added three plates to the pile of six she had placed on the table. "Because our shearers are not very rough or sweaty, not like those men this morning." She turned her mouth down with distaste. "The fat one wore really stinky clothes. Even Miffy backed away from him."

"Not everyone has a chance to wash each day," Rose said. "You mustn't despise those less fortunate. If we ate with the men, it *would* save work," she continued without taking a breath between the two subjects as if they might be a single thought—and they might well be. Ella knew her sister did not consider a shearer her equal.

"Let's do it, then."

Rose considered. "Unless it rains,"

"I'm sure we won't see rain for quite a while."

After lunch, eaten with none of the hilarity Ella normally heard from the shearer's table, Ella left for the stables. She hoped the men would learn to relax in the sisters' presence and she hoped that Rose would begin to see them as good people rather than uncouth men who should be offered a fine example of formal manners.

She almost sidestepped when she saw Cal carrying Vianna's saddle. Her footsteps slowed as she wondered why the dratted man had left the shearing shed.

"So you're going to practice jumps?" he asked Vianna as Ella neared.

"Miffy gets out of condition if I don't keep her in training."

He spotted Ella. "And is Miss Ella going to practice jumps, too?"

She had Papa's flat-brimmed felt hat on her head. "I'm just going out for my daily constitutional." Self-consciously, she walked past him, snagging a bridle from the stables and palming the crumbled lump of sugar she used to bribe the second stock horse to come to the fence. When caught, she took him to the mounting block, tethered him, and fetched her sidesaddle.

Cal, hands in his pockets and leaning against the wall, lifted his eyebrows. "I thought you might ride one of the chestnuts."

"We don't use them as hacks." Ella swung the saddle over the horse's back. "Normally Jed alternates with each of the stock horses, but today I need—want—to take this horse out." She wriggled her hands into her leather gloves, trying not to glance at the breath-stealing man.

Vianna, already mounted, rearranged her skirt over her boot tops. "The mares are lovely, aren't they?" she said to Cal. "They're a matched carriage pair. Papa won them in a card game. They're Ella's. He left them to her in his will. He left me a painting of Mama." She looked pleased.

Cal checked Vianna's cinch and handed over her crop. He left without saying a word.

"Why was he here?" Ella asked her sister in a whisper.

"Oh, I asked him to help lift my saddle."

"Gracious, Vi. You must have saddled your horse alone a hundred times." Ella left to retrieve the roll of fencing wire and the cutters as soon as Cal was out of sight. "He can't see me, can he?" she said to Vianna, who awaited her.

"Who?"

"Cal. I don't want him to know what I'm doing. I can't spend my life letting a stranger do our work."

"What work?"

"Mending fences. I thought I would see if I could repair a few. Cal saved me from riding into Noarlunga to buy another roll of wire, which spared me the embarrassment of having to ask for credit. Therefore, if I can get onto this horse, I expect I can do everything else."

"Why wouldn't you be able to get onto the horse?"

"You'd know why if you helped with the bucketing." Ella cinched her saddle girth. Now, on inspecting the stock horse, she wondered if the bay had grown two hands taller since the last time she'd ridden.

"I collected the eggs, I set the table for lunch, and I took the chestnuts out this morning," Vianna said in a hurt voice. "My arms are little. Rose should help you with the heavy work."

"Her arms are little, too." After tying on the wire and slipping the cutters into her pocket, Ella mounted with an overdone groan.

Vianna smiled. "Oh, Ella, you're not truly going to repair fences?"

"Cal has already given Jed enough jobs to last for days."

"I wish we could keep him." Vianna put up her hand to adjust her tiny riding hat. "He looks just like a fairytale prince."

"Good gracious," Ella said in a superior voice. "I'm shocked, Vi, truly shocked to hear such a shallow sentiment—we certainly can't keep him." She shot her sister a mischievous grin.

Vianna laughed. "I *knew* you thought he was handsome, too. Rose doesn't. She says no man is worth thinking about."

Ella stared into the distance, wondering what had brought about Rose's disdain and wishing she could agree. For the past few days, her thoughts had been almost fully occupied by the handy shearer. If he would only be here for two weeks, before she shriveled into an old maid, she would have a chance to wallow in the presence of an attractive man—perhaps even flirt if given half a chance.

Her chest ached at the thought.

Chapter 4

Ella rode with her sister past the woolshed and parted with Vianna at the gate of the holding yard. After following the boundary fence for some fifteen minutes, she found a section of broken wire. With the tool Cal had shown her how to use, she pulled the ends together, though not easily. She fixed the next four faults a little faster. Most of the wire had been snapped at the top.

On the fifth repair job, she slid from her horse and saw the perfect explanation as to why. At the top of the incline, a mob of kangaroos leaped the fence. The first five found no impediment. The sixth hit the top. The wire didn't break, but the kangaroo stumbled like any jumper who had misjudged the height. Unlike most other jumpers, however, the marsupial picked himself up and sped off even faster than he had approached the fence.

She couldn't imagine how high or how strong a fence would need to be to keep out kangaroos. Many times she'd seen them leap even higher, and many times she'd seen them throw themselves continually at a fence until they'd conquered the invader and left the defenses useless. Fence mending would be a constant for anyone who made a living on the land. However, for a woman who had mastered the rigors of laundering, mending fences was a mere physical task. She laughed, socking her fist into her blistering palm.

The sun rose high in the sky. Eucalyptus oil scented the air and the haze hovered around a group of trees. She heard the pad of hooves and saw Jed approach on the other stock horse. Papa had often commented on the stockman's ability to find him whenever he wanted. Ella stood waiting, wondering what sign she'd left of her movements for Jed to track her so easily.

She shaded her eyes with her hand. "Is there a problem?" she asked as soon as he came close enough to hear.

He shook his head and gave his wide smile. "Sheep where Missy say. Do Missy's fences now." He swung off his horse.

Stretching her aching back, she smiled. "I'd appreciate help. It's hard to pull the wire and twist it at the same time."

She and Jed led their horses to the next part of the damaged fence. He spotted two sheep that had escaped into the bushland and followed them on foot. Soon the sheep stood on the right side of the fence. Jed pulled the wire tight and Ella twisted. When her fingers grew too tender, they changed jobs. They finished for the day at the eastern boundary, and very little wire remained. With no money and with the account at the local store embarrassingly overdue, she would have to barter for more.

She glanced at the sun and sighed, focusing on the food preparation she needed to do for the evening meal. "We'll go back now," she said to Jed.

He grinned and mounted his horse. As Ella followed suit, Jed dismounted and raced off with a whoop. Ella watched him leap over the fence and run with long, loping strides until he disappeared.

Within a few minutes, he returned with a dead rabbit hanging from his belt. "Good tucker," he said with his habitual beam.

By no means had Ella mended all the fences, and the work left to do would be exhausting. She grinned back. Now that she had been taught how, she could finish the task in the next few days.

* * * *

The ubiquitous mutton roasted and the vegetables sizzled. The daylight would last another couple of hours. With the outside table ready for the evening meal, Rose wrote letters and Vianna cut scraps of fabric for her doll's clothes. Ella, her mood lightened by her successful day, joined Cal, who had promised her a lesson in shepherding. He looked indefatigable. His shirt was fresh, he smelled of soap, and his dark hair was wet and slicked back. Not only was he wildly handsome, but he was also patient enough to continue teaching a pupil whose ability was, at best, untried.

The dogs, under Cal's control, separated four ewes from those shorn during the day and herded the grouped sheep toward the temporarily empty woolshed paddock. Jed would bring in the next mob tomorrow. When the sheep stopped inside the fence, Cal said, "Tell the dogs to sit."

"Sit." She wished she and Cal had not lost the familiarity of last night. A little relaxation, a smile, a touch, or even a joke would have been appreciated. Instead, he acted like the taskmaster of this morning.

The dogs pranced around, stirring drifts of dry soil. "Be definite."

"Definitely sit, dogs," she said sternly, placing her hands on her hips. Amazingly, they did. "Oh, this is easy. Stand."

Cal shook his head and laughed. "Heel." He glanced at her in mock reproof as they moved to his side. "Tell them to stay."

"Stay."

"Now, we want them to move the sheep two by two back through the gate," he said, but the atmosphere had changed. Cal had adapted to her jaunty mood and seemed ready to be amused. He induced the dogs to do as he wished by a series of commands no more complicated than sit, stay, down, and heel.

By the time the sun had diminished to a glare behind the bordering pines, Ella had control of the dogs. She would never match Cal with her practical skills, but she tried hard to meet his standards. She and the dogs, with Cal sauntering behind, took the sheep back to the woolshed paddock.

"I'm very pleased with myself. I should be able to teach Jed to do that quite easily. You have a rare talent for getting the best out of people. Have you ever thought about running a property of your own?" She glanced at his broad shoulders and averted her gaze. His maleness caught at her insides and set her pulses fluttering.

"I hope to do that, certainly. My own way."

"I suspect you never do a thing any other way," she said matter-of-factly. "Is running a property your plan for the future?"

He brushed his fingers over his chin as if considering. "Not for my immediate future, no."

"It's hard to get past immediate futures," she said, watching Girl angle her head beneath Cal's hand to receive a pat. "If you're like me, you want to do everything yesterday."

"Like find your rich husband?"

She passed through the gate, which he shut behind her. "Women with rich husbands don't have to learn how to herd sheep."

"And they live in smart houses in the city."

"Have you ever been to the city?"

He nodded, leaning back against the gate, one heel hooked on the bottom rung. "My mother lives in the city. Every year she finds me a new wife."

"And how many do you have now?" She rested a palm on the fencepost, smiling at him, conscious of his strong jaw, his sculpted cheekbones, and her own breathing.

He smiled back. "None. The females that suit her don't suit me."

"And what sort of females suit you?"

"Are you testing my flirting skills?" he said with a hooded glance at her.

His unexpected response dried her mouth. She held his gaze. "Perhaps I'm testing mine."

He inclined his head. "Most of you females seem to have it down pat."

Encouraged by his banter, she lifted the closing wire over the fencepost and lingered. "Ah, I understand. You're nursing a broken heart. Some woman trifled with you and then she married another."

When he neither moved nor answered, she wondered if she'd guessed correctly. What sort of woman had broken his heart? Obviously one who didn't appreciate a man with looks, humor, ability, intelligence, and apparent ambition. Cal could go anywhere and be anyone. He wouldn't need to consider, using no particular example, a woman with no income, no special talents, blistered and scratched hands, and at least one dependent sister.

He turned slowly to stare at the shorn sheep, resting both elbows on the top of the gate. "When do you plan to do the dipping?"

Her eyes shifted to his bared forearms, sinewy, muscle-hard, and tanned, and she groaned. "I suspect you think I don't have enough to occupy myself."

"The best time for dipping is after shearing."

She put her hand over her heart. "I swear that the sheep will be dipped sometime in the next two weeks."

"Does Jed know how to dip sheep?"

"He used to help Papa."

"You could probably help him."

"Ladies don't dip sheep."

"Ladies don't repair fences." He took her hand in his, stroking his thumb across her reddened palm and examining a blister. "I assume that's what you've been doing today."

She drew a shivery breath, leaving her hand in his, remaining so still that the moment expanded to significance. "Jed doesn't have time to do all the tasks you set him. I've needed to help."

"Did you rake under the woolshed?"

"Someone had to, as you said."

He gently turned her palm over and stroked the pad of his thumb across a new scratch. "Do you have the recipe for the dip?"

She heard herself breathe out. "No, but I'm sure you do."

With her hand in his, he turned to face her. The strength in his stance contrasted with the softness in his expression. Her heart began to pound erratically.

"No woman has trifled with me and broken my heart," he said, his thick lashes shading his eyes. "Do you see that as a fault in me?"

"If you have a fault, I'm yet to find it."

"Why do I assume that is not a compliment?"

"Why indeed? No mere female could possibly understand the workings of a man's mind."

He glanced at her from beneath his lowered lids. "Our minds are simple—we need only food, and sleep, and one other thing."

"Money?" she said, removing her hand from his hold with great reluctance.

"Two other things."

"Respect?"

"Don't tease me, Ella."

"Ella? Did I say you could use my name?"

"I'm not a flirting man. There's only one thing I want from a woman."

She knew exactly what he meant, and she wished she could feel offended. Instead, she experienced a curl of heat low in her belly. "It's nature, though, isn't it? There's only one thing a ram wants from a ewe."

He took a sideways view of her expression. "I don't think your father would like to hear you talking this way."

"Perhaps if he hadn't died, I wouldn't be. I would be inside the house pressing flowers for my album or sketching a design for an evening gown. I'm changing with the circumstances, Cal. Didn't you say I should?"

"Perhaps I'm not your best adviser."

Her eyes prickled. She dashed a wrist beneath her nose. "You're the only volunteer I've had thus far. I never expected to be left with a debt-ridden farm. Once I had everything, including a social life and two parents. You wouldn't understand. You have a mother and you can go where you please and do what you please."

"You have to make the best of what you have."

"Did you read that in the shearer's manual? I'm trying—you can see I'm trying." She faced him defiantly. "I wish I'd been born a man."

"I wish you had, too." He didn't move. The expression on his face told her that he controlled himself rigidly.

"Don't worry. You don't need to continue educating me." Her chin lifted higher. "I can manage without you."

And suddenly the tension dissipated. He glanced at his feet. She could swear he was hiding a smile.

"I've been ungrateful," she said stiffly. "I should thank you, yet again."

He lifted a palm to stop her speaking. "You're bothering me, Ella."

She turned her face away from him. "I won't bother you anymore."

"It's not something you have control over. It's the effect you have on me."

"I know I speak too bluntly, and I know I argue way past the point of no return. Papa said I'm far too tactless but that most people could see that underneath I have a good heart."

"I'm sure your father knew you better than I do, but I don't agree. I think you are a delight and a constant temptation. And that bothers me, for I have no choice other than to resist you."

She stared at him, gaze wide, her blood rushing so loudly she was sure he would hear. She tried to concentrate on breathing. Her body thrummed with awareness. He looked taller, darker, and more dangerous with the sun behind him. Without a doubt, everything about him lured her, from his self-containment to his utter stillness. The dogs frolicked at his feet, but he ignored them. Girl nudged his leg, but he pushed her snout away. She stared at Ella with sorrowful eyes. Ella heard the pitiful bleating of the sheep and a loud "cawing" she identified as a nearby crow.

"Ella," Cal said softly, lifting a hand to her hair and catching a flyaway tendril between his fingers.

Her skin seared where his knuckle brushed her cheek. To herself or him, she whispered, "We shouldn't."

He cupped her face between his calloused hands. His fingers slid into the sides of her hair and with careful thumbs, he caressed her cheeks. "No, we shouldn't. But just this once in my life, I want to be irresponsible."

She only had time to soften her lips before his mouth angled across hers. She closed her eyes and he began to kiss her, slowly and gently. At first she felt the tingling there, but heat spread slowly throughout her body.

She shifted her hands to the muscles of his back and pressed her body against his, thrilled by his hard strength. Although willing to admit to excitement, she couldn't get comfortable. He appeared to have something in his pocket. She wriggled. The more she wriggled, the deeper his kiss. He moved his hands down her to her buttocks and lifted her up against him. Her body pulsed with sensation.

Wanting to experience more, she moved her hands to his chest. When she'd faced him in his soaked shirt, she'd seen his perfect form, but she needed to touch him. His heart thundered against her palm and somehow his strength, his stability, and his lack of hesitation bred confidence in her.

She slid her hands to his behind and became another person, a hot, heavy-breathing bundle of desire. His rounded tightness and shifting muscles thrilled her. The stronger a man, the safer a woman felt. She made a sound of need.

His hands moved to cup her breasts. Standing on tiptoes, she let her body beg for every caress she could get, for she wanted more. She shifted her hips, not knowing how she could press any closer. His mouth lifted from hers and pressed against her cheeks, her nose, and her eyelids. He breathed as heavily as she, and his heart thundered exactly like hers.

No doubt he too wanted more. "This is probably no time to tell you," she said in a husky murmur. "But you have rocks in your pockets, and if you are going to kiss a woman you should be aware of her comfort."

His face nestled into her neck. "My Lord," he said in a strange voice. "I thought you understood about rams and ewes."

"I do." She stilled. Her cheeks flamed. "I simply hadn't applied it..."

He kissed her cheek, holding her upper arms. In a deliberate movement, he took a step back. After a moment of utter stillness, he nodded as if saying goodnight and walked off, the dogs trailing behind him.

She touched her cool palms to her face. The heat didn't subside. Gathering her skirts, she ran back to the homestead understanding that he hadn't treated her either as a lady or a station owner.

He had simply shown her what a man wanted from a woman.

* * * *

With the evening meal cooked and ready to be served and the daylight waning, Ella dressed in a dark brown taffeta she'd had fashioned two years ago so that she could attend formal functions with Papa. She presented herself in the kitchen and took her apron from the hook behind the door.

"My," Rose said, staring. "You look very fine. Perhaps I ought to have a gown made in that color...after we get our money, of course."

"And after we have bought the house?"

Rose took the serving spoons from the dresser drawer and made a sound of agreement.

Ella breathed out with relief. "If you want your inheritance to take to your husband, Vianna and I would be able to buy your share of a house somehow."

Rose gave a cynical smile. "I won't be marrying a man who wants my money. I have a very ambitious godmother. She has watched over me carefully these past two years. Men are more calculating than one supposes." From the cupboard beneath the dresser, she took out the biggest meat plate and a covered vegetable dish, both gold-edged white china. "For a shearer, you would be a good catch. Be careful. That said, perhaps Vi should come out of black, too."

"And what about you? When do you plan to come out of black?"

"When we get back to the city." Rose glanced down at the beautiful black silk she wore. "I won't have any use for these when I start enjoying life again."

Ella sliced the meat. When Rose married, and nothing could be more certain than that event, life would continue as Papa had preordained. Ella would, possibly, take care of a few nieces and nephews in addition to Vianna. She couldn't be a good catch for the handsome shearer who thought she was a delight, who kissed her as if she were a temptation, and who walked off when he discovered her inexperience. He wanted to dally with a woman but not one who expected marriage. Fortunately, she couldn't marry a poor man, but the chance to be someone's delight and their temptation didn't come every day.

Rose piled the vegetables into the dish. "Where is that lazy child? She ought to be helping us."

Ella went to the hall doorway and called, "Vianna!"

Vianna came out of the drawing room. "I was just getting my music ready for tonight. I thought I would play for the shearers after dinner," she said defensively.

"I'm sure they would be very pleased." Ella scraped the gravy into the boat. "Take this out and the vegetables, Vi. You go out, too, Rose. I won't be much longer."

Cal took one glance at her sophisticated presentation and seated himself at the other end of the table. Instead of being fazed, she was satisfied. If he sat by her, she would be unable to control the tremble of her hands and the clench of her throat.

She watched him when she thought he wasn't looking, noticing that the other shearers treated him with unusual respect, following the lead of Alf, who also watched him when he thought no one was looking. Cal apparently impressed males just as much as females. Vianna lurked around him like a cat wanting to be stroked, but Rose let her brief interest rest on Ned, who had a tendency to tweak his moustache whenever she glanced at him. Ella, unfortunately, didn't have an effect on Cal.

Finally the meal finished, and she washed the plates. Rose wiped. Dusk lowered outside. She saw Cal, Girl at heel, leave the men's quarters and stroll behind the woolshed, heading for the river, possibly meaning to take a swim.

For the next ten days, she planned to be a woman rather than Papa's daughter. For the rest of her life, she would be the responsible spinster guardian of her younger sister. She would never again meet a man who said she was irresistible. Her first chance was her last.

After putting the plates away, she took a sheet of paper from the dresser and wrote a quick note for the local dairy farmer, Nathaniel Lannock, who took his milk to the township every morning, filling the empty cans he passed along the way. Since Papa had died, Mr. Lannock had kindly delivered the milk to the back door. Clattering and bumping with her heavy load, she half-dragged the knee-high empty can to the front gate.

She returned past the apricot and plum trees, their fruit picked last month, the apples and pears with a couple of months to go, and the heavily laden peach trees. She skirted behind the stables and the woolshed.

Tonight, she intended to see if, despite her inexperience, she could lead Cal into temptation and deliver him from evil restraint.

Chapter 5

Cal, accompanied by Girl, circled past the billabong. The crackling leaves beneath his feet released the heady fragrance of eucalyptus oil. He needed to get away and cool himself off. Tonight, Ella had dressed in a dull brown gown that instead of rendering her invisible, did the opposite. The rigid cut contrasted with the lush curves beneath, causing him to think of nothing else. Had she been older or more experienced, he wouldn't feel guilty about his attraction to her. Not only did she amuse him, he wanted her gown unhooked and his hands all over her lithe and luscious body. First, before he had his way with her.

Without distracting himself, he would be aiming for far more than flirting, but this was practical Ella with big beautiful eyes, a mischievous mouth, and no man to protect her. He had a responsibility to his upbringing to treat young ladies with the respect they deserved, and she deserved more than most. She worked like a drover's dog from dawn until dusk despite being largely unskilled. Tonight's meal was overcooked, the meat was tough, the vegetables were watery, and the gravy was almost solid with lumps. Lord help them all for the next few weeks.

He removed his boots and socks. The sun had died, casting a soft gray over the treetops. Night birds rustled through the undergrowth, searching out grubs. He loved this land of his birth—the soft cream of the stones; the warm ocher of the soil; the restful blues and greens of the growth; and the pastel whites, grays, reds, and pinks of the timber.

Although the summer flow was low in the river, the water raced past fresh and clear. Reeds filled the edges. Dwarf gums, pink gums, and stringy barks grew a few feet away with a lower canopy of acacias and tea trees. He scooped his shirt over his head and found a hefty twig, which he slung into the water. Girl leaped after for her regular game.

About to remove his trousers, he heard a crunching of dry leaf litter. He turned and saw Ella approach. His mouth dried.

"Are you planning on taking a swim?"

"Yes," he said firmly. "I'm also planning on removing all my clothes and so you might want to leave."

She remained on the bank near his shirt and shoes. "I don't know what I might want to do. These days I only know what I have to do. My papa was a remittance man. Do you know what that is?"

He tried to read her expression but couldn't, so he paused by the water's edge. "Someone who is paid to live elsewhere by his family."

"In a nutshell. My father was born in England and he had an inheritance from his grandfather. He gambled the lot away before he turned twenty-five and met my mother, with whom he fell instantly in love," she said, her gaze resting on his face. "Without the guarantee of an income, they couldn't marry, and so his father gave him yearly increments for ten years to move to this new colony. They bought this property with my mother's inheritance."

He swept his hand through his hair. "Why do you tell me this?"

"By the time my mother was a little older than Rose, the only thing of value she owned was her jewelry." She stared across the river. "When Papa died, he left all her jewelry to Rose. Everything, down to the simplest chain. I suppose that would be some sort of tradition, to leave the most valuable possessions to the oldest daughter?"

"Like primogeniture?"

"Rose would never sell an item and perhaps Papa thought I might."

"If he wanted to keep the collection together, he would leave the lot to one daughter," he said finding the conversation puzzling.

"Is that how a man thinks?"

He nodded, having no idea if that was how her father thought.

"I was so hurt," she said. "Silly, really, when I know Rose would look far more beautiful than I in Mama's diamond set. I'd assumed he left her the best because he loved her best."

He put one hand to the back of his neck, frowning. "I don't know how valuable the diamond set is, but I'm quite sure that your father, being a mere man, applied logic when he decided on the carriage pair for you."

"Which would you have given me?"

"Both," he said promptly and wished he had held his tongue.

She aimed a rather conscious smile at him. "Because I'm irresistible?"

"Because I don't have either and it's easy for me to say."

She walked slowly over to him, lifted her palm to his upper arm, and watched her fingers skim lightly against his hot skin. He tightened his bicep in order not to let her touch effect him.

"I thought you were going to remove your trousers," she murmured.

He groaned inwardly.

"I might be inexperienced, but I'm ready and willing to learn anything you care to teach me." The backs of her fingertips whispered across the hair on his chest.

His flesh tingled and his heartbeat accelerated. All too tempted, he lifted his hand to the wisp of hair in front of her ear and tucked the lock behind. "You need to keep yourself for your husband."

"I don't have a husband."

"I'm not rich enough for you." His thumb brushed the side of her face and he noted the burnished gold of her lowered lashes.

"Foolish man. I don't want to marry you."

"You say that now." His voice was gruff with amusement. "But if I got you into trouble, what choice would you have? Or I?"

She raised her gaze.

At that moment, Girl bounded out of the water, raced up to him, and dropped a stick near his feet. She stepped sideways, planted all four feet firmly in the sand, and shook her coat, sending a cool spray of water over them.

Ella gasped and stepped back.

With the woman he shouldn't touch out of his reach, and without her hair stirring against his cheek, her hand wandering over his skin, he could think. He'd known from the start she was out of bounds.

Drawing an agonized breath, he turned quickly, dropped his trousers, and sprinted through the water. He dived under and swam to the middle of the river. Girl joined him, grinning. He cupped her chin. "Good, Girl."

But for Girl's distraction, he might have given in to his lust. Even now his body disagreed with his decision, though he could deal with that. Glancing over to where Ella had been, he noted she had gone. With luck his rejection of her offer would keep her away from him in future. He hoped so.

He didn't know if he could reject her again.

* * * *

Half an hour later, he presented himself back in the quarters. The men had organized themselves a game of two-up. They'd set their lanterns in a circle. The floor vibrated with their stamping and calls. Almost unseen, he stretched out on his bed and watched.

Instead of Ella's subtle floral scent, he had the pleasure of Ned's pomade, Benji's sheep-smelling shirt, and the foot odor of nine bootless men. Instead of being propositioned by a very desirable young female, he heard Frank's long story of how his Aunt Abby had a rotten tooth pulled by a traveling salesman while pennies thudded to the floor and men shoved at each other to see which landed first, the heads or the tails.

"You're back," Alf said, gathering his winnings. Ned glanced up, smirked, and took the bets for the next throw. "Do you want to join in the game?" Alf sat beside Cal on his bed, making a wad of his pennies in a crushed handkerchief.

Cal shook his head. "I'd rather get some sleep."

"I suspicion you don't gamble. Mr. Beaufort now, if he was still alive, he'd be in here like a shot, winning everyone's wages or losing his own shirt—it didn't matter no-how to him." Alf had shorn on the same properties for twenty years or more. "Used to have a yellow gig and a whole stable o' horses. I b'lieve he sent Miss Rose off to the city to see if she could make his fortune." Alf winked. "Marry into money, you know. Instead she's back here cooking."

Cal didn't give a damn about the lovely Rose, who had a pair of bored eyes. Nice looking she might be, but her conversation consisted of polite comments and impartial words. She couldn't combat his normal seriousness with an apt comment the way Ella did, and she lacked Ella's vitality. Although Cal appreciated that Rose helped in the homestead, he doubted she had ever considered helping Ella with the real work. "I suspect she didn't find a husband in the city because none could afford her."

Alf chuckled. "She'd be expensive. Gowns o' silk, she wears, and very fine. No man with the sense o' a lamb would miss that. Reckon you didn't."

Cal *had* missed noticing Rose's gowns. Ella dressed well but normally she wore cotton. Tonight she might have been wearing silk, but she didn't need silk. She could ensnare a man with her smiles and stay him with her willingness.

If he continued to help her, she would repay him with her only currency—herself. Only a cad would accept that from an innocent when he knew he planned to leave.

"Nevertheless, with her looks, she would have caused quite a stir."

Alf slanted him an impartial glance. "You would reckon so."

"Her sisters will, too."

"Don't reckon you would be fixing fences and training dogs if you didn't think that."

Cal grinned reluctantly. "The youngest is a baggage."

"She's a small 'mount spoiled. That's to be expected. Ho. Tails, tails." Alf rose to his feet and thumped Benji on the back. "Good lad. You almost won back your pay."

Cal lay back with his arms behind his head. He thought he should catch up on his lost sleep.

And try not to think of Ella's mouth on his face, on his chest, on his... He groaned and rolled over onto his stomach.

* * * *

Ella arrived back at the homestead, wondering how awkward the moment might have been but for Girl. Although she had not expected to be refused, she knew Cal still wanted her. She wished she hadn't told him of her hurt over the inheritance. She had sounded jealous of her sister, which in the matter of the jewelry she had to admit she was. After all, she would scarcely own a carriage any time in the near or distant future. If Papa had meant her to keep those horses as a reminder of him, she likely couldn't. Better a simple chain she could wear around her neck.

A lamp still burned in the drawing room, an area she kept as highly polished as the day Mama had died. A red velvet sofa and a set of armchairs; side tables; and an ornate, glass-fronted bookcase stood down one end of the room and the other held Vianna's piano, at which Rose sat. "Judging by the time you took, I would swear you counted each and every peach in the orchard."

Ella faced her sister without mentioning where she had been. "Rose, I rode along the fence line today. I should have done so months ago." She deposited her behind in the armless velvet chair, watching her sister finger the piano keys while she listened. "The posts are rotten. Wire is down everywhere. Where the fences are not breached, there's no grass, and where they are, the loose sheep wander far and wide. They've made bogs of their water holes and hideouts in the scrub. I imagine plenty have disappeared."

Rose shrugged. "Tell Jed."

"He can't do more than he does and we need him to help the shearers. He has to bring in the sheep and take them back to pasture, a time-consuming job that is utterly necessary to our future plans. I can help him. I know what needs to be done. With just a few improvements, we can make this place more saleable."

"If you want to oversee the property, do so," Rose said in a dismissive voice. "I suspect you need to get this place out of your system. You'll soon see what Papa tried to teach you—that women are the weaker sex."

Her father had taught Ella little more than the fact that, as a daughter, she was of value only on the homestead. She could, however, work on the land, weaker than a man or not.

Nevertheless, she didn't go to sleep that night deciding which fences needed to be attended to first. Instead, she plotted how she would convince Cal to change his mind and romance her.

* * * *

Edward wasn't a man to fuss or complain, but he'd had the worst two nights' sleep of his entire life and in a hotel only six hours from home, detained by a broken carriage wheel before he'd barely started his journey.

He'd spent his first day asking questions in the bank and making investigations around the town while trying to stretch a back aching from sleeping on a mattress that he would swear was stuffed with gumnuts. He doubted the blankets had been aired in a twelvemonth. Even a cat couldn't be left in a room as small, and if he'd had to wait any longer for this morning's overcooked breakfast, he might well nigh have fainted from starvation.

"You ate half a loaf of bread before your chops came," Sam said with indignation. "And your bed was no worse nor mine, and mine was as good as I've slept in."

"Ha," Edward said, easing himself down on a high-backed hall chair in the lobby of the Caledonian Inn. "That's what I mean. My bed was no better than yours. I should have had the best." As the owner of the biggest private holding in the colony, comprising a homestead the size of a small town, a horse stud, a cattle stud, a dairy, a townhouse, and various pockets of housing in the city, he was used to no less.

"Yes, y'honor," Sam said through clenched teeth. He threw up his hands and walked up the hall and out into the sunlight.

"Mutton chops," muttered Edward, outraged. He lifted a foot to rest on his overnight valise. "I own most of the sheep in this part of the world. I should have been given beefsteak. They know who I am."

Almost thirty years ago, he had arrived in this colony from England with money in his pocket and a will to make more. Now he owned enough well-fenced sheep to cover the horizon. Not only that—after a heated discussion two years ago with his grandson, Charlton, he'd let the lad have dams dug and wells sunk on his property. Fortunately, this added expense had more than doubled his profits.

He leaned back, half-closing his eyes, squinting through the doorway at the bright early morning sunshine. A dray pulled by sixteen oxen and carrying bales of wool passed. The driver walked along beside. Dust swirled a foot high, and a magpie picked for grubs in the roadside grass.

The light from the doorway dimmed, heralding Sam's return. "The lead horse has cast a shoe. Give me your valise. I'll put it in the coach. We won't be leaving for another hour."

"Cast a shoe? Cast a shoe?" Edward was more irritated with each word he uttered. "Another hour? What am I supposed to do for another hour?"

"You could drink yourself into a better temper in the taproom," Sam suggested, smartly removing the valise and himself.

Clamping his lips, Edward pushed to his feet and strode to the taproom door. He entered a slate-floored room that stank of hops and mold and echoed with emptiness. A middle-aged barmaid wiped down benches.

The only other patron was a young, painted female dressed in a limp purple gown. She sat on a stool by the taps, her head in her arms. "'Nother port," she called in a slurred voice.

The barmaid walked behind the long bar, poured a glass, and slid the liquor down the length. "There you are, Ruby. And that's your last. What would you like, sir?"

"A glass of ale."

"Ruby," the barmaid had called the female. Edward had heard the name mentioned by his stockmen after they'd been in town, therefore he knew her to be one of the local whores.

Ruby lifted her head, opened one eye, and focused on him. "You're young Mr. Lynton's pa," she said in a cockney accent. She had a receding chin and thinly plucked eyebrows.

"I'm his grandfather." Edward clamped his lips. Henry, his son, had died in his twenty-sixth year. Being young and rich had killed him. Drunk, he'd died after engaging in fisticuffs over another man's wife. He'd died in one of the most beautiful parks surrounding the city of Adelaide, leaving his young wife and his five-year-old son.

Twenty years had passed but Edward still regretted letting Henry leave the land so that he could become a Rundle Street farmer, a gentleman with a city office on that illustrious street of commerce. None knew better than Edward that satisfaction came from work, not chasing paper trails of money.

"You have the look of him." Ruby upended her glass, poured the contents down her throat, and turned to face him. "Tall and 'andsome," she added with a calculating smile.

Edward straightened. "You know him?" Although surprised, he was careful to sound as if he didn't care.

Ruby lifted her greasy locks from the back of her neck, preening. "*Oi* know all your men. And they know me."

The barmaid, a woman with a thin mouth and dun-colored hair scraped back into a small knot, made a sound of disgust. "I don't think young Mr. Lynton has once given you the time of day."

"Time wouldn't be of no use to me," Ruby said in a triumphant voice. "A shillin' is what *Oi* ask. No more." She cackled like a woman twice her age and flicked her head, indicating the barmaid. "Her daughter, Betsy, she charged more than half his wage."

"Get out of here, Ruby," the barmaid said in a deadly undertone. "You're drunk and you stink."

"*Oim* stayin'."

"I'll pick you up and throw you out."

"*Yew* don't own this place. *Oim* tellin' *yew*..."

The barmaid moved from behind the bar. Ruby slid off the stool. Part of her hem trailed across the floor as she wobbled out into the street. Any dignity she once might have possessed had been lost long since.

The barmaid picked up a wet rag and began wiping the bar as if to scarify the wood and remove any trace that the whore had existed. "Betsy wasn't a prostitute," she said to Edward through tight lips. "If he gave her money, it was no more than he should. Before she met him, she was a good girl."

Edward shrugged. A man with Charlton's looks and expectations would turn the head of any female. "If he had his way with her, I hope she was cleaner than that one." He inclined his head toward the doorway.

"I just told you she was a good girl. He ruined her."

"Got her with child, did he?" Edward asked, as if interested. If Charlton had, it was no more than Edward expected. The boy's father had been a rake, too. Just because Edward hadn't seen a wild streak in Charlton, didn't mean Charlton behaved like a gentleman when he went out on the town with the lads. "Can she prove it's his?"

"No," the barmaid said. "She didn't have a baby. I told you, she's a good girl."

"What is this conversation about, then? I thought you said he gave her money."

"And so he did." The barmaid folded her arms. "I don't know why, if he didn't ruin her."

Edward spread his hands.

"She left here two months ago with twenty pounds."

"Now I know you're lying. My grandson didn't have twenty pounds to scratch himself with."

"And you as rich as the queen?" She gave a mirthless grin. "Don't try gammoning me."

Edward scowled. He paid for anything his grandson wanted, which never seemed to amount to much. Charlton saw no more cash than a ditchdigger. His father, Henry, had taken the sum he wanted whenever he wanted money. Edward had kept his purse closed after his son died. If Charlton had given the girl twenty pounds, he had given her his hoard. More fool he. He raised his eyebrows. "Another ale. And put a head on the next."

He thought she would have liked to slide the drink at him, hoping he would catch the slops in his lap, such was her expression, but one of the benefits of being a rich man was that most people didn't dare annoy him.

"She's gone." The barmaid's mouth turned down. "To Victoria. If she'd stayed, one day she could've 'ad my job."

"Well, obviously the girl is a fool," Edward said with sarcasm, glad to have the last word.

The barmaid stared at him. "And Ruby doesn't charge a shilling. On bath day, the best she can get is sixpence."

"Ready to roll." Sam poked his head into the room.

Edward dropped a coin on the bar to pay for his ale and followed Sam out of the Inn. "Tell the driver we'll stop in Kingston."

Whether Betsy was a good woman or a bad woman didn't matter to him. He'd heard she'd left with twenty pounds. If she'd left with Charlton, the twenty pounds would have been superfluous. This meant that Charlton hadn't gone to Victoria. Edward hadn't really supposed he would, but he didn't appear to be in Adelaide, either, or his mother would have heard.

"The lad wouldn't be in Kingston. What would he do there?"

"Despite what you think, I am not chasing after Charlton. My grandson can go to hell for all I care."

"That's billycock and you know it. I saw you the morning the lad disappeared. A greater fuss you've never made than when you thought he might have been thrown from his horse."

"A natural enough assumption."

"So don't tell me you don't care."

Edward had cared, even after Charlton's horse returned, stirrups neatened to the saddle so as not to flap when galloping unridden. However, Edward knew by this that Charlton had left of his own accord. He tightened his fingers into a fist. "Damn him! And damn his pettifogging arguments!" Should Charlton imagine he could force his grandfather to concede by prancing off like a girl, he would soon learn to rethink his actions.

Never would he subsidize Charlton in the same lifestyle that had killed his father. Never. Edward pressed his lips into a firm line. He chased no man. From Robe, he would travel to his town house in Adelaide.

Edward bore the bone jarring and the harsh heat. His head, aching since he'd heard that Charlton Alfred Langdon Lynton had little or no money, now throbbed with tension.

Chapter 6

The morning sun glowed pale yellow in the clear blue sky as Cal took his first sheep from the pen.

Frank sharpened his shears. "See the woodpile?"

Before Cal had entered the woolshed, he had noted the heaped pile of split wood near the kitchen. "Jed's been busy." If Miss Rose had half Ella's gumption, she could do enough for the day in half an hour or so. The stockman had more important tasks than making small logs into kindling.

"Not Jed." Frank's grin widened, showing his big, square, gapped teeth. "Ned. He thought he'd test to see if Miss Rose would be impressed enough to spare him a kiss or two."

"And was she?" Cal lifted his sheep to a sitting position.

"Not so's you'd notice." Frank pushed his whetstone into his pocket and eyed Cal sideways. "I told him he might need to mend a few fences, maybe, afore she got around to kissin' him."

Cal stilled for a few seconds, exploring Frank's words. When the implication hit him, his jaw tightened. Ned must have seen him kiss Ella. Now he understood why the man had continually smirked at him last night and had even nudged him once. Ned had told Frank, and if his gossip spread farther, Ella's reputation would become grist for the mill. He straightened pugnaciously. "The next man to make a joke of me will get what he is asking for," he said loudly to Frank.

"No one's makin' a joke of you."

"Well, keep your mouth shut. If a certain lady wanted to rebuff me, that's her choice."

"Rebuff you? I didn't hear about no rebuffin'."

"Told you so," Alf put in. He threw his first fleece to the sorting table where Benji, standing and listening, spread out the wool. "I've known Miss Ella for years. She wouldn't be encouraging the attention of no shearer, not her."

"Ned said he saw the whole thing," Frank mumbled, hesitating by the pen door. "Looked like a thorough kissing to him."

Cal rested his fists on his hips, lifting his eyebrows. "As long as he sticks to that story..."

"Mind you," Alf said with complacence. "If Ned wants to think he might earn a kiss for chopping the wood, I don't think we should set him straight. The little ladies can do with all the help they can get."

"Ned don't usually tell stories." Frank glanced uncertainly from one to the other. After a sigh, he shrugged and pulled his first sheep out of the pen.

Satisfied that he had stopped any gossip that might eventuate, Cal worked until smoke-oh, when he joined the others on the log seats outside. Only Alf spoke.

"She went out early this morning." He indicated Miss Vianna, who rode past to the stable yard where she dismounted. "Said she needs to practice riding for the local show—uses the paddock behind the billabong. It's set up with barrels and planks for jumping."

Cal shrugged, watching the child tie her pony by the reins. Turning his back on her, he faced the fire, noting the steam drifting from the billy-can.

"Not like Miss Ella. She's a worker, that one. Make a good wife for a man on the land. She keeps them stables nice, too."

"The stables?" Cal filled his mug with steaming black tea. "I thought the horses were Jed's responsibility."

"He don't do no more than the sheep. Don't have time for nothin' else."

"She does the mucking out? The grooming?"

"The lot. Her and Miss Rose have split the jobs between them. They want Miss Vianna to be good at reading and writing and such." Alf shrugged. "The gentry aren't like us working people."

"Most of the gentry *are* working people," Cal said before he could stop himself. "Or so I've observed."

"Worked for a lot of them, have you?"

"Not a lot, no. But for quite a while. Not many people get rich in this country if they don't work. It wouldn't do the child any harm to take on a few more tasks."

"You oughta tell that to Miss Ella."

"Family relationships are not my area of expertise," Cal said with a twist of his mouth.

Alf raised his eyebrows. "And if she rebuffed you, she wouldn't listen to you anyway, would she?"

Frank, Ned, and Tommy stared at Cal. Fortunately, at the same moment Girl nudged him. "You think we should get back to work?" He squatted beside her and pulled her ears, then quickly downed his hot drink.

"Girl is really pretty," said a female voice behind him. Miss Vi, wearing a smart pale blue skirt and jacket, leaned down and held out her hand to Girl. "Prettier than our dogs." She had left her pony standing saddled in the sun.

"They look much the same." He rose to his feet, remaining by the fire while the others returned to the woolshed.

She wrapped her hand in her skirts when Girl didn't respond to her. "She is shinier."

"I brush her every day."

"Ella brushed ours this morning." She concentrated on her shoes. "They're with her now while she waters the fruit trees. She's trying to learn how to handle them."

He ran his hand over his chin, as if considering. "I suppose they can round up the dropped fruit."

She offered a quick smile. "They're resting, just like your dog does when you don't keep her busy."

"Girl does plenty without me telling her. She enjoys the rewards of completing a hard day's work."

Without asking what those rewards might be, she scanned his face. Although delicately pretty like Miss Rose, the way she chewed at her lip indicated that she was not as sure of her charms as the oldest Beaufort. "Would you look at my pony's foot? She has something stuck in her shoe and I can't get it out."

"Did you try?"

Alf coughed loudly. "I'll be getting back to the shearing now." He shuffled off.

She twisted her fingers together. "I did try, but I've never done it before, and I didn't like to bother Ella. She's always so busy."

"I'll see what I can do for your horse if you go and see what you can do for your sister."

She stared at him.

He didn't move. "Do we have a deal?"

"I'm not strong enough to be of any use. I can't carry a full bucket of water." She took a step back, looking defiant but sounding unsure. "And she doesn't like me spending time under the hot sun."

"I suspect the orchard sun is no hotter than the paddock sun in which you ride."

She concentrated on her feet. "I don't like outdoor work."

"I suspect Miss Ella doesn't either," he said gently. "Do we have a deal?"

She heaved a breath, then she nodded. "I can't let Miffy suffer when I only have to do something I don't want to do. If you can't help her, though, our deal is canceled." She raised her chin and took two steps backward. "Do you think your dog would like to come and play with our dogs while you shear?"

He thought of telling the child that Girl preferred being with him, but Miss Vi's view of work was that play was better. And Girl might like a slack moment for all he knew. "I don't see why she shouldn't be given a social outing once in a while." He accompanied Miss Vi to the stables. "But she won't leave me unless I indicate to her where I want her to stay. First I'll look at the hoof."

"I think she might have fun," the child said seriously. "She played with them after they had their bones this morning."

"Ah, that's life, isn't it?" He untied the pony and took the reins in his hands. "Like is attracted to like."

"I don't know. I've never had anyone to be attracted to, not my own age. I would like a friend, but we need to live in the city before I have a chance of finding one."

He walked the pony a few steps and noted the limp. Stopping, he lifted the left front leg and spotted the trouble. He took out his pocketknife and eased out a jammed twig. It fractured into splinters on the ground. "The hoof might be tender for a while." He removed the saddle, leaving it on the mounting block while he opened the gate to the stable paddock. He ushered Miffy through. "Don't ride her again until you are sure she's lost the limp."

"Now I'll do as I promised." The child watched him hang the bridle over a hook, then she led Cal toward the orchard at the front of the house. Suddenly she picked up speed and ran ahead. "Ella," she called in a clear voice. "Girl is coming to play with Paws and Patch and Petunia. Cal doesn't mind. See? He's not a slave driver."

Ella straightened. She wore a hat like an empty cushion tied to her head and gloves that came to her elbows. "Dear life, Vi. Whoever said he was?" Her guilty blush gave her away.

Cal controlled his urge to smile, remembering that during their last encounter he had rebuffed her. Staring at her, he pushed his hands in his pockets, outwardly watchful but inside so charmed by this woman that he wondered how he could keep her at a distance. With his voice even and his expression bland, he said, "No, I don't mind if Girl has time off. I'll tell her to stay with the other dogs. She won't take any notice of you."

As if offended, Ella looked down her nose at him. "I know how to give orders in a definite voice. You taught me well and I'm really quite good with the dogs now."

He shook his head, unable to keep his expression stern. "Your voice doesn't matter to a deaf dog. Girl obeys signals."

Ella glanced at Girl. "What's the command to stay?"

"A flat palm. Come is to tap the leg. Go is to point. Other than that, she reads body language."

"I think it might be rather convenient to be a dog and deaf."

He nodded. "Very perceptive." Girl, although well trained, could be the very devil when she found questionable smells to roll in or wanted to chase small, furry animals. At those times she used her deafness to advantage. "If she doesn't want to know what I want, she refuses to look at me."

Ella caught his gaze and glanced away. She and Girl had much in common. Cal lifted his hand and made a circling movement with his arm, which meant Girl needed to do a round up. She realized he meant the other dogs and before he got her into trouble, he indicated with an upraised palm that he meant her to stay with them.

"Very clever." Ella lifted her hair off her damp neck. The knot had loosened. One tendril clung to her skin. "Even I understood that instruction."

Perspiration shaped her gown to her body. This woman who sweated over the land, chased sheep at night, and didn't mind being seen not at her best was unutterably desirable. A trail of perspiration wandered from her throat to her cleavage. He breathed out slowly. "She'll stay."

He walked off, wishing he didn't want Ella. Doubtless he'd been too long without a woman. Betsy had been perfect for a man who didn't intend to settle down. She'd been readily available, she didn't talk when he was tired or disgruntled, and she didn't spend his money. She didn't want anything from him other than his presence, or so he had thought. When she'd heard he intended to leave, she'd indicated that she had hoped he would be her ticket to a better life. She'd wanted to leave with him.

He'd doubted she'd loved him, despite her protestations, and he knew she would be a drain on his resources, mental and monetary. More logical was to make her a gift of the money he had after she said she could make a go on her own in the millinery business. He had no cause to disbelieve her. She'd neither been a drinker nor a dreamer.

A business of one's own was the most worthy cause a person could have, in his opinion. Some found independence by sheer hard work. Some managed to be born into the right family. He, who had worked hard and who had been born the heir to a grand estate, had not been trusted to make business decisions. Therefore, he had left to pursue his own worthy cause.

He strolled back into the shearing shed. If he increased his shearing rate, perhaps he could leave the Beaufort Station sooner and forget the too appealing Miss Ella faster.

He sighed. He could do the first, but the second seemed not at all likely.

* * * *

Edward stared out of the carriage window, again impressed by the southern valley area. He'd rarely seen this land brown and dry. Although the entire colony had borne the six-year drought, the hilly pastures here seemed not to have suffered as badly as inland.

Along the main road, cows stood under trees, swishing their tails contentedly, and newly shorn sheep grazed. Kangaroos ran from the scrub and disappeared into the leafy camouflage.

The carriage heated. Sam snored beside him. The old fool should have stayed at Farvista, where he could sleep all day and not annoy people. Edward began to feel hot and tired and older than Moses. He leaned out of the carriage window, hoping for a fresh sea breeze. His previous journeys to the city had not seemed to take so long.

Ahead, a pack of border collies raced hither and thither across the road. The coachman slowed. Edward made a sound of disgust. The dogs should have been working, not gamboling their lives away. Sam stirred and opened his eyes, moving along the seat and glancing out the same window.

"Are we there?" he asked in a voice like a rasp. They'd planned to stop in Noarlunga for the night.

"Maybe another hour," Edward said through his teeth. "We're being held up by dogs on the road."

One of the dogs streaked past the carriage after a rabbit. The rabbit wheeled, veered across the road, and dashed under a wire fence. The dog leaped over the fence in pursuit. "Girl," Edward said to himself. "Sam, that's Girl. Damn it, she knows the carriage but she didn't stop." He yelled to the dog but she wouldn't hear him. "Sam," he repeated, beating his fist on the outside of the carriage door to let the driver know he wanted to stop. "That was Girl."

"Looked like her," Sam said in a strange voice as the carriage lurched to a halt. "But them collies all have similar markings."

"The dog went onto that property. We can ask in there."

"We can ask what?"

Edward clamped his lips, staring out the carriage window, trying to sight the dog through the trees. In what looked like a small orchard, a blue-gowned worker and a fair-haired child were carrying buckets of water to the trees. The child dragged her bucket, bumping out liquid with every step. "We could ask for a glass of cool water."

"We got more'n a gallon here, iffen you should want to wet your mouth. If you was wanting to know the whereabouts of a certain young man and you found him, what would you be wanting to say to him?"

"I would want to ask a certain young man what he was doing on that holding for three months while at home..."

"You know the answer. You told him he could leave if he weren't satisfied. If the owner there is giving him the run of the place, that's why he'd be there."

Edward narrowed his eyes. "You know that was Girl, don't you?"

"Coulda been. She ignored you the same as she always did." Sam's mouth softened. "Mr. Charlton's the only person she heeds."

Edward rapped on the carriage door. "Drive on," he called in a strangely husky voice to the coachman.

* * * *

While Girl waited for him on the bank, Cal swam across the river and back again. He cooled off but didn't manage to exhaust his desire for Ella. On the way back to the homestead, a faint trail of smoke from the Aborigines' cooking fire tainted the dusky sky and the muttered yabbering of the natives carried through the trees. As he passed the woolshed, he noticed a crack of light through the door. Alert, he tied his shirt around his waist and walked up the ramp. At first he could only see the lit oil lamp. Then he spotted Ella. She stared at the piled wool bales.

"Counting your profits already?" He leaned against the doorframe.

"Oh." Startled, she put her hand on her heart and turned. "I wanted to see how much we had, but I don't suppose it does any good. It simply makes me feel better to know that this amount of wool has already been clipped."

He moved inside the shed. The lamplight gave her a shapely silhouette. The outline of her hair looked gold and her face was shaded in mystery. His blood raced through his body. He slowly moved toward her, seeing nothing but the glow in her eyes and the gentle curve of her cheek. His heart pounded. His good intentions died. He wanted her in his arms and he wanted her mouth on his. He wanted her under him.

He reached out and grabbed her into his embrace.

"Oh, dear life," she whispered, sliding her arms around his neck. She stretched her body to fit with his.

For a moment he held her pressed against him, experiencing the softness of her womanly curves and the fact that she had no misgivings. The warmth of her response made him ache with desire. She didn't tease, she didn't bat her eyelashes, and she didn't try to strike a deal before letting him touch her.

He dropped his mouth across hers, needing a tender moment. A few minutes of sensitivity on his part would no doubt satisfy him as much as giving in to his baser needs.

However, his need arose and hardened instantly. He opened her lips with his, tasted inside her mouth, and tried to remember his last thought. He lost all coherence. Backing her up against the wool bales, he used his body as persuasion. Never in his life had he taken advantage of an innocent. Well aware of his strength and size, he usually let the woman of the moment set the pace.

With his lust foremost, he wondered if he would let her go if she fought him. She didn't fight. She clutched his buttocks as if she couldn't have him against her firmly enough or long enough. Groaning, he lifted her onto the nearest wool bale. She reacted with surprise and expectance. Girl watched him with her tail slowly wagging. Pointing to the door, he waited for her to walk outside, then he swung up beside Ella, irrevocably drawn by her soft smile. His caution dead and his pulse erratic, he gathered her against him.

She settled her palms on his chest, nestling her face into his neck. She sighed. His hands stroked her down her spine to her delightfully rounded behind, which he cupped, easing her into his pelvis. He wanted this woman with a hunger that astounded him. His body responded to his urge, heating. He rubbed his cheek across her hair, hesitant but determined.

She leaned back and examined his face, reaching up a hand to cup his cheek. Pleasure and confidence glowed in her eyes. His breath shortened. He'd known from their first kiss he could have her. From the start she responded to some unknown quality of his. A link between him and anyone was rare, but without words he had rapport with her. This woman was a rare prize. He wished he had the right to her.

His lips met hers. She tasted as sweet as she looked. He rolled slightly, taking her with him. The jute bed was coarse and the stench of lanolin was pervasive, but lust conquered all. His legs separated hers and he tugged her blouse out of the waistband of her skirt. Her flesh slid hot and smooth beneath his hand, exactly as he had imagined. Her mouth moved on his, parting. Her tongue teased against his lips. The tickle caused a fire in his belly. He wanted her and badly.

Rolling again, he settled on top, shifting his hand to her breast. His thumb rubbed over her hard, puckered nipple. She made a long, low sound. He lifted his mouth from hers, kissing her chin and her throat. She arched back. Urgent, he slipped his hand from her breast and began unbuttoning her blouse. A fine muslin chemise separated her flesh from his eyes. He pulled a blue ribbon at the neck and tugged at the gathering. The material loosened, she wriggled, and he exposed her fine, pale breasts.

With a husky growl, he pressed his mouth to the soft bulk, holding one in each hand. His lips slid to the side, trailing to her pale pink nipple. He moved his tongue across and around. She clutched at his hair, digging her fingers into his scalp, offering murmurs of encouragement. Knowing exactly what he wanted, he covered her nipple with his mouth, dragged and teased, gaining pleasure from giving pleasure.

He couldn't mistake her invitation. She enjoyed what he did and showed him with her hands, cupping his head, stroking his neck and ears, digging her fingers into his shoulders. Her knees lifted and her feet rested on his calves. Perhaps she hadn't done this before but she had the best of female instincts. She had the best of female attributes, humor, intelligence, and ability—everything he wanted in a woman.

He liked her and he desired her. What could be more perfect in a male/female relationship? Involvement, perhaps, but he'd never seen the point of emotional involvement. Nor had he ever let himself lust to this extent. He again lifted his mouth to hers, rubbing the skin of his chest against the wondrous lushness of hers.

Her palms flattened on his back. When he glanced at her face, he saw that her eyes had taken on a sleepy, seductive appearance. Her lips were fuller, redder. With an almost languid grace she gave him kiss for kiss, appearing to indicate that wherever he led, she would follow.

However, she'd given him a lead he couldn't help but follow. She kept him snugly within the clasp of her thighs—not that he had any intention of chastely lying by her side. He meant to be between her legs but he wanted to be thrusting inside her. He moved his hand to the hem of the skirt stretched tight over her lifted knees. He pushed the fabric, sliding his hand down her thigh to her bare behind.

His insides clenched. Although few women wore underdrawers, he imagined she would. Using his palm, he absorbed the delight of her naked flesh, her satin skin, lightly muscled. Lifting a little, he bunched her skirt over her hips. She now lay beneath him bare to the waist and completely exposed at the chest, exactly as he'd imagined her too many times. He only needed to undo four trouser buttons and he could sate his desire.

He glanced at her face. She had closed her eyes.

"Look at me," he said in a low voice.

Her eyes slid open. "It's real, isn't it? What we're doing?"

"We're not doing anything yet."

"I suppose we should stop before...?"

He challenged her with his gaze. "Before?"

"Before I find out why people get married."

"Finding pleasure has little to do with marriage."

"In your world, perhaps. In my world, women who beget children without the benefit of clergy are forever shunned."

"I'll beget no child on you."

She closed her eyes again. "You're asking my permission to go farther."

He clenched his jaw. He'd never meant to ask permission, but in his heart of hearts he'd known he couldn't take what he wanted from this young lady. Whether or not they conceived a child, he would leave her unchaste, taking with him her best bargaining tool for marriage. Desperate he might be, but not mindless. "I'm not asking your permission. I'm telling you that I won't be doing anything that would cause a pregnancy. I will go as far as I can but not there."

She focused on his face. "Such feelings I have for you," she said in a shaky voice. "I want... Well, I don't yet know what I want, but you're making me want it far more." She gave a helpless laugh. "I want to know your body. I think about it and I ache. I crave and I don't know what I crave, though I know where I crave."

He pressed his lips across hers. "My body is yours. Touch me. Anywhere. But start here where *I* crave."

He turned aside and took her hand from his back, sliding it to the juncture between his legs. The anticipation made him grow tighter, harder than he'd been before. He hoped he wouldn't make an idiot of himself, but if he couldn't have fulfillment inside her, he would take any other substitute.

She chose to rest her hand where he indicated. After a moment's hesitation, her fingers explored, finding his length, his width. He let out a breath, afraid to move, hoping she wouldn't stop. Her touch didn't ease him but at the moment he could only choose stimulation, anything other than being told she'd rejected him in favor of her purity.

He stopped her when he knew he couldn't take any more without wanting to undo his trousers.

She stared into his eyes. Her lashes lowered.

He rested his forehead on her shoulder. "I think about your body, too. But the difference is that I know what you want." He couldn't suppress a wry smile.

She turned her head aside and gave an embarrassed laugh. "I'm beginning to know what I want, too."

His throat tightened. Her face was lovely in the glow from the lamp, and her hair had spread beneath her head. She combined the mystery of the female with the known quality of sex. He shifted his hand from beneath her buttocks and smoothed his palm across her triangle of hair. She gasped. For a moment he cupped her there, feeling her heat. Then, with a pounding heart, he slid his fingers into her moisture. Her head snapped back, her eyes widened and she breathed through her mouth. Her face looked pale and her eyes dark. She moistened her lips. Her legs parted farther.

Using light, teasing strokes, he encouraged her to respond to his touch. Apparently she enjoyed what he did and just as apparently, he didn't bring her to fulfillment. He could tell she was fully aroused but she didn't seem to know how to let go. She reached out with her hands and ran her thumbs over his nipples. And suddenly arched and called out his name.

He stilled his hand. He breathed harder than she. Her completion pleased him. He gathered her into his arms while her breathing steadied, while the pounding of her heart calmed. And found that he didn't want to let her go. "I would like to lie with you throughout the night," he said in a whisper.

"That can't be." She pulled back from him.

"No."

"You did know what I wanted."

"You see that as a fault?"

"I see it as a sign that you are experienced with women."

He sat up. "I'm not a philanderer, if that's what you ask."

"I am glad to hear that." She tugged at her skirts, covering her legs.

"Nor am I a marrying man," he said carefully.

She hid her expression by buttoning her blouse. "I don't want marriage. I need advice for this place far more."

He noted that her fingers had stilled. "You let me pleasure you because you want me to help you?"

For a moment she remained silent, then she fixed her gaze on his, smiling lightly. "A favor for a favor. Isn't that how you think? As I was saying, you might know if I should plant feed or if I should leave an extra pasture for the sheep." She smoothed her hair and swung off the wool bale. "Sleep well," she said casually as she picked up her oil lamp. She left him in the dark.

He gritted his teeth. He wouldn't sleep until he'd eased himself, and if she knew anything about men, she would know that she'd left him fully aroused. Making his way to the door, he rubbed the heel of his palm on his forehead.

She didn't know anything about men other than the one thing he'd taught her. A favor for a favor.

Chapter 7

Edward slept better that night than he had for the past three months despite his hotel room in Noarlunga being no bigger than the one in Robe. He ate his breakfast with more pleasure. The appreciable difference in his mood came about because at last he knew the whereabouts of Charlton. Sam smirked and said, "I told yer so," at least twenty times.

Before Edward's carriage left for his final destination, Adelaide, he took a stroll past the local police station, the butcher, the baker, a supplies' shop, and a grocery to reach his destination, the bank. He merely had to mention his name to be ushered into the manager's office, a pokey little room with a window scarcely the breadth of a man's shoulders.

"Mr. Canavan," he began, taking the chair offered. "If you can accommodate me, I'm interested in an investment." He stretched his legs as he stared around the room, noting the shelves cluttered with loose pages and notebooks. He hoped the man's bookkeeping was better than his sense of order.

"Land?" Mr. Canavan, a slim young man with an overlarge forehead, asked. "Or a business? I can help you with either."

"I saw a parcel of land on the way into town last night, a place the other side of the Onkaparinga River. An orchard by the look of it. A holding called Beaufort."

Mr. Canavan leaned forward. "That would be the Beaufort place. Right up your alley, you might say. The owner died six months back and the heirs would likely sell for the right price."

"The price couldn't be righter than when they have a buyer. What price would they expect?"

"The mortgage needs paying." Mr. Canavan stood, walked to one of his shelves, and pulled out a packet of papers tied with a ribbon. "The discrepancy between that and the value would be in the vicinity of one to two hundred pounds. I'd say the owners would accept four hundred pounds with the stock, more or less."

Edward tapped his cheek. "I don't need the place, not at this time. I will, however, think on it."

And think he did. He left the town wondering why Charlton had hidden himself on a steeply mortgaged property a minute fraction of the size of the land he would one day inherit. He wondered how long Charlton had been there. However, for the first time in three months, Edward not only knew where his grandson was, but he also had an excuse to visit the area regularly, having shown interest in the small parcel of land.

Not many young men could leave a place like Farvista and be happy elsewhere. Had his grandson remained patient longer, Edward would have signed Farvista over to him, but during a long-running argument over one of Charlton's many ideas, Charlton had said, "I don't need your name to succeed," by which he meant, "I don't need you."

Hurt, of course, Edward had retaliated by saying, "In that case, you won't need my money either."

Perhaps Charlton needed neither. But hasty-tempered Edward needed Charlton.

Property owned alone was of no use to anyone.

* * * *

Ella sat opposite Cal during breakfast. Justifying her reaction after his expert lovemaking last night, she barely glanced at him. As a confirmed spinster, she couldn't afford to take the episode seriously. She couldn't marry; therefore, a momentary encounter might well be accepted as a favor for a favor.

Although she could control her eyes, her insides thrummed with awareness. Beneath his clean but wrinkled shirt was a hard male body composed of the long, shifting muscles of his back, a rocklike abdomen, and tight buttocks. For one moment her gaze met his. His expression, as unreadable as ever, nonetheless caused an ache inside her, a yearning she couldn't control.

She breathed out, finding her toast suddenly too dry to swallow. Her first experience of his body had to be her last. Better she resist his attraction, for the man would leave in little more than a week and she would have no choice other than to forget him. She'd not been compromised, nor had he at this stage. Though he'd explored her body, she'd barely touched his. Better she didn't even consider doing so.

She cleared the breakfast table without knowing she had, without noticing that the men had left.

"Did Jed kill and skin those two lambs yet?" Rose asked in the kitchen.

Ella concentrated on her hands in the dish of hot water where she washed the thick white plates. She blinked, remembering that on the second Thursday of each month, Rose and Vianna took a trip to Noarlunga for supplies. "He put them in the trap and they've been sitting covered with wet burlap since before breakfast. Not five minutes ago, I saw him harness one of the chestnuts, and if you don't mind, I asked him to tie the other one, too. You can get the hostler at the hotel to change them over before you come back. Both need exercise, and I won't have time today."

"Of course I don't mind. I'm only glad you'll serve lunch for me. Are you sure you don't want us to stay and help wash the breakfast plates?"

"The sooner you leave, the sooner you'll be back. I'd rather wash plates than prepare the evening meal. I need to get the seed potatoes planted today, and that will be a long job."

"After the butcher buys the meat, I'll be able to pay cash for the flour and sugar. That way I won't need to get into a discussion about our overdue account at the grocery."

Ella shook her head, smiling. "You have the knack of twisting that poor, sweet grocer around your little finger. Any man, in fact."

Rose gave an unconcerned glance. "Not any man. Only those I don't care about." She checked the bread dough she had left for Ella to bake for lunch and went to fetch her hat and gloves.

By the time she returned, Ella had almost finished washing the dishes. She'd been mulling over Rose's last words, hearing the slightly bitter tone. "Have you met a man you care about?" She tried to sound diffident rather than curious.

Rose shrugged. She wore a black straw pillbox hat tied with a wide black bow. A bunch of black and white feathers curled high at the back, and with her blond hair smartly arranged in a perfect knot, she looked truly elegant.

"Did something happen to you in the city that you didn't tell me about?"

Rose paused and took a deep breath. "Nothing I want to discuss." She smoothed on her black kid gloves.

"Did you fall in love, Rose?"

"Love! I met a fine, handsome young man who needed a wife with money. He made no bones about his poverty. While I was trying not to be *too* flattered by his proposal, Papa died. Then I realized I didn't have the inheritance I thought. A woman with younger siblings and no money is of no use to an ambitious man."

"If that was his attitude, you're better off without him."

Rose tightened her mouth. "Vianna," she called. "Are you ready?"

Vianna clattered into the kitchen. "I wish we didn't have to take the meat with us. It stinks. Oh, and my shoes are growing tighter. I'm going to need a new pair soon." She stared with significance at Ella.

"I don't know how we can make you stop growing. Stop feeding you, I suspect," Ella said, escorting her sisters to the door.

"That's mean. I'm sure you buy new shoes when yours begin to pinch," Vianna said over her shoulder as she ran to the trap waiting by the stables.

Ella's gaze met Rose's. Rose nodded. "We'll have to."

When the trap left, Ella dealt with the laundry but not as quickly as she would have liked, for she had a bundle of shirts from the shearers to pole out, too. Finally, with time to collect water for the next day's laundry, she turned her gaze to the stable pump. Frowning, she hurried over to the stockman, who had dug a trench from the pump and along the side of the track, almost as far as the house. "Jed, whatever are you doing?"

The stockman lifted his sweaty black face. "'elp Missy," he said proudly. "Mr. Cal, 'e say trees need ribber so Missy don't carry buckets no more."

"Ribber? River?"

He indicated with his hands. "'ere." Running his bare toe along the dry soil, he marked out a path, showing where a trail would veer to the orchard. The line branched off between each row. "'ere. Ebbrywhere."

"And if I just let the pump run long enough, this ditch will fill?"

"Jed pump ebbry morning and no more Missy buckets."

"It's brilliant, Jed. How clever you are. There's quite a natural slope here. Did you think of this yourself?"

He shook his head, still grinning. "Mr. Cal."

Ella debated going to thank Cal but decided she ought to keep away from him. Aside from that, if she interrupted him in the shed, the other men would stop to listen. Had he wanted a song and dance performed, he wouldn't be Cal.

She left Jed to his chore, knowing that if the idea worked, she would save many hours each week. This would make dipping possible for her and Jed, perhaps next Monday. She knew the regular spot Papa used in the billabong paddock.

After inspecting the dipping trench, she noted that the wooden lining had lifted in places and the sloped run on either end had lost a few rungs. By the time she returned to the house, morning smoke-oh had ended. She put the bread on to bake, taking this quiet time to dust the house. When the delicious aroma of the cooked loaves filled the air, she put them on the table to cool. Then she collected the shirts and cloths from the line.

Finally, she found time to brush her hair into as neat a knot as she could and set the cold meat and loaves on the table. She rang the dinner triangle. As the men arrived, she spooned relish into dishes and sliced tomatoes and onions. Her eyes wet and with a slight sniffle of self pity, she took these outside. She sat, blinking, with not another thing to do.

The bread had been cut neatly and the meat sliced into the thinnest and most elegant portions she'd seen since Papa had been in his best mood. "Oh, my," she said, clasping her hands in front. "To whom do I owe my thanks?"

"Ned did the bread and Cal did the meat," Alf said complacently. "Two proper ladies' men they are, that's for sure. Didn't know we had such talent on the team."

"Stands to reason," Benji said, his mouth disdainful. "Men who can shear have to be able to cut a fine line. Should we serve ourselves?"

Ella nodded. The less formality, the less work for her, but not only that—the constraint eased. The men talked freely and entertainingly. While avoiding Cal's gaze, Ella heard everything she did and didn't want to know about sheep, shearing, packing, classing, and wool auctions.

Cal maintained they needed their own auctions in the colony instead of having to send the wool to Victoria. He sat at the other end of the table, completely at ease. Unfortunately, every glance she took at him made her want him more. He filled an emptiness inside her she hadn't known existed.

In the early afternoon, the shoppers finally returned. Vianna brandished her new shoes with a pout of her mouth. "They fit but they're sturdy enough to march to Noarlunga and back a hundred times without showing any sign of wear."

"I would have loved to have bought jeweled slippers for our princess," Rose said with a droll glance. "But I didn't have a choice. They only had boots in her size." She folded the wrapping neatly. "I couldn't pay cash for our groceries because the lambs were small, the butcher said, and by the pound he could only pay us four shillings for both. I used the account—again." She shook her head. "I would have been too embarrassed to offer four shillings when we spent one pound, two and six."

"And those men who stopped in here the other day, the fat one and the thin one, they were in Noarlunga, too." Vianna's curls swung onto her face when she jerked off her bonnet. "They came over and petted the chestnuts. It's funny how much they like horses, and it's even stranger how much the horses don't like them. Judy bit the thin one. I didn't blame her. He still smells."

"You smell. He stinks," Ella contradicted automatically.

Vianna lifted up her nose and flounced out of the room.

"I didn't mean she stinks," Ella said, staring in dismay at the empty doorway.

"She's cross because she wanted pretty shoes, not practical boots. I told her she could have what she wants when we live in the city."

As Ella put a portion of the new flour in a small sack for Jed, she wondered if they weren't making too much of living in the city. She doubted their lives would change dramatically with a simple shift of abode. They would still have to scrimp, and they would still have to worry about money until she found a job.

After she had finished ironing the men's shirts, she inspected Jed's ditch. She experimented by pumping the water until a flow filled the nearer section, and she then watched the stream travel about thirty feet before soaking into the earth. She wasn't sure the idea would work, but she didn't have time to fill the whole length.

"Watering would be better with a hose," Cal said from behind her. His dog nudged between them. "But you don't have one. Failing that, a pipe would be good, too."

"We don't have that either."

"We, er... I know of a house with bricked half-drains for the run-off after the rain. That would be your next best bet, but I think once the water has run along the trench a few times, and the mud has been baked dry in the sun, the stream will flow quite well."

"I'm sure you're right." She moved to the other side of Cal to continue watching the water flow. "You usually are, blast it."

His dog moved between them again. He patted her without seeming to notice. Ella glanced Girl and noticed a smug, doggy grin.

"Girl is quite a competitive female." Ella stepped back to her original place beside Cal, and again the dog separated them.

"She likes to have my attention. She has no one else." Cal squinted at his dog, as if thinking. The meal's triangle rang. He turned, then he stopped, catching Ella's glance with a smoky stare. "As you can imagine, deaf working dogs are not in great demand. The stable master wanted to put her down. I wanted to see if I could train her. I proved my point, but I failed Girl. I should have remembered that a trainer's job is to teach self-reliance to his pupil. Instead, I gave her dependence. I won't make that same mistake again. Independence is too precious a thing to be ignored."

Ella stood, watching him stroll away. Independence was easily enough achieved for a male. For her, a woman, she needed money first.

* * * *

Ella woke just after dawn, yawned and stretched, rolled out of bed, and pattered barefooted to the kitchen. She filled her bedroom jug with heated water, which she took back to her bedroom.

After tipping one cupful of water into her basin she soaped herself all over. Then, she stood in her basin on the floor. Her breath eased out with pure pleasure as she poured the rest of the water over her body, letting a waterfall flow from her shoulders to her toes. This shower of water in the morning always woke her and put her in a state of true contentment.

After dressing in one of Mama's old, faded, hand-me-down gowns, she lit the fire under the laundry copper. With Rose she prepared the day's breakfast.

The men arrived clean, neat, and not too talkative, except for Ned. "Sky's gray," he said, morosely. "If the rains come, we won't be shearing, not if the wool's wet."

"Predictin' don't do no good," Alf answered. "We'll just wait and see."

By the time breakfast finished, black clouds hovered over the hills. Ella put a small load of laundry in the copper. The boil began just as thunder rumbled. She poled out the steaming wash as fat droplets of rain hit the ground, skidding every which way in the dry dust. Before filling the clothesline, she waited for a pause in the downpour.

The holding yard began to empty as the men pulled inside as many sheep as possible. Spotting yesterday's shear sheltering in a white huddle near the woolshed, her skin prickled. She rubbed at the goose bumps on her arms while she waited for Jed to arrive with the next mob.

More than uneasy, she sprinted inside for an umbrella. With her skirts gathered in one hand and the umbrella in the other, she raced through muddy puddles past the woolshed, past the curious sheep, and along the stirring billabong. She ran through the scrub to the river and along the riverbank to the Aborigines' camp. She might have dashed through or past because she raced quite a distance and found nothing, no sign a camp had ever existed. Numbering at least twenty, the native men, women, and children had disappeared. She sped around in circles until, finally out of breath, she let the tip of her umbrella rest in the sand while she leaned over, gasping for air.

The tumbling river reflected the heavy black sky. Eyes hot and chest leaden, she hauled the umbrella over her dripping head and clumped back to the homestead. After stamping most of the mud from her shoes outside the woolshed door, she finally entered, her smile watery. Only two of the yarded sheep remained unshorn. Tommy took one and Frank the other. The rest of the men, in various attitudes of relaxation, ankles crossed, hip shot, leaning against the wall or sitting on a rail, turned in a synchronized motion toward her.

"Good morning," she said, inelegantly wiping her wrist under her nose. "I see you've run out of work. For now, I can't supply you with any more, but I'll leave soon and round up the sheep for tomorrow." She took a deep breath. "You all may as well go into town for the day."

"The sheep'd be too wet to shear anyhow." Frank frowned. "Ned was right. He oughta be a weather forecaster. He'd make more money that way, a'cos he's a mite slow as a shearer." He grinned at the mustachioed lothario.

The men didn't move. She pushed strings of wet hair off her face. No doubt she looked like a crazy woman, holding an umbrella over her head indoors. Slowly, she lowered the shelter, watching droplets of water plop on the floor.

Cal straightened. "Where's Jed?"

"I don't know." Her voice cracked. "They've gone walkabout. The camp has disappeared. Jed didn't tell me he was going."

"Does he usually?"

"I'm not usually the one who has to worry about this." Slumped, she indicated the woolshed that already had upward of eighty bales of wool standing near the loading bay.

"Right," Cal stepped forward. "Since I won't be shearing and since I don't make money when I don't shear, I'll come with you to round up the sheep. That is, if you let me borrow one of your stock horses."

"Of course," Ella answered, feeling the bones in her face disappear. She blinked hard. "You'd be very welcome."

"I don't want to go into town." Ned tightened his belt. "Nothin' to do there. I'll take one of them Clydesdales and go out with you as well."

"Me, too." Frank grinned. "That'll be a rare treat, riding one of them sofas."

Ella's throat clogged with emotion. "I'll just go and change." Infused with new energy by these generous shearers, she turned and dashed off to the homestead.

"Jed's gone walkabout." She passed Rose in the kitchen. "We're going out to get the sheep, Cal and Ned and Frank and I. I don't know how long we'll be."

The next time she raced past Rose, her sister held Papa's hat and his oil slicker in her hands. "Be careful." She looked serious. "I don't want you to catch a cold."

The horses plodded through the drizzling rain to the first paddock. "The sheep from the farther reaches are here." Cal edged his horse nearer to hers. "Jed brought them in yesterday. He put those we've shorn into the long paddock. You won't have to go to the trouble of collecting them again before the dipping."

"It's a shame he's gone. Lately, he has had some amazingly progressive ideas."

He ignored her irony. "By my calculations, you would have about three thousand more head to shear, and if we collect as many today as we can, I can help collect the rest on Sunday. I don't plan to go to church on my day of rest."

Ella and the team rounded up well over two thousand sheep and put them in the paddocks around the billabong so that, with the stragglers they expected to find, they would be watered and yet still close enough to transfer to the woolshed paddock. Ella wished she had Cal's head for organizing. Failing that, she wished Papa had left instructions in his will, but perhaps his plan had never been this one. The last time he'd been present for shearing, he'd had three stockmen. The sheep could have been brought in and taken out any time.

However, shearing had to be halted until the next day. Ned, the forecaster, thought the weather on Saturday would be fine. "They'll dry out overnight," he said with confidence. "Reckon it'd be close to ninety already and it's bound to be hotter tomorrow."

Although she would have liked to bring in the last of the sheep, Ella didn't have time that day. Nor could she dig her potato patch in wet soil.

"Though it probably doesn't matter," Rose said while they prepared dinner. "With luck we'll be gone before the harvest anyway."

* * * *

That night, Ella stirred with sweaty dreams. She woke in time to see the predawn, ghostly haze. Outside the magpies warbled their morning songs and a flock of corellas screeched in delight about their morning raid on the fruit trees.

She yawned and stretched and rubbed her eyes. A new day; an old loneliness. Cal wouldn't touch her again, fearing she expected marriage. Her dreams of his mouth on hers and his confident hands on her body were merely that, dreams.

She fumbled out of bed, struggled into her dressing gown, and made her way to the outside amenity. After that, she took her warm morning wash and, freshened, she dressed.

The meat scraps from the previous evening's meal sat under a cloth on the kitchen table. One dog yapped a greeting as she walked toward their enclosure. The night before they'd been as restless as she, barking at the full moon, no doubt.

Again, she yawned as she set their dish inside their yard. Each dog had been tethered on a long rope for added security. Papa had insisted. This morning the ropes were tangled. "Dancing the maypole last night, were you?" She was answered with wagging tails, doggy smiles, and an attempted lick on her hand.

She untangled the ropes and set the dogs free. They raced to the food, whuffling happily. For a moment she stood and watched. The life of a dog seemed uncomplicated—food, work, sleep—just as her life would be when Cal left. She pushed her hand through her hair, taking the weight back from her face and staring forlornly across at the stable paddock.

She couldn't see the Clydesdales. With rain possible, likely one of the men had put them under shelter last night. She wandered over to the stables. No friendly nickering greeted her. She heard no shifting hooves. She smelled chaff and oats, horse and leather. She saw farming implements, saddles and harness, but no horses.

Standing, hands on hips, she frowned, worrying her bottom lip. Outside, she scanned the surrounding area. Not even a bird tweeted. With a fluttering in her chest, she inspected the paddock fence. The posts stood, sturdy and implacable. The gate was shut. Although tracks in the dust indicated hooves and booted feet, yesterday the men had saddled and used the horses. The tracks told her nothing.

Her entire body began to shake. Alf had taken on a new shearer for the first time in years, a man who knew more about her station, her horses, and her craving body than anyone else in the world. This man whose surname she didn't know had shown interest in her when no other had. He knew she had no support and too much pride.

With her heart resounding loudly in her chest, she scrambled to the men's quarters and then stood hesitant and short of air by the door. Inside, the floorboards creaked. Every nerve in her body stretched. The door eased open.

Cal stood there, alert, familiar, eyebrows raised in query.

She'd never seen such a glorious sight in her entire, fearful life. Hand at her throat, she ached with relief. He wore trousers only. His wavy dark hair was mussed with sleep and faint stubble shaded his jaw.

"I heard you with the dogs," he said, perhaps in explanation for his state of undress. He moved out of the quarters, shutting the door quietly behind him.

"I don't know if I'm fussing about nothing," she murmured, unable to meet his questioning gaze. Someday, she would forgive herself for thinking a man as honorable as Cal had stolen her horses, but right now she deserved nothing but contempt for distrusting him. "But I can't find the horses."

"Which horses?" He rubbed his hand in his hair as if to tidy himself and took her farther from the quarters. Clearly, he didn't want the other men to hear them talking. "What's the time?"

"Almost dawn. Well, dawn." She noted the orange hue of sunrise creeping from behind the hills. "I can't find *any* of the horses."

"The Clydesdales are in the stable paddock. I saw them last night."

"They're not there, nor in the stables. None of them. The chestnuts and the stock horses can't open the doors to their stalls, let alone a heavy stable door. Nor can Miffy. And the Clydesdales couldn't leap over the paddock fence."

He rubbed his hair again, but the crow's nest he seemed to be aiming for settled into crushed velvet. "Let's take another look."

Comforted by his presence, she watched as he inspected the stables and the paddock. He also carefully inspected the tracks by the gate. "Here. A side-worn riding heel," he said, squatting down and running his forefinger over the print in the dust. "Not mine. Not Frank's or Ned's. Too large to be yours."

"And Jed doesn't wear shoes."

Standing, he scanned the ground ahead. "Come with me."

She hadn't noticed the scuffled tracks leading down to the river.

"I can pick out five or six horses in this group," he said, slowly following the traces. "And two men. As none of the shearers left the quarters last night…" He stopped, hands on his hips, and faced her. "Your horses have been stolen, Ella."

Chapter 8

Ella couldn't form a lucid reply. She stood, staring at the man whose advice she relied on far too much, the man she expected to fix all her problems, and realized she had to face reality. Running the station was now impossible. Turning, she walked off, heading back toward the homestead, desperate to be alone with her whirling thoughts.

Cal swiftly moved in front of her, stopping her in her tracks. "So, do you think one of your neighbors will let me borrow a horse?"

"They don't know you." She examined the tall, dark, handsome stranger, whose full name she had never asked. "Cal. Just a single, anonymous name. Just one. Do you have another?"

"A few others. Alfred. Langdon." He scrutinized her face. "I need a quicker way to follow the thieves than on foot, and I need to leave while the tracks are still fresh."

She shook her head. "That's a job for the police. Mr. Lannock will be here soon with the milk. I'll tell him that our horses have been stolen and ask him if he can inform the authorities."

"The matter is more urgent than that. The sooner I leave, the quicker I'll catch up with them. Unlike them, I don't have to match my pace with a couple of obstinate Clydesdales."

"Of course. The Clydesdales. If you don't get them back, you won't be able to leave when you finish shearing." Her mouth twisted.

"And if we don't get your horses back, you won't be able to continue your station work."

She stared over his shoulder to the paddocks dotted with the white, newly shorn sheep, to the homestead with the spiral of smoke issuing from the chimney, and then to the road beyond that followed the seashore to the city. "What work? You only need to shear the sheep we brought in yesterday and then you will have to leave. And so will my sisters and I. We won't be staying. I've done my best to manage with one stockman, and I was willing to try with no stockman, but I can't cope when if it's not one thing, it's the next." She firmed her face. "A life on the land is not for me."

His eyebrows lowered. "How can you leave? What will you do for money?"

"We'll sell the sheep." She evaded his gaze.

"No one will buy five or more thousand sheep in a drought year. You'd be lucky to give them away."

"They can die out here for all I care." Her voice cracked. "Each day we live on this thankless property we run up more debt. We can't pay the money we owe until we get the wool payment. So, until then we will comply with Rose's godmother's request to stay with her." Clamping her lips, she turned.

"Ella." He stopped her by a grip on her shoulders. "If you get your horses back and if you sell your carriage pair, you'll have enough money to buy your own house in the city. Your horses are your greatest asset."

She gave him a hard, cynical smile. "A couple of horses will bring perhaps twenty pounds. I couldn't find a hovel for less than a hundred and you know it."

"You would make at least two hundred guineas for that pair. I know someone who just last year bought a pair of grays not half as fine as your chestnuts and she paid two hundred. They're in great demand. All the ladies want matched pairs."

Her eyes fixed on his and her mouth dried. "Two hundred guineas? Are you sure?"

He nodded.

She swallowed. "In that case, I'll have to go out and bring them back."

"Not you. I."

"No. They're mine. Papa left them to me." Turning, she strode off to the homestead.

Cal dogged her footsteps. Unwilling to let him help, she ignored him. Within moments they reached the corner of the house, each as determined as the other. Then she heard the clop of hooves and the rattle of cans and saw the local dairyman turn his milk wagon through the front gate. With Cal, she waited until the horses clinked to the veranda.

"Good morning." Ella looked up at Mr. Lannock. She used a shaky hand to indicate the stable paddock. "We had horse thieves during the night, we think."

"Are you sure?" Mr. Lannock climbed off the driver's seat and dragged a can from the back. The container landed with a clatter. He stopped and stared at Ella with a concerned expression on his long, melancholy face. "Your horses could have wandered off. Them fences of yours are none too sturdy. I've been meaning to send John over to help Jed fix them."

"Cal—this is Cal Langdon by the way—overseer—repaired the stable paddock fence a week ago." She reddened with her mauled explanation as to why a stranger stood implacable by her side. "This morning he found tracks indicating that the horses were led away. I plan to get them back, make no mistake."

The older man reached over and shook Cal's hand. "Nathaniel Lannock." He pursed his lips at Ella. "And how do you expect to do that, Missy?" He planted his chapped fists on his hips.

"I'll send some men after the thieves." She shot Cal a silencing look.

"How, if they've taken your horses?"

"Perhaps I'll ask..." She cleared her throat. "If I can borrow a couple of yours."

Mr. Lannock nodded. "I'll do better than lend you a couple of horses. I'll send John and William."

"No need," Cal said, firming his jaw. "It's my job as overseer."

Lannock rubbed his bristled chin. "Maybe you're needed here."

"He's invaluable, just as John and Willie are invaluable at home. Thank you for your generous offer, but if we could borrow the horses that would be far more help than we ought to expect of you."

"Glad to be able to do something." Lannock's gaze flickered to Cal's bare chest.

"She woke me the moment she discovered the horses were missing." Cal spared Ella the awkwardness of an explanation for his state of undress.

Mr. Lannock came to his decision and, lifting his chin, said, "Hop up on the wagon, then, Langdon, and I'll take you back to my place to fetch the horses."

"I'll put on a shirt and shoes, if you don't mind waiting a minute or two." Grabbing the milk can, Cal hauled the weight to the back door.

Ella sighed with relief that Mr. Lannock had accepted Cal as the overseer. Her steadiness of character might be maligned in this very small community if Mr. Lannock jumped to erroneous conclusions about a young lady attended by a half-dressed man so early in the morning. The gossip would only be repeated with more relish if she accompanied that same man out into the bush for who knew how long.

The shearers had begun to stir, but Cal would doubtless offer them some explanation as to what had happened. Ella had barely entered the kitchen when she heard him and Mr. Lannock clatter down the driveway in the milk wagon.

"Our horses have been stolen," she said without preamble to Rose, who stood bent over the kitchen fire. "Cal is borrowing a couple more from the Lannocks, and we'll chase the thieves. When the police arrive, you must send them after us."

Rose glanced at her with disbelief. "Stolen? Who would steal our horses?"

"They took the Clydesdales, too, which is why Cal is coming along with me. I thought I should go alone because we lost five horses, and the shearers only lost two, but Mr. Lannock wouldn't have let me take his horses...and I don't have time to argue." Ella eyed Rose, hearing every objection without a word being spoken.

Rose slumped on a kitchen chair, staring at her clasped hands. With a sigh, she raised her face to Ella's. "You can't go after the thieves. What will you do if you find them? They won't take a bit of notice of a man and a young woman, and they certainly won't give back the horses simply because you ask."

"Should we not try just in case we fail?"

"I don't want you endangered. We need you, Vianna and I. Let Cal go alone. He could take Papa's rifle and—"

"Rose!" Ella said, shocked. "We can't expect a total stranger to risk himself for our horses. Until a few minutes ago, I didn't even know his full name."

"If he said he would..."

"He takes over far too often. And I can't let him. I am responsible for the land and the livestock. I won't relent, Rose. Since needs must, I'll take him with me, but I certainly won't leave the whole thing to him."

"And what if you need to stay out overnight?"

Ella shook her head. "He seems to think we can catch up with them quickly."

"But if not, you can't spend the night with the man."

"Cal wouldn't touch me," Ella said, her voice firm. "I gave him the opportunity, and he rejected me."

"You gave him the opportunity?"

Ella moved to the hall doorway. "The wasted opportunity, as it happens. I'm not even sure the man likes me as much as he likes telling me how to run my life. As far as I can tell, the efficiency of stations interests him more than desperate spinsters."

With no time to waste, she left to change into her riding clothes. Cal, elusive and mysterious, had saved her life, eased her workload, and done his best to teach her station work. She could trust him, none better. Yet, for one brief moment this morning, she had suspected him of having far more dastardly designs than lusting for her body—she had suspected him of ingratiating himself so he could steal the horses. Had he done so, he would have disappeared.

Perhaps she wished him gone. The man was too helpful, too willing, and growing far too necessary.

* * * *

Edward slowly climbed out of the carriage onto the gravel driveway. He and Sam had rested a day outside Adelaide and had left early this morning to avoid traveling during the heat of the day.

Although he hadn't sent word of his plans to Irene, Charlton's mother, he expected her to accommodate him. After all, he owned her fine mansion, a gracious building fronted by the city parks of Adelaide, and he had supported his daughter-in-law in luxury since the day she had married his son. He didn't need to rap on the door. The carriage had been heard. A maidservant ushered him and the silenced Sam into Irene's august presence.

"Edward! My dear. And Mr., er, um." She rose to her feet. Although in her middle forties, she had the waist of a seventeen-year-old and soft, white, youthful skin. Edward didn't doubt she used cosmetics, but none showed, and as usual she was impeccably dressed and groomed, her dark hair lifted in high curls.

"Just call him Sam. Or Mr. Edyvean. Not Mr. Erum."

"You look tired." Her face held no expression.

"I'm old. You'd look tired if you were my age." He indicated the chair to her. She sat again, straight-backed, her graceful white hands folded in her lap as he lowered himself to a plump sofa by the carved marble fireplace. Sam stood near the window awkwardly. "Sam, go to the gardener's cottage and see if they can put you up. Failing that, come back here and you can have the best guest bedroom."

Irene tightened her lips. "Bespeak a room for Mr. Edyvean in the coach house and make up Mr. Lynton's room." The young hovering maid stepped back to the doorway. "And bring us tea."

"No tea for me, ma'am. I'm more comfortable with the outside staff. Sides, I won't be getting no 'oliday like m'lud promised me if I have to stay where he can see me. I'm off to the coach house." With that, Sam backed out as if in the presence of royalty and disappeared.

Edward allowed himself to grin.

Irene raised her eyebrows. "You don't usually take a holiday at this time of the year. Surely this is your busiest season on the station."

"This year is different. I don't have the lad to worry about. I don't have to watch him running my place to a standstill."

She shook her head. "My son is the most competent man I know. So you imagine he's here in Adelaide, do you?"

"I know exactly where he is. Sam and I passed him along the way. And I can tell you that he'll be back at the station with his tail between his legs quicker than you can say 'pardon me.'"

"Oh?" Irene's lovely face showed not a single crease. "And where did you see him?"

"I didn't see him. I saw the dog. Girl's never more than a couple feet away from him and so he was there, on a station just short of Noarlunga, a run-down sort of place. My guess is that he's been hired to ready the property for sale. He'll be wanting to use all his fangly-dangly new ideas, and he won't give in until those ideas utterly confound him. Then he'll come home knowing where he's best off."

"I doubt he would leave to be the manager of a station. He was already one, wasn't he?"

"Who knows why he left? He certainly didn't confide in me, but if he left thinking to put in place that wool auction idea of his, he would soon have changed his mind when he saw the lie of the land, so to speak. Without more than a moderate amount of cash or an extraordinary amount of goodwill from growers, enough for them to deliver their bales to whatever destination Charlton designated...and then wait month on month hoping he could convince agents to travel from Victoria to Adelaide, he would know he didn't stand a chance, which I told him months ago." He laughed. "You can't put an old head on young shoulders. Upon my oath, without using my name he wouldn't get even one agent to travel from Victoria."

"Then again,"—Irene rested a forefinger on her cheek—"I'm a comparatively influential woman with more than a moderate amount of cash. I wouldn't be averse to advancing him something to start his own business."

"You wouldn't," Edward said, aghast. "It'd be like Henry all over again. You wouldn't put your only son in that sort of danger!"

"I happen to think that with my blood running in his veins, too, he would be more resistant to temptation than his father." Irene raised her eyebrows, staring a challenge at him.

Edward sat in silence, breathing his outrage into the hot still air. Irene was a rich woman because of his generosity. When Henry had died, Irene wanted the lad with her in the city. Edward wanted the lad in the country where he would come to no harm, but his schooling had been so important to Irene that she had mothered him during the term—no boarding school for the young Lynton—and she had sent him to Edward for the holidays.

To obtain control of the situation, Edward had convinced Irene to take advantage of the town house. He allowed her an income befitting her status as the mother of his heir. As she had inherited a house, a parcel of land, and an almost defunct business from Henry, she had a little money of her own but not, Edward thought, enough to make her independently wealthy. "You invested wisely, did you?"

"Very wisely. I'm not a spender."

"Not of your own money, no." He slid his gaze over her gown, a rose silk with more folderols added to the skirt than he had seen on his grandmother. "Is that a new painting over the console?"

"Relatively. The console is new, though. Do you like it?"

"Is it mine or yours?"

"Yours."

He sighed. No one could accuse her of less than good taste. Although she'd recently refurnished the town house in the new Italian style, the gilding didn't appear to be overdone, and the mahogany nicely set up the old walnut. The walls in the sitting room had recently been painted yolk yellow, the silk curtains being of a similar hue, a nice contrast to the marble pillars and the white moldings around the doors and windows. A couple of mellow Persian rugs protected the polished jarrah floors. In all, he admired the room and her taste. His son's smartest move had been to marry her.

"Well, since you are not in Adelaide searching for my son, I hope you will enjoy the social season with me."

"Social season? In January?" he said with a curl of his lips.

"The social season resumes whenever I decide to hold a ball," she answered with gentle rebuke. "And I will be hosting one in February. I had hoped Charlton would be present. I have found another young lady I would like him to meet."

"Perhaps that's why he disappeared. He's never been interested in any of your young ladies."

"True. I simply haven't found the right one. But this one is very respectable, related in some way to Mildred Cameron. Do you remember her?"

"Vaguely. An ambitious little widow."

Irene smiled. "A charming woman, very charitable. She has a niece, or goddaughter, who is astonishingly beautiful and not too forward. I think she might be to Charlton's taste. He dislikes those who gush over him, not only because it's bad form, but also because they might be more interested in his inheritance than in him. However, the young lady under discussion has repaired to the country to recuperate, Mildred says, and is not expected back until February, hence the reason for the ball."

"Interesting." Edward rose to his feet. He couldn't imagine any conversation he would rather not have than one about prospective brides for Charlton. "I'll change out of these clothes and pay a visit to my club."

He washed, made a change of clothes, and left knowing that a bite to eat at his club and a glass or two of sherry would relax him almost as much as had his sight of Girl two days ago. Although he was full of bluster, until he saw the dog his mind hadn't been eased about Charlton's safety. The heir to some hundreds of thousands could have been taken for ransom. The dog's presence reassured Edward. No one would take her but Charlton, and if she lived, he lived.

Nevertheless, he didn't definitely know that his grandson, possibly the only person in his life he truly cared for, intended to stay on the Beaufort Station. Before Charlton had left, he'd been adamant about beginning wool auctions in the colony. Edward could testify, even if only using recent events, that Charlton, once on a trail, rarely deviated.

Chapter 9

The sun sat high in the cloudless blue sky, and nary a breeze stirred the hot air. Tight with tension, Cal rode ahead of Ella, following the thieves' tracks to the river. Without a doubt, the obstinate creature should have stayed home with her sisters. Tracking the thieves alone would have been a welcome reprieve from this now untenable situation of temptation dogging his tracks. Not only that, Ella would hold him up. She had already wasted almost an hour.

When he'd arrived back at the homestead with the two borrowed horses, she had kindly informed him she would allow him to accompany her, then she'd finished packing for the trip. After one look at the mountainous pile of heaven-knew-what, he gritted his teeth. "Let me go through this." He grabbed her first bundle.

He hauled out a bag of tomatoes, a few potatoes, two onions, the end of a cooked leg of mutton, and Hessian-wrapped chunks of raw meat, which caused him to stare.

"For your dog." She raised her chin.

He carefully set the fresh food onto the veranda.

"Don't unwrap that," she said in a squeak as he began to untie her second bundle. "It's a change of clothes in case we have to stay out overnight."

"Nothing's surer than we'll have to stay out overnight. What's in this one?" He toed the next.

"A billy packed with flour, salt, sugar, and tea. A skillet, a sharp knife, a turning fork, knives and forks, plates and cups. A jar of mutton fat."

"That's good. We'll keep that and the water bags. Pass me your bedroll."

She gave him two soft woolen blankets, beautifully folded, and a feather pillow. He put the pillow on the back veranda, too, and shook out her blankets. Into her staples bundle, he tightly wrapped the cooking implements and dry goods. Then he compressed her change of clothes and strapped the whole thing together. "You can't take your pillow. This is more than we need. If you would consent to stay behind I could travel faster."

Her eyebrows lifted. "If at any stage I see I'm holding you back, I'll return. And so will you. I won't allow you the responsibility of endangering yourself for my horses. And that's that."

Clenching his jaw, he snatched his belongings from the quarters and tossed the pack and the water bags over the saddle of the sturdiest horse and Ella's bundle onto the other. He didn't doubt her competence. He doubted that if the neighbors found out about her being alone with him overnight they would hold their tongues.

Rose, carrying a Springfield rifle, opened the kitchen door. While Cal stewed, she waited for Vianna, who brought over yet another package, this one wrapped in calico. "It's a loaf of fresh bread and sandwiches for lunch." Vianna smiled anxiously. The sheen of unshed tears glittered in her eyes. "You will find Miffy, won't you?"

He took a deep breath. "I'll find her and get her back for you."

Rose made an "ahem" sound. "And this is Papa's gun."

"So I see." He strapped the unwanted food to his bedroll.

She passed the rifle to him.

He passed the weapon back. "If this is the only protection you have, keep it." He gathered his reins. Since Rose had not offered paper cartridges or percussion caps he also doubted she knew which end of the rifle to point, but with the shearers a distance from the homestead and only an eleven year old for protection, she might see a firearm as a comfort. If not, he hoped she wouldn't use the thing as a threat. In his view, anyone who carried a rifle had to be prepared to take a life, human or animal.

"Take care of Ella." Rose stepped back.

He nodded curtly, having noted Rose's raised chin and polite smile. Concern for her sister appeared to be lacking. Not for the first time, he wondered if she were totally self-centered or merely emotionless. "I intend to."

If Ella meant to go, she would have to keep up. He set a cracking pace along the riverbank, hoping to make up time on the thieves. The undergrowth, reeds for the most part, and the overhead trees rustled as they passed. In places, the silt gave way to rocks. Needing to guide the horse through, he dismounted. Ella did, too. She didn't complain, but her fair cheeks flushed with the effort.

His horse suddenly shied, snorting.

Out of the corner of his eye, he spotted a lone native standing with a bundle of spears. He tightened his reins, controlling the nag and pulling his horse over to protect Ella, who cannoned into him.

"Jed." Smiling at the stockman, apparently oblivious of his weapons, she said, "What are you doing here?"

"Help Missy find 'orses," the stockman replied, his face grim.

"How on earth did you know we'd lost them?"

"Tracks." He pointed to the ground ahead of them.

"Aren't the tribe on walkabout?"

Jed scratched his chin. "Wait. Two days. No more."

"Jed is an amazing tracker," Ella said to Cal. "Do you think you can walk back? He'll need your horse."

Cal stiffened. "I certainly won't let you go into the bush with Jed and not me."

She narrowed her eyes.

"No 'orse." Jed grinned at Cal. "Track." Using his spears he pointed ahead. Without another word, he ran off at a quick lope along the river's edge.

After a hesitant pause, Cal followed on horseback. The aborigine followed the same trail as Cal would have and the pace remained swift for a couple of miles. Ella trailed behind, mightily put out judging by her reluctance. Then Jed stopped. The sun's rays glittered like etched gold on the river. Ella ranged beside Cal and together they watched Jed examine the flat bed near the water.

"What do you see?" Cal asked Jed, his voice careful.

"Fire 'ere." Jed pointed to a smooth area of silt covered with dry leaves. Stirring beneath with his bare toe he found blackened ashes. He stood, searching the surrounding shards of rock, and found a scattering of burned twigs. His teeth flashed white in his black face.

"Last night?" Ella slid off her horse, glancing at the thick bushland hiding the hills. "If they started from here at first light, we'd be eight hours behind them. We can't catch them before dark." Her posture slumped.

"They'll be more weary than we are. I suspect they took the horses no earlier than midnight and no later than two or three. It's three hours to here from the homestead. They can't have had more than a few hours of sleep. Therefore, we'll be traveling the faster." Cal let a tide of cooler air under his hat and readjusted the angle.

"But if they're trying to hide their tracks, they're expecting to be followed."

"Of course they..." Cal began before noting the drained expression on her face. He swallowed his impatience. "We've been following clear tracks the whole time. They haven't crossed to hide their trail. At this moment we can see where they laid their bedrolls in the scrub, and we can see where they tethered the horses to the trees." He pointed to the unmistakable sign of the horses' presence—a pile of trampled manure. "They only wanted to hide their fire, hoping any searchers couldn't work out how far ahead they are."

"I hope that means they're not as far ahead as I suppose." Ella bent and massaged each of her smooth white calves in turn, drew a deep breath, and prepared to remount.

"I'm sure they're not." Relenting, Cal took her reins. "I think we could rest for a bite to eat and a cup of tea, couldn't we, Jed?" He estimated the time to be around midday, judging from the angle of the sun.

Jed nodded and clattered his spears to the ground. He started a neat and economical fire while Cal fetched fresh water from the river. Girl stayed at heel as she always did in an unfamiliar situation, lapping water from the river and staring ahead as if scanning their intended route. Ella unpacked the sandwiches. After a long-lashed gaze at Girl, she tapped at the side of her leg.

The dog, acknowledging another person for the first time in Cal's living memory, pricked her ears and moved forward. Ella gave Girl a sandwich and patted the dog on the head. The dog sat and blinked at her, letting her tail slowly stir the soil.

"That's because *he* wouldn't let me bring meat for you." Ella gave Cal a quelling glance.

"We'll catch her a lizard later." He reached for a sandwich, feeding the avid hunger that eventuated after a period of intense concentration. Mutton. Again.

At home, on his grandfather's property, they ate mutton but they also ate beef and pork and large plump hens, eggs, and fresh fruit from their home farm. Even their workers had a far more varied diet than the Beauforts. Cal had had a good life.

Since the age of eighteen he'd worked toward his future, assuring Farvista would run efficiently when his grandfather sat tuning his harp on a throne-like white cloud, criticizing every one of Cal's actions. Although he craved more responsibility, he toiled day and night, thinking he had to prove himself. He had never expected a wage, assuming himself to be his grandfather's heir. Money seemed unimportant when he appeared to have everything money could buy—except autonomy.

Nothing had shocked him more than to hear from his grandfather's own lips that he'd never earned more than his board. In his wardrobe at Farvista sat fine cotton shirts, well-cut jackets and woolen trousers, cravats, brocade waistcoats, and leather boots as soft as butter, all of which, according to his grandfather a month before Cal had left, were his to wear only while living with Edward.

"Whom will you leave this to when you've passed on?" Cal had asked with a sweep of his hand across the property.

"I'll decide that in the fullness of time." Edward had flattened his shaggy eyebrows into a frown. "I might yet divide the place up."

"So my care of the land counts for naught?"

"Be grateful you've been taught to put in a good day's work. That's my legacy to you." Edward had stamped off.

Instead of being the heir to a vast property, Cal owned only a deaf dog. He'd left a month later, his legacy from his grandfather standing him in far better stead than his custom-made saddle or his leather-bound books. Now independent and with his ideas set into motion without using Edward's money or name, he was well on his way to proving himself worthy of his grandfather's respect. Only when he had succeeded would he face his grandfather on equal ground.

More dissatisfied than he supposed, he rose to his feet and strode to the river's edge. Grabbing up a stone, he flung the weight as far as he could across the water. Ella had endorsed his grandfather's assessment. Like Edward, she hadn't trusted him. She doubted his ability to retrieve her horses without her supervision. *This* from a woman who, until a few days ago, scarcely knew the boundaries of her own land.

He hurled two more stones before he admitted to himself that half his frustration with her came from knowing he couldn't satisfy his physical desire. The retrieval of the horses meant her security. If she didn't trust him, as he meant to do with his grandfather, he would prove himself by confronting the horse thieves for her and removing their ill-gotten gains.

That resolved, he wiped his sandy hands on his trousers and trod back to the others. "Do you know this area?" he asked Ella, who sat cross-legged with her skirt tucked around her, making finger pictures in the sand. Her hair gleamed gold in the sun.

"We passed our last fence quite a few hours ago. We're on Crown Land now."

"Does that mean you have never been past your last fence?"

"I've been to Willunga. As a matter of fact, I've been to Adelaide, too. But, no, I've never been in this direction, not that I know which direction we face now because of the bends and twists we've been following with the river."

"I suppose you've never been fishing either?" Snagged twigs patterned the clear water with vee-shaped ripples. A flock of sulfur-crested cockatoos gossiped while they gathered grass seeds. One, reminding Cal of a child hanging by his legs, swung upside down on the shredding bark of a river gum, creaking a call that sounded like "watch me, watch me!" in the way of an attention-seeking child.

"No. Papa thought, that is, he had a great dislike of water."

"Have you ever eaten fish?"

"To deny myself that pleasure would be taking my dislike of water to pointless extremes. I'll make the tea."

"Maybe we'll have fish for dinner tonight. What do you think, Jed? Good tucker in the water?"

Jed nodded enthusiastically.

"Good." Cal accepted a mug of tea from Ella. "Because I'm relying on you to show me how to spear a fish. I've never done it, though I'm quite an expert yabby catcher."

Jed stared at him in query.

"A yabby." Cal spread his hands about eight inches apart, wondering how to describe the freshwater crayfish. "Two claws, hard shell. We catch them with bait on a piece of string, or that's what I did when I was a lad."

"Yabby," Jed repeated with disdain. "Woman get." He thumped his chest with his palm. "Man get big fish."

Cal grinned. "Right. Ella can be the yabby catcher."

She gave him a wary look but didn't answer. Instead, she rose and rinsed her cup at the water's edge. Cal followed suit with his. Within minutes they'd repacked and set off again.

Before too long the gorge started to rise on either side of the river. The flow of water grew narrower and faster. Ella stuck closer to his side than Girl. Once she came so near that her leg snagged his. His entire body quickened. He dismounted, his concentration lost. For some time he'd been trying to trail Jed, who had run farther and farther ahead until he had disappeared from view. He'd left no tracks, and Cal could see no tracks from the stolen horses either. He stopped Ella's horse.

"What's wrong?" Ella too dismounted. Not only did his lust for her increase hourly, but also did his liking, for she let her horse rest as often as possible. The gelding took the opportunity to tear at the grass growing head height on the steep embankment.

"I've lost the trail. Stay here and I'll check in the scrub."

She shivered. "Not on your life. I don't want to be left by a river alone."

"This river isn't dangerous."

"Ha. Bunyips are everywhere. 'Wither thou goest'... Well, you know what I mean."

He put his hands on his hips, scanning her expression. Since she knew Bunyips were imaginary she must be afraid of snakes. "Come on then, but I warn you it's a fair climb. We'll tether the horses down here. That will be easier than dragging them up and urging them down again."

The grassy knoll was steep and they arrived at the top with dirty hands and breathing heavily. Ella kept close by Cal as he searched the surrounding bushland for a sign of organized passage. He found nothing. Had he been told that no foot before his had ever touched this area, he would have believed every word. The scrub grew thickly with stringy bark trees that had spread from their bases as if to let the sun shine through their growth to the ground below. In groups, river gums, resplendent with cream and burgundy streaks throughout their lengths, presided over the land.

"We are agreed that no one has passed through this area?"

She nodded, gazing at him as if she needed to read his expression.

"We'll go down to our horses and backtrack."

"You don't think the thieves might have crossed the river, do you?" Her voice rose on the last word as she slid down the knoll behind him.

"It's the only conclusion. Unless they veered off in one of the rocky areas."

As if he couldn't hear the anxiety in her voice, he led his horse along the muddy embankment, scanning for tracks. He saw only their own, distinct because of Girl's paw prints.

"I think it's about half an hour to the last rocky area," Ella said from behind him. "So we will have lost another hour."

The shadows had lengthened. He wanted to find the trail before dusk and a good campsite before nightfall. Most of all, he hoped Jed would return. He didn't want to be left alone overnight with a woman who repaid favors with the delights of her body.

They arrived at the rocky area she had mentioned in about the time she had estimated and he saw their tracks. "Stay there and don't move." He passed the reins of his horse to her. "If there is any sign here, I don't want to miss it." He had to backtrack to the very beginning of the riverside rocks to see the last trace of the thieves and the Beaufort horses.

From there he inspected almost every blade of grass on the embankment and found nothing. He peered at each rock along the shoreline. Some had been disturbed but he couldn't say that hadn't happened as he and Ella had passed through the first time. With intense concentration, he checked again and found a path of rocks leading into the water. He scanned the surrounding terrain and discovered rocklike indentations in the silt. Lifting his head, he said, "I think they moved the stones from here and made a nice little hidden path into the river."

"And then they crossed." She led the horses from her instructed position, staring to the other side of the river. "It's narrow here and deep."

"I would say they swam across."

"Which I can't do."

"Not a problem." He smiled tightly. "You can go back to the homestead and have a good night's sleep."

"Hmm. We should arrive back at about midnight."

"You, not we."

"Oh? I should ride along this uneven trail in the dark alone?"

He narrowed his eyes. "If you'd set off with Jed, you would be alone now."

"I don't plan to swim across a river in my riding clothes."

"Stay on your horse. He can swim. You can cling on."

"The saddles will get wet. The food will get wet. That's a very silly idea."

"You have two choices," he said, with forced patience. "You can go back now and leave me to go on. Or you can come with me, in which case you'll need to cross the river because I plan to cross the river here, where the thieves did."

"I'm sure we can find a shallower place to cross."

"We've lost an hour as it is. This is the place we should cross."

"Why are you so determined to make me go into the water?" She leaned back, crossing her arms.

"You could take the other choice. If you're not prepared to follow the trail, you shouldn't have come. You should be at home where you belong."

With a firm expression, she mounted her horse.

"Where do you think you are going?" He grabbed her horse's reins.

"To find a more suitable place to cross."

"Give me the food bundle."

"You cross here and I'll cross wherever I can find shallower water. If you meet me on the other side—"

He dragged her horse over to his and leaped into his saddle. "Give me the food bundle, damn you."

She glared at him. "Damn *you*," she said distinctly. "While I have the food, I know you'll meet me."

Experiencing a flare of justified anger, he leaned over and snatched her bedroll. "Trust me," he said through gritted teeth, clasping the food bundle under his arm.

He clapped his heels to his horse. At the same time, he jerked on her reins. Her horse balked, almost sitting on its haunches. He gave a war whoop and tried again. With a roll of his eyes, her horse went from a standing start to a bolt into the river. Screaming, Ella clung to the saddle with both hands. His horse followed and together both animals sped into the water, churning foam before them. Holding the bedroll at shoulder height, he twisted the reins of Ella's horse around his wrist.

"Leave go," Ella shrieked. "Let me be. Let me be!" She tried to grab back her reins, but his hold was firm and his mind set.

The water flowed above his knees. Ella sat rigidly clasping her saddle, her eyes clamped shut, her forehead creased, and her mouth stretched. Girl swam behind, struggling slightly to keep up. The river held no mystery for her. She swam with Cal every day. Ella's fury doused his, although he doubted the river was more than five feet deep. He felt only a gentle tug of water as the horses swam.

His horse stumbled slightly as his hooves touched the river bottom. Soon both horses walked on the rocky silt as if they too swam every day. Girl braced her feet and shook off her excess water. Ella sat, head lowered and gasping. Water dripped from the skirt of her gown. "I'll never forgive you for that." Her eyes flashed with fury. "Never."

"So, you're wet." He shrugged, puzzled by her overreaction. "You'll be dry within an hour."

She lifted her head. "Don't speak to me. I'm far too..." Her breathing came in short bursts. "Mad."

Now annoyed, he planted his fists on his hips. "I wonder how you think I feel, knowing you thought I might steal your food. I'd say we're quits."

He passed back her reins. Without another word, he began looking for tracks. Finally he vindicated himself. Farther up the river, he found the trail they had lost.

Chapter 10

Ella knew her failings and she couldn't credit that Cal had forced her into the water against her wishes, that he had been so determined to have his way when she couldn't have made more obvious the fact that she could find a suitable crossing.

In a loaded silence she stayed with him as he stalked the tracks he had found. She saw only the most obvious signs, blatant hoof prints in the silt or, in some cases, boot prints. Cal noticed far more. Where the trail veered into the bushland he examined broken twigs and once, when the terrain appeared completely undisturbed by man or beast, she saw him lift off a bush a strand of hair long enough to be from the tail of a horse. Every now and again she deliberately stilled her hands, which had a tendency to tremble.

When the dusk cast a gray pall over the landscape, he lost the trail. "We'll camp here for the night." He stopped his horse in a flat stretch of dry summer grass.

Every bone in her body ached, including in her toes. She'd spent more than ten hours on and off her horse, and for the past two hours she'd had to walk or ride in squelchy leather boots only because a bully had insisted. At least he'd kept the food dry. "Your wish is apparently my command."

She glanced at the oval of short grass surrounded by tall trees. Clear water flowed not fifty feet away. She slid from her horse and removed her saddle. Cal removed his. He unpacked the rope halters, which he substituted for the horses' bridles, and brushed his horse down with a handful of fresh leaves. She followed suit. As the horses began to graze, she shook her saddle blanket to freshen the nap, as he did.

"I'll light a fire." He began to collect small twigs.

Determined to express nothing other than indifference, she collected a bundle of a more substantial size and dropped the broken branches beside the dry leaves he persuaded to smolder. He fed the smoke until a slender flare built into a crackling red flame, while she unrolled her blankets, finding the packed billy.

He held out a hand. "Let me take that."

She passed the blackened tin to him and he left to collect water. She had the inclination to sit with her arms crossed, but instead she set out the cooking implements preparing to fry the remains of the bread in mutton fat. The sun had disappeared behind two hills and the air smelled dusty. Not a leaf rustled; not a bird called. She wiped at a trickle of perspiration in front of her ear, feeling the grittiness of her skin.

Cal came back with the water and two forked sticks to suspend the billy over the fire. "If you don't mind, I'm going to take a swim while the water boils." He uncurled himself from his squat by the fire.

She nodded. Hot and dirty she, too, would enjoy a good wash. Not, however, in a river. "Don't let me stop you doing as you wish."

He turned and, with Girl following, strode to the river. On the bank, he stripped off his clothes. Ella watched, knowing she stared, knowing the thump in her chest comprised half admiration, half reluctant desire. The back view of his naked body, broad at the shoulders, lean at the hips, stood starkly white against the dark flow of the river. Like the last time he had stripped in front of her, he displayed no coyness, and this time no haste as he waded into the water. At knee depth, he finally dived.

She hugged her legs and cushioned her cheek on her knees. Nothing seemed real. Never had she imagined she would sit and watch a naked man cavorting with his dog in a river. Cal surfaced and threw a stick for Girl. She brought the plaything back to him time after time, as if she hadn't walked close to twenty miles that day. Ella could hear Cal's laugh and she could see his broad grin. He loved being in the water and he had no fear. Perhaps if Papa hadn't continually warned his daughters about the dangers of drowning, she would be relaxed in the river, too.

While she had privacy, she walked into the bushland and found a discreet place to relieve herself. Upon her arrival back at the campfire, Cal had finished his swim. He stood by her blankets wearing his trousers, rubbing his chest dry with his shirt. His nipples had beaded into tight dots. Her abdomen clenched. This man appealed to her in a physical way that seemed doubly hard to bear, given that he wouldn't act on his attraction to her. She lowered her head and turned away.

"I would like to bathe, too," she said in a low voice. "If you could promise not to look."

With an impassive face he pointed. "There's a pool of water in that outcrop of rocks. It's shallow and likely warmed. If you undress there, even if I try—and I won't—I shan't be able to see you. I'll warn you if I see a bunyip lurking."

"Very funny." She stood, collecting a cake of perfumed soap and her clean blouse. Her lips bundled, she strode toward the rock pool. If Cal believed that bunyips, rather than being out of her depth, frightened her, well and good. Not anxious to reveal her cowardice, she wouldn't explain.

She sat on the flattest of the rocks and removed her soggy boots and stockings, glancing in his direction. He squatted to fuel the fire, appearing to have no interest in her. With hasty jerkiness, she removed her clothes, curious as to why her fascination with his male body wasn't reciprocated by his equal fascination with her female body. Her chest emptied with a soft sigh.

After sliding into the foot-deep, tepid water, she washed all over. She rinsed, staying where she sat. The water had a relaxing effect on her tired muscles. When she leaned back and stared at the darkening sky her mind emptied. For a few minutes, she did nothing but slowly scoop water over her shoulders and flex her toes. Then, she filled her lungs with the hot night air and stood, sluicing the water from her body. As he had, she dried herself with her blouse and dressed in her fresh one. She also took the opportunity to wash the blouse and stockings she'd worn and, swinging them casually, walked barefooted back to the campfire, collecting river sand between her toes.

He made the tea while she draped a couple of nearby bushes with her clothing. Maintaining her resentment of his autocracy, she sat on her blanket, placed her boots by the fire, and ungratefully sipped from the mug he handed her. "Since you don't cook, I suppose I will be allowed to fry the bread."

"Wait." He threw the dregs from his mug onto the ground. "I'll try to catch a fish." Pushing one hand deep into his pocket, he pulled out a rolled piece of twine ended with what was obviously a fishhook.

"A man for all occasions," she commented dryly.

"I have amazing things in my pockets." His gaze hooded with mystery. "Aside from rocks."

Her eyes met his in sudden surprise.

He stared back, shrugged as if his revelation was of no consequence, and walked off.

She sat gazing after him. His dog, far better trained than she would ever be, followed him without encouragement. For a moment she wondered if convincing her of his disinterest after that episode in the woolshed was a way of convincing himself. She leaned back on her palms.

No doubt he had a reason for withholding his attentions from her. When she forgave him for the river episode, she might decide to stop accepting his decisions.

* * * *

Cal knew he had made a big mistake. He hadn't expected Jed to disappear. Although he could feed himself off the land, or go without if necessary, he couldn't expect Ella to do the same. She was bone tired, any fool could see that, and she hadn't recovered from being hauled through the river, another mistake on his part. She hadn't minded the wetting; she simply didn't like her objections being overborne. Nor did he and he would consider that in the future.

If he could only catch a nice big fish as a peace offering, and if he could only treat her like another man... "Pah." A swirling twig jerked in surprise and sidled away. "If I thought she was another man, I wouldn't be standing here trying to impress her by stocking her dashed larder. I would..." He clamped his mouth. Had he been alone, he would eat the fried bread and tomorrow catch a bird, or a snake, or a lizard, or whatever came to hand and eat without another thought. Many a time he'd been out for a week or more with his grandfather's stockmen living off the land during the sheer boredom of watching sheep day in and day out.

The wilderness wouldn't last forever. Tomorrow or the next day he would pass a settler's cottage or farming land and he could easily enough ask for food. No traveler was sent away empty-handed in this harsh land. But here he stood, dangling his line into the river, hoping that a deluded fish would see his worm-baited hook as a temptation because a woman with a mind as quick as January challenged his masculinity. Rocks in his pockets! "Pah."

He shouldn't have told her. Nor should he have imagined her undressing and washing. He visualized her smooth white body and the satin of her skin. The recollection of her response in the woolshed heated his blood.

Tonight would be endless. He would see her eyes closed in sleep and he would long to savor her scent, her curves. His line straightened. Lost in thought, he almost let the twine slide between his fingers. At almost the last second he came to his senses and held on. Without too much difficulty he landed a small fish. Within minutes he landed the second. Relieved, and with the daylight almost gone, he took his spoils back to the campfire. One fish still jerked.

Ella glanced at his offerings and averted her head. "Will the fish take long to die?" She wrinkled her nose.

"No." He whacked each fish on the head with a piece of wood and, without ceremony, cut off their heads and filleted them.

She warmed the pan and melted the mutton fat into which he dropped the scaled fish. Rinsing his hands with the cooled billy water, he watched possibly the four smallest fillets of fish he'd ever seen curl as they cooked. "We'll have lizard for breakfast," he said in a curt voice. He wouldn't apologize for the sparseness of his catch. She shouldn't be here.

"We have flour. I'll be able to make pan scones."

He grunted. She served the fish on two plates and they ate them with the last of the bread.

"That was nice." After stretching, she put the billy on to boil again. She leaned back on her elbows, appearing less hostile. "A few years ago we went to a town picnic in Noarlunga. I ate an apple fried in batter with sugar and cinnamon sprinkled on the top. I thought it was the most delicious and original treat I had ever tasted. We had never had anything other than fresh or stewed apples before that, but since then we haven't grown any healthy apples. A moth burrows into them each year and they spoil. I imagine there's a trick to keeping the moth away but I don't know it. Do you?"

He spread his hands. "I've never had anything to do with orchards. I told you before that the only business I know is sheep."

"And you're so good at what you know that I can't imagine why you are working as a shearer. What exactly did you do before you joined the team?"

"Regular sheep-tending duties."

"But you weren't the manager of a station."

"No."

"Talk to me, Cal. Tell me why you weren't the manager."

"Because the place had a manager. He had his nose in everything and he didn't want a second opinion."

"Did you leave because you had a second opinion?"

He nodded.

She put her head on one side as if considering, then she sighed. "We are, at the moment, an hour farther behind the thieves than when we started. That's my fault, I know. I also remember saying that if I'm holding you back, we won't go on. But I'll do better tomorrow, I promise, and we'll catch up that hour and more. I find that not doing as well as I intended spurs me to try harder."

He absorbed her words and knew them for the truth. One of her admirable qualities was her ability to muster herself and move forward.

"Good," he said roughly. "Because whether you continue or not, I will. I promised your sister I would get her pony back and I don't mean to renege on my word."

"Most commendable," she said in a tone indicating she meant the opposite.

"Isn't that what you would expect of me?"

"It depends." She gave him a sideways, almost challenging glance. "When your promise suits me, I hope you will be honorable. When it doesn't...dear life, Cal. I don't see a problem in you changing your mind. Flexibility in all things, I say." She stood and brushed down her skirt, although she had no sand in particular to brush for she'd sat neatly on the blanket to eat. Taking a deep breath, she placed her hands on her hips and faced him. "But you are so determined to go where you think you ought to go because of giving your word that today you forced me to do something that..." Her voice shook and her palms slowly wiped down the sides of her skirt in an unconscious gesture of nervousness. "It wasn't necessary for me to go through that part of the river."

"It was no more than six feet deep."

"No matter the depth, I dislike being in water. It...makes me worry."

"If you don't face your fears you'll never lose them."

"You faced my fears. I didn't, and I haven't lost them. Today you taught me little more than to be more wary of you."

"It's a lesson well learned."

"Don't be silly. You can't want to keep people away from you, even though your only promise to me was somewhat along the same lines."

"We don't need to discuss that."

"We're alone."

"All the more reason for me to keep my promise."

"Which is what I said in the first place. It's easy to make promises when the outcome suits you."

"How does the outcome suit me?"

"Because I don't appeal to you."

"Who said you don't?"

"So you don't deny it?"

He rubbed his fingers along his stubbly jaw, not certain whether a lie or the truth would serve him best. Her eyes glistened brightly as if the answer meant much to her. "I *should* deny it."

"You should apologize for frightening me today. And you should promise not to do so again."

"I'm sorry about the wetting. I was single-minded and thoughtless. I promise not to force you into the water again. There. Are you happy now?"

She took two steps toward him and lifted her bare foot, placing her toes on the center of his chest. He instantly braced but she stared straight into his eyes. "Really, I should push you flat on your back to show you what I think of your high-handed action."

"You couldn't."

"Perhaps. But I might get a lot of satisfaction out of trying."

Her foot rested right over his heart. She had a half smile on her face, which showed up one endearing dimple near her mouth. Not for a single moment did he doubt she was flirting with him and not for a single moment could he prevent himself from responding. Very slowly he lifted his flattened palms from the blanket, silently daring her to manhandle him.

Her lashes lowered and her smile took on a hint of mischief. He relaxed and covered her toes with his hand, meaning to put her foot and her influence over him at a safer distance.

Her knee flexed and she pushed him flat on his back.

Unfortunately, she came tumbling down, too, with her loss of balance. She sprawled atop him, one knee bent on his chest and the other pressed beside his waist. Her hands rested on either side of his head.

She laughed. "You're at my mercy now, Mr. Langdon. Never challenge a middle child. We learn early not to let bigger or smaller people influence us. The only thing that influences us is keeping balance." Her lovely face hovered inches above his and she laughed with delight. "And when you pull us off balance..."

"You land with a thud heavy enough to stun an elephant," he said, knowing that again she had disarmed him. Certainly she flirted with him, but in such a lighthearted way that he felt at peace rather than on his mettle either to put her off or compete with her and win.

She moved her knee off his chest and lifted, preparing to stand. "Let that be a lesson to you."

"I will." He tried not to smile. "I won't ever force you to do anything you don't want to do because I know I'll get the same treatment." His hands moved to her neat behind, which he cupped in his palms, wishing he sounded threatening rather than husky. "But if I want the same treatment...?" His gaze met hers.

Her lips parted slightly and a familiar rush of desire flooded him. The exact situation he had feared was about to develop and he could have avoided it without any awkwardness had he not been an impressionable male. His hands slid to the small of her back and he angled his head to take her mouth with his.

A black shadow loomed behind her. Cal sat up, pushing her sideways out of danger.

Jed stood there, dangling two rabbits from one outstretched hand. "Find good tucker." He grinned.

Chapter 11

Jed sat with a look of comic appreciation on his face while Cal skinned and gutted the rabbits.

"How many men would you say we're tracking, Jed?" Cal offered the scraps to Girl.

Jed held up two fingers. "Men." Then seven. "'Orses. Not far. 'Ills 'igh." He pointed into the darkness.

"Will we catch them tomorrow, do you think?"

Jed nodded. "Rum."

"They're drinking?"

"Finish one bottle. Catch tomorrow."

"We've already eaten. Do you want me to cook the rabbits for you?"

Jed grinned as if Cal had made a joke. "You keep. Jed eat bush tucker." With that, he faded off into the blackness.

Cal called after him, "Do you want a blanket?" The only answer was silence.

"I expect the rabbits will make good eating tomorrow if we cook them now." Ella glanced at the corpses as if she didn't quite know what to do with them.

And so Cal pierced them with a stick and let them roast over the flame. The flare from the fire spread for some distance. When he finished he doused the flame with soil.

Ella covered the meat with the bag and sat opposite him. "Do you have brothers or sisters?"

"I'm an only child."

"Are both your parents alive?"

"Only my mother."

"Do you support her?"

"She has a private income. However, she will inherit some money in the fullness of time."

"Which you, as an only son, will naturally inherit from her?"

"I imagine so. However, I don't expect her to pass away any time in the near future. Are you looking to borrow money from me? I don't have any, I can assure you."

"I don't want to borrow any money when I can't pay the debts we already have," she said in a cross voice. "I'm trying to find out your mission and I know you have one. Where do you mean to go from here?"

"I'll leave the team after this job and then go on to Adelaide."

"But whatever you plan to do isn't pressing?"

"It's pressing, though I don't work as hard as I can here because I shear faster than most. If I worked at my top speed, I would take money from their earnings. As you can imagine that would cause annoyance and I would prefer to be employed at this stage. I need money for what I plan to do."

"What do you plan to do?"

He leaned back, lengthening his body, resting the upper half on one elbow. "Investigate the feasibility of setting up wool auctions in South Australia." He crossed his outstretched legs at the ankles. "It seems to me that there's good money to be made by keeping our profits in the colony."

She picked at the blanket near her knees. "It's a good idea. Where do you expect to start?"

"I have started already. While I've been traveling with the team I've been getting the support of the woolgrowers. On our last day here, I'll discuss the matter with you, too, though I must warn you that not all have agreed to send me their clip."

"What will you do with the wool?"

"Some months ago I arranged a loan with a reputable bank owner for the hiring of a warehouse. I'm to come up with half the money this month. He will guarantee the remainder as long as I can fill the warehouse within the following three months, during which time the shearing season will end. Benji is considering the position of my wool classer. As soon as I arrive in Adelaide, I'll talk to auctioneers. I've had the whole thing organized in my head for some time."

"So, you'll be a townie soon?"

He nodded. "I see myself as a factor. I'll set the wheels in motion but I won't stay for the ride." He moved her boots from beside the dying fire. "They're dry now. Keep them near you while you sleep."

She straightened the laces and put her boots to one side. "I can see you dressed in a suit, and you would look impossibly handsome."

"In a suit?" His brows drew together. "I look the way I do now."

"Yes, impossibly handsome. You look that way no matter how you dress, or don't dress, but in a suit you would have every young female in town chasing you."

He didn't answer. Her compliment pleased him. He didn't know how he looked to women. When his name had been Charlton Lynton, women had flocked around him. He didn't assume his attraction came from his outer appearance and his mother had been quite clear on her opinion of his charm.

"Learn some conversational skills," she had told him, "for the Lord's sake. You can't spend your life explaining about sheep and property sizes. Ladies want to be told they look pretty and gentlemen want to talk about their business interests. Relax, Cal. Life is far less serious than you suppose."

To him life *had* been serious. He didn't want to impress by calculation. He wanted to be seen as a man with integrity rather than a man who could buy any opinion he chose with his grandfather's money. Ella knew him as only the man she saw, a shearer, an itinerant worker.

And she'd said he was impossibly handsome!

He certainly liked the assessment given that she meant she didn't have an eye to what she thought he might inherit—which was, of course, nothing in the foreseeable future. "Do you think life is less serious than I suppose?" He drew up one knee as a casual armrest.

"Probably not, though a few months ago I might not have thought that. I think life is very serious now." Her nose wrinkled. "It's all very well to talk about money not being important, but without funding, money is irrefutably essential. Dreams are built on having enough money. And if we don't seriously put an effort into earning money, we *won't* realize our dreams."

Gazing at her he decided he'd made another mistake. He'd thought he would prefer no woman to others. She'd said nothing earth shattering. She'd expressed her thoughts. That they echoed his thoughts was no revelation either. Many people thought the same way. In this colony dreams of money and advancement were nothing new. Immigrants moved here to chase their dreams in this utopia of the south. Her words in themselves didn't influence him. The whole of her did.

Her physical appeal had impressed him from the start. His first glance at her had constricted his breath. From her first reluctant words, her humor had been apparent. Her smile came from within and easily. She worked with a will, showing a responsible attitude toward her family. He'd noticed those attributes over the past week. Today he'd realized she didn't hold grudges. She forgave quickly. She'd forgiven him the river episode long before he'd apologized. She didn't know how to make anyone feel small or lowly. She connected with everyone around her.

The mistake he'd made was in assuming that she was simply another attractive woman. He certainly wanted her—although he doubted he could describe that as emotional involvement. His protective feelings might be masculine instinct. He might be able to explain away his interest in her as unemotional, and would probably have to, for if the tangled thoughts in his head meant that he might have begun to love her, he would have to cut off those thoughts right now.

He had nothing to offer her. She needed money to get out of debt and off the station. Possibly he could support her while beginning his business but he would have to make a commitment that wasn't so simple. In the deal, he would also get her sisters. While he didn't want to think of them as deal breakers, he knew he couldn't provide for four people and carry on as he planned with the wool auctions.

Ella had fallen, dripping, into his life at the wrong time.

Three months ago would have been more convenient when he'd assumed he was his grandfather's heir; when he'd expected to take over the running of a successful business. If he'd fallen in love then, he could have married produced one or two children, assuming that he would in time fill his grandfather's shoes. He would have ranged between living with his wife at Farvista or in the city, depending on the call of business or various festivities, just as his father had done. He would have worked hard to keep his wife and children comfortable, knowing that he had his grandfather's sanction of trust and respect, knowing that he was no grasping dependent. Now he knew otherwise, and now he had nothing but his wages and his hopes.

He thumped his fist on his knee and stood, wishing Ella back at the homestead.

Her eyes widened. "What did I say?"

"Nothing that any other woman doesn't think. Money is the be-all and end-all."

He grabbed his bedroll and moved as far as he could from her, while keeping close enough to protect her if she needed him.

He couldn't see her face as she settled down to sleep. No doubt he'd hurt her. He'd wanted to hurt her. Obviously the only way he could protect himself from her charms was to set her against him.

He couldn't afford to begin thinking that meeting Ella might be the most important event in his overly complicated life.

* * * *

Ella woke stiff and sore, hearing the irritating rattle of pans. Opening one eye, she saw Cal squatting by the smoking fire. She closed her eye again and groaned.

"Are you awake?"

"No." If she'd had a blanket handy she would have pulled the thing over her head. The nearest blanket, however, sat hot and rumpled under her hair. She'd used it as a pillow, the weather being hot enough for her to require no covering.

"We need to make an early start. I'm making damper."

She sat up and stared at him. The man had no end to his talents. "Perhaps you could make a round of cheese to go with it," she said grumpily.

"First I'd have to catch a wombat and milk it."

"I wouldn't put that beyond you."

"Wouldn't you?"

"I've never slept on the ground before." She rubbed her shoulder. "It doesn't make a person wake up in the best of moods."

"You're the one who decided you had to come. You've made your bed, so..." He raised his eyebrows at her. He had not shaved, but he had brushed his hair back from his face. His shirt was fresh and she was a crumpled wreck.

She sighed and rested her cheek on her knee. From there she could see Girl lying under a red gum, tongue lolling. The river quietly lapped at the sandy banks. A flock of ducks swooped in showing their turquoise under wings and began sifting for food on the top of the water. Pelicans joined the ducks. They, too, sifted and fished. The bird life in the area saw no threat from humans. Nor did a poisonous brown snake sunning itself in the dappled shade of the graceful river trees. She glanced at the reptile but didn't mind sharing the bushland with one of the native inhabitants. Pulling the tie from her braid, she began untangling her hair.

"You have two fenced paddocks not far from the homestead," he said.

"More orders for me, Mr. Langdon?" Given the impossibility of their future relationship, an impartial subject was a reasonable enough way to pass the time.

"One is your hayfield, which by the look of it has been unplanted for the past few years. The other is the billabong paddock."

"I don't know why Papa didn't plant last year. Perhaps he couldn't bear to ask the Lannocks for the loan of their plow and bullocks when he knew he owed them money."

"You have a hand-plow in the stables. Why didn't he use that?"

"I don't know. Perhaps he didn't know how." She reached for her comb in her bundle. "Do you think we should bother to plant feed before we leave?"

"If Jed comes back before the rains. But first you'll have to finish the fencing."

"And the dipping." She combed through her hair, watching him watch her and enjoying his fascination.

"No rest for the wicked," he said in a husky voice.

"Perhaps I've been wicked." Glancing at him from under her lashes, she twisted her hair into a simple knot on her nape. "But it's a normal wickedness, surely?"

"If you mean that episode in the woolshed, nothing like that will happen again."

She met his gaze. "And you only need to say it won't happen and it won't?"

"I learned to discipline myself at an early age."

She stood and walked to the bank of the river. Her bare toe stirred the edge of the water. Turning to face him, she said, "Perhaps I don't admire that sort of discipline. It speaks of a cold heart. Aside from that, you're rejecting me and it hurts."

He shrugged. "I'm sorry you're hurt and I'm sorry you feel rejected. But you must see that a physical relationship between us is inappropriate."

"I have no intention of throwing myself at you. I'm not exactly desperate." She gave a tight smile. "If I wanted a husband, I don't doubt I could find at least one during my first year in the city. More than that would be greedy, as you previously mentioned."

He stood. "You're being too modest, Miss Beaufort."

"I scarcely know the meaning of the word." In a dramatic gesture, she flung her hand out and accidentally knocked off her hat. The brim settled with a thud. She stepped toward her headgear.

"Leave it!" He leaped forward.

She cut past him. He snatched at her arm, hauling her backward. Stumbling, she clutched him for balance, amazed to see her hat begin a jerky dance. "Oh, my." The tail of the brown snake writhed beneath the hat.

"He looks very nice in your chapeau," Cal said, gentling his grip on her upper arm. "I think now is not the best time to grab the shade from him."

"Possibly not." She stayed in the circle of his arms. "Though perhaps I could hurry him along if I tell him flat brims are a passing fad."

He gave a soft laugh.

The snake, acting as affronted as a snake could, wriggled from beneath the brown felt and whipped off into the scrub. They stared at the now vacant headwear. For a moment Cal stood with his hands on Ella's waist while she breathed in his sun-warmed skin, wishing she could keep him with her always. With a soft smile she raised her hands and settled them around his neck. He stared into her eyes, gripped her upper arms, and lifted her away from him.

"Beautifully done," she said, stark with disappointment. "You could have kissed my forehead in an avuncular way, but that might have been a little patronizing. And you're not capable of being patronizing, are you, Cal? In every situation, you always do the right thing." She noted the pump of a vein in his neck and, turning, she strolled back to the fire. "We can start out again as soon as we've eaten. Am I really holding you up?"

"If I'd been alone, I would have left by now."

She drew a resigned breath. "I'll go back. If all we can do is grouch at each other, we'll waste too much energy."

"You'd trust me to retrieve your horses?"

"Cal, I'd trust you with the rest of my life. No. That came out wrongly. I'm not proposing marriage to you. I'm saying that of course I'd trust you. I simply thought it wasn't fair to leave you to do something I wasn't prepared to do myself."

"You're not qualified to camp out and detain horse thieves."

"How do I gain that sort of qualification? By sitting at home with my sewing? Look, when you've gone I'm going to have to do many things I've never done before. And I'm sure you weren't born on a horse yelling 'stop, thief.' I'm sure you didn't walk past dry grass and say 'hey, presto, fire, light yourself.' I'm certain flour and water didn't leap into your hands saying 'I'll be damper when you cook me.'" She sat cross-legged by the plates. "And I bet the first time you slept on the ground you woke up aching, too."

"I can't imagine why you would assume any of that." The glimmer of a smile softened his mouth.

"Do we have to be mean to each other? I said I'll go back and I will."

"Would you consider marrying me?"

She stiffened with shock. "What?"

"I'm not proposing. But would you marry a man who had not a penny to his name?"

Very slowly, she gathered pleats in her skirts. "I'm in mourning."

"You're evading the question."

"I haven't thought of marriage."

"With a poor man. A moment ago you were talking about your prospective rich suitors."

"I don't see how I can think of marriage while I have my sisters to provide for. If I left them, they'd be worse off than they are."

"Why would you leave them?"

"Wouldn't I follow my husband wherever he led?"

"What if he led you into further poverty?"

"I wouldn't like it," she said bluntly. "No one dreams about going from bad to worse."

"'For better or worse,' I think the promise is."

"Given the choice, I'd take 'better.' And 'richer.' There, now are you happy? Have I made it clear that I don't think of marriage with you?" She snatched at her towel and went to the rocky basin to have a quick wash.

Her eyes prickled. She knew that that they'd both been talking about the same subject—their attraction to each other. She knew as well as he did that they couldn't have a view to marriage. Not every woman, however, wanted marriage or nothing.

When she went back, he was prodding a blackened lump in the fire with one booted foot. "The damper's ready." He rested his gaze for a brief moment on her mouth.

For an even briefer moment she closed her eyes. "The sooner we eat, the sooner I leave." She tried to hide the need he so easily aroused in her.

"You can't leave, as you know. You couldn't make it back in under a day and if you don't, you'll have to sleep out alone. I can't let you do that. You've come this far and you'll have to continue."

"I've passed the point of no return, have I?" She picked up the plates, wondering about her phrasing—*point of no return* in their journey or the point of no return in their relationship?

Chapter 12

Finally, the aroma of sizzling bacon wafted into the study. Edward wondered if the lady of the house would manage to be present for breakfast, but Irene emerged as undisturbed as usual and as perfectly groomed, hair curled like a bunch of grapes down the back of her head. She wore pale lilac, a color that aged her. Edward pondered saying so but realized that as she didn't look a day over forty, the aging effect hadn't quite caught up to reality.

"Good morning, Edward. A fine day." She sat in the chair he pulled out for her.

The dining room had been papered in cream and white stripes. Curtains in pale green framed the French windows, which had been opened to show the view of green velvet lawns and shade trees. He wondered if Irene had put in the croquet lawn she had discussed with him last year. If so, the area must be to the right. "Day indeed. You've missed the best part."

"You remember, don't you, that I have planned a garden party this afternoon?"

"I remember."

"And you will be here?"

"I said I would, didn't I?" Last night he'd refused, but Irene said how strange not to attend a garden party held at his own house when people knew he had arrived a few days ago. He didn't care what did or did not look strange or what people thought, but he finally decided that among Irene's chattering friends he might hear something useful. Therefore, he planned to arrive back here after his meeting with his lawyer.

An hour later, after being ushered into Mr. George Pennysmith's paneled office, he sat in an upright, uncomfortable chair beside Pennysmith's heavy desk.

"All is well with my affairs, I presume, or you would have contacted me. Do you have news of Charlton?"

"None." Pennysmith, a man in his late forties, slight and slim, with dark hair thinning on the top and a girlish pink mouth, affected surprise. "Why? What has happened?"

"I simply wondered if he had dealings with you. He had a business idea in the offing. He might have tried to obtain finance through you."

Pennysmith blinked at him. "Some three months ago I found three or four men with money to invest and put him in contact with them, if that's what you are asking."

"That is, indeed, what I am asking. And did any invest money in my grandson?"

The lawyer pulled at his earlobe. "Young Mr. Lynton has not kept me informed."

Edward lowered his eyebrows. "What exactly did you discuss with him?"

"Little more than I'm discussing with you. He paid for my time, which I found surprising. Normally I render my account to you."

Edward stared straight at the man. "I would like you to supply me with the names you gave him."

Pennysmith frowned. "I will send you a list. You are at your usual town address? I hope you and your grandson haven't found my recommendations in any way lacking."

Edward stood. "I'll expect to see the list sometime this afternoon."

Edward strolled down Rundle Street a comparatively satisfied man, interested to hear that for his proposed venture Charlton had paid for the services of the lawyer and not left his grandfather to foot the bill. The lad had ethics not considered by his father. While the lad stayed away not costing Edward a penny, he would certainly learn on which side his bread was buttered.

Either that or... Edward took a deep breath. He couldn't give up his investigations of Charlton. If the lad honestly preferred his independence and if he honestly wanted his own business, as long as Edward held the purse strings Charlton would be safe enough. Edward squinted in the unremitting sunlight.

He would listen to the lad's ideas when they met again.

* * * *

Ella watched Cal drop a steaming chunk of torn damper onto her plate. She ate from the center to the blackened crust on the outside, appeasing her appetite quickly. "Shall you save some for Jed? He might arrive for breakfast."

"He came back before you awoke, ate the rabbits, and has gone on ahead. He said he'll mark the easiest way because the gorge is steep. I've an idea we'll be leading our horses most of the time." He tossed the crusts to Girl and she swallowed them whole.

"When we catch up with the thieves, what will we do?"

"Take back the horses." He had already watered and saddled their mounts, which stood in the shade of the trees, blinking patiently. The rays from the sun burst through the canopy, dappling the ground. This day promised to be as hot as the last.

"Do you think taking them back will be so easy?"

"Roll your pack. It's time we left."

Ella strapped her pack onto her horse, experiencing her first glimmer of apprehension. When they caught the thieves, how would they force them to give back the horses?

She rode behind Cal, noting his uncompromising back and his broad shoulders. He seemed as one with the outdoors. His steadfastness matched the solidity of the red gums. His size and strength were undiminished by the vast areas, and his natural assurance echoed that of the untamed land.

If she'd met him six months earlier, before her father had died, and he'd proposed marriage she might have said "yes." With Papa there to care for his other daughters, she could have accompanied Cal to the city and would have borne his poverty with him. The many money-saving hints she'd learned in the past few months would have stood them in good stead.

Now, of course, she couldn't leave with him or help him. After the sale of the property, only the debts would be resolved. Her wool-clip money had to be used in conjunction with her sisters' if any were to survive financially. Without one of the portions, the other two would be in dire straits.

Their best chance now was to get back her horses and sell them.

Cal didn't speak to her and she didn't appreciate his attitude. He hadn't proposed, and she wouldn't accept anyway. Therefore, she saw no need for his high-minded principles.

About a mile along the river's edge, the scrub thickened. The visible trail shifted to the dense bushland and wandered farther and farther from the river. The hills grew higher. To mark the way, Jed had jammed broken branches into tree forks, although the trampled grasses clearly showed where a large group of horses had traveled the day before.

Dry branches snapped and cracked under the horse's hooves. Her sweaty fingers toyed with the reins. Girl raced through the undergrowth, mainly following Cal but circling back occasionally to check the lagging Ella. The sun rose higher in the sky. Tall and indomitable, Cal dismounted from his horse.

"The branches are too low. We'll have to walk single file."

She nodded and dismounted, too. No longer could they maintain a straight path. The track twisted through thick scrub. Clumps of tiny native orchids grew in the shade of the trees. She walked on little starry yellow flowers and exotic berry-bearing creepers and she climbed over fallen logs, all the while urging her horse along, too.

Cal stopped. "Tired?"

She shook her sweaty head. Her back ached and her legs hurt but she had no intention of holding him back.

"The gorge is over there."

She stared where he indicated, mutely, noticing a patch of blue sky.

"We need to rest."

She dropped her horse's reins. The horse stayed, tossing his head, jingling his bridle. Her blouse stuck to her back.

Cal passed her the water bag. "You first."

"No cups?"

"This is not a Sunday picnic."

She swilled, wiped her face with the back of her hand, and walked to where he had pointed while he drank. "Cal," she called in an awed voice. "Come and look."

He moved to her side. The gorge fell sharply a hundred feet or more, a split in pink rocks with a clear-running river below. Delicate plants grew out of the crevices, softening the perfect profile. She'd never seen anything quite as beautiful in her life. The air smelled fresher here, another atmosphere, cooler.

She glanced at Cal. He held out his hand to her, removing the stalemate of their situation. In the surrounding splendor, she moved into his embrace. Her hands slid around his neck and her body molded against his. She heard him sigh, and their lips met. His hands contoured her against him. With a mind emptied of everything but him, she slid her fingers beneath his collar; then, breathless and hazy, she took her lips from his. She leaned back to examine his expression, trying to read his thoughts.

He looked half desirous, half rueful. Her palms settled on his hot skin and his chin brushed across her hair, slowly, tenderly. He smiled at her and she knew she loved him. At that moment, she thought her heart beat only for him and she smiled back. His mouth relaxed, but his expression veiled. Almost too slowly to bear, he put her away from him. With a guiding hand, he escorted her back to their horses.

She walked with him along the marked trail, her energy renewed and her heart light. His calmness, his thoughtfulness, and the gallant way he tried to take care of her might be admirable, but she didn't want to be left with only a memory of gallantry. She wanted to be a woman who'd once loved a man who desired her and had even spoken of marriage, hopeless though that was. Without an experience of love, she would live a life of regret.

And Ella Beaufort didn't intend to regret a thing.

* * * *

Edward stood with his hand on the veranda railing, gazing at Irene's garden party guests. A string quartet played under the shade of a group of oak trees. Edward shifted restlessly.

He wore the required morning suit but would have preferred to be dressed in a cool cotton shirt and comfortable trousers. Although he'd been born to the drawing room, he didn't care for formality, whereas Irene, the daughter of a minor clergyman in England and raised respectably middle class, had all the graces of an aristocrat.

Dressed in an elegant, peach-colored, rustling gown trimmed with black lace on the neck and sleeves, she drifted over to Edward. One delicate white hand held her full skirts from the first step of the veranda. "Do come and mingle, Edward. Perhaps you would like to meet Daniel McLaren. He was a school friend of Charlton's and he has just arrived with his sister. Let me introduce you."

Edward put his cup on a marble-topped table and descended the two slate steps leading to the lawn. No longer left with an overview, he heard snippets of conversation as he followed Irene to the center of the formal garden, where thin sandwich triangles, small cakes, and bite-sized canapés had been set out on a lace tablecloth.

"Grace," Irene called authoritatively. A sandy-haired, slender young lady dressed in green turned from a group conversation. "Bring Daniel with you and meet my father-in-law."

Grace, balancing a small, frosted cake on a plate and a cup of tea in one hand, scanned Edward. She had unusual green eyes that tilted at the outside corners. Turning to a young man with the same eyes but redder hair, she indicated with her other hand that she would take his arm. He obliged instantly.

Irene made the introductions. The McLarens discussed the superiority of the weather, the excellence of the entertainment, and the need of the colony to be governed firmly. Edward recognized that, although attractive, the brother and sister would only ever echo the sentiments they heard around them. Neither would say a word out of place but each would appear to be contributing original thoughts.

After Edward and Daniel had discussed the latter's school days and his membership on the cricket team with Charlton, Miss McLaren asked, "Did you bring your grandson with you?" She discovered an interest in her glove buttons.

"Not this trip," Edward answered.

"I suppose at this time of the year he would have too much to do at the farm."

"The station," Edward contradicted carefully. "A farm is a place of diversities, varied stock perhaps, or stock combined with grain growing. A station has but one main aim—the breeding of sheep or cattle."

She glanced up at him and fluttered her eyelashes. Her rouged mouth curved. "I think that Charlton explained the same to me. I should remember these things. But Daniel says that ladies have too much to occupy their heads as it is—what with remembering which hat they wore the day before so that they don't wear the same one two days in a row." She poked her brother in the shoulder with the handle of her parasol.

"She's not serious," her brother said with an indulgent smile. "If I'd ever made such a fatuous comment I would have only been referring to her rather than to ladies in general. I don't find ladies to be any more empty-headed than males as a rule."

"But gentlemen don't like ladies to have a head for business." The shade of green Miss McLaren wore was similar to her catlike eyes, making her coloring more significant.

Her manner annoyed Edward. "Gentlemen like ladies who like them," he answered. "But I'm sure most would like the lady of their choice to understand their business, too."

"And I'm sure most ladies would try as long as the gentlemen didn't expect them to share those same interests. Don't you agree, Mrs. Lynton?"

"Henry and I shared common interests. Unfortunately, they weren't his father's." Irene glanced sideways at Edward.

"In which case it was very generous of Mr. Lynton to let you go your own way," Grace said with an odd flicker of boredom. "As I'm sure he would do with his grandson."

Edward tensed. He certainly hadn't allowed his grandson to go his own way, not if he meant to start a business. In the years they'd worked together, he'd seen no sign of flightiness but the lad had never been given his head, a mistake Edward now realized. Until Charlton knew some independence he couldn't prove himself, and until he returned Edward couldn't make reparation.

"As for ladies being interested in business," Daniel said, taking the conversation back to the former subject. "All very well as long as they don't expect to compete with men."

Grace laid a hand on her brother's arm. "And with progressive ideas like that, my dear, you'll be a great success as soon as you find a job worthy of you."

"Daniel has some skill in accounting," Irene contributed almost absentmindedly. Edward wondered if she'd been mentally restocking the buffet plates in the gazebo. "Indeed, his first job out of school was to work in the Bank of Adelaide."

"They passed me over for promotion." Daniel raised his chin. "I had no choice but to leave. Since then..." He spread his hands.

"Our father allows us a small income. We manage." Grace gave yet another pat to her brother's arm. "If all else fails, I'll contrive to marry a rich man—you can be sure of that." She laughed to show she'd been jesting.

"Irene," said a pleased voice. "It's too kind of you to invite me here, too kind. And you must give me the recipe for your curried egg. It's too, too delicious." A short, round woman about Irene's age, dressed in dark burgundy with a matching hat, stretched out a hand to Irene. "My, you look beautiful. Doesn't she look beautiful?" She included Edward and the McLarens with a gentle gesture.

Irene gave an amused smile. "You're angling for a donation to Saint Matthew's Orphanage, I suspect, Mildred. This is Edward, my father-in-law, and Grace and Daniel McLaren, whom I think you know. Mrs. Mildred Cameron."

"Yes, yes, we all know each other," Mrs. Cameron said, not quite turning her back on Daniel McLaren. "In town for the summer, are you? How too, too lovely. I believe it's very hot in the country at this time or so my goddaughter Rose writes. And dusty."

"Oh, and how is dear Rose?" asked Miss McLaren in the tone of someone who hoped for bad news.

"She'll be back in Adelaide within the next month, I vow. She and her sisters plan to sell their property."

"And then they will set up in a great mansion of their own."

Mrs. Cameron's smile fell. "I suspect they'll choose something more modest. They're not expecting to sell for more than a pittance, you know, what with the drought and sheep costing a bare shilling each."

"A pittance?" Grace said in a surprised voice. "In that case, I have to say I think it's a blessing she broke off—"

"Enough." Daniel ran his fingers through his groomed hair, destroying its direction. Without taking leave, he turned and walked off.

Grace stared after him. Her smile retained none of its former glitter. "Oh, dear. I didn't mean to upset him."

"If you can think of a job for him, please do, Edward," Irene said calmly. "Perhaps he might apply himself in the near future."

Edward frowned. He had neither the inclination nor the time to aid a young gentleman he barely knew. His own grandson, using none of his connections and no money but that he earned, was managing without handouts.

"And where does your goddaughter have this property?" he asked Mrs. Cameron, who stared in the direction young Daniel had taken with her eyebrows drawn together.

"Rose is just outside Noarlunga. The Beaufort Station. You might have passed it on your journey to Adelaide."

Edward was even now considering buying the property where he'd seen Girl rushing about. "And she lived in Adelaide for some time?"

"Oh, yes, for the past two years. Perhaps you heard Irene speak of her?"

"The day you arrived, Edward, remember?"

Edward scratched his neck beneath his starched collar. "The young beauty?"

Irene nodded.

So, they were speaking of the female Irene meant to pair with Charlton. The eager young buck had discovered the lady on his own. However, the young beauty was practically penniless. She would like a rich husband every bit as much Miss McLaren would, every bit as much as any female on the marriage market would. Charlton was, no doubt, often sought for his inheritance. Edward rubbed his chin.

The lad wouldn't tolerate such cupidity. That his grandfather knew. The lad would accept a love match and nothing less. Edward could speculate but he didn't know Charlton's feelings about Miss Rose Beaufort. He preferred not to think that Charlton, as a punishment, had decided to stay away from a fuddled old man who loved him.

If the lad wanted the lady, Edward would make sure he got her.

Chapter 13

Ella led her horse through the thick bushland. The animal balked and stalled whenever possible. Ella's arms ached. She longed to rest but, although uncomfortably sweaty and bone weary, she knew she had to go on. Cal couldn't afford to waste any shearing days and it was late Monday already.

Ahead of her, the strong, tireless Cal strode past a flock of rainbow lorikeets, which barely shifted to let him pass. Wondering what so occupied the birds, Ella dropped her horse's reins and investigated a scrawny shrub with prickly, arching canes and saw native raspberries. She picked one and popped the small fruit into her mouth. The taste was every bit as delicious as a cultured raspberry.

Glancing ahead at Cal, who appeared to have no interest in resting, she unpacked the billy and emptied her depleted dry goods, which she tucked back into her bedroll. With quick fingers, she raided the raspberry plant, almost filling the container while Girl sniffed at the birds' leavings. The lorikeets jiggled anxiously. Any other bird would fly off in a panic if a human invaded their territory, but lorikeets, as she'd noticed when they stole her orchard fruit, seemed to realize that if they hopped out of reach they could remain safe from a woman even if she ran at them with murderous intent.

Finishing, she gathered her horse's reins and hurried to catch up to Cal, who waited for her not far ahead. Girl slumped on the grass.

"We should probably water the horses," Cal said as she moved abreast. "I can see the river through there. We appear to have walked down the side of a hill."

"Good. I'll wash these raspberries and we can eat them. Could we make a small fire for a cup of tea?"

"I don't want to waste the time. We've done well today. The tracks we're following look fresh." He pointed to a pile of moist manure. "We can stop tonight for a proper meal if we've made up time." He led the way to the river.

She handed him her horse's reins and stooped to swish the fruit in the water. Girl found a lizard, which she munched with relish. While the horses drank, Cal filled the water bags. He tethered the horses to a tree and leaned against the sturdy trunk, waiting for her with his ankles crossed.

"Here, have some." Smiling, she scooped out a handful of dripping fruit. "They're gorgeous. They taste like real raspberries."

"They are real raspberries." Instead of taking the fruit from her, he lowered his head and ate out of her hand. "They're good." He stared straight into her eyes and without warning grabbed her into his arms. "And I can't be, any longer. I've thought of nothing but this all day." His lips took hers in an urgent kiss.

Desperate to hold him closer she circled her arms around his back, sloshing the water from the billy over his shirt. He straightened, ending the kiss, deliberately placing the can onto the ground. "Where were we?" His eyes darkened with desire as her scooped her into his arms again.

He kissed her with a hunger she reciprocated. Her body arched into his. She clung to him, pressing her lips to his, opening her mouth for his hot, demanding tongue. He lifted her, turning her in a half circle so that her back flattened against the tree trunk. Without taking his mouth from hers, he slid a hand into the opening of her blouse, found her breast, and cupped and stroked. His thumb brushed over her nipple, urging a peak, which he teased under his palm until her entire body throbbed.

She had no control over her actions or her sounds. Noises of encouragement and pleasure came from her chest and throat. Her body stretched to fit with his. She rocked her pelvis, wanting the hardness between his legs to fit between hers. The sensation excited her beyond thinking. He dug his fingers into her buttocks, firmly holding her in the position that gave her no relief—only more burning frustration.

Her hands worked his shirt out of his trousers and her palms pressed against the taut, moist skin of his chest and his back. She loved the flex of his muscles as he moved, so strong, so utterly masculine. The tang of eucalyptus, released by the heat of the day, added to the heady atmosphere. Two large magpies flew overhead, their wings loudly scything the air. She so badly wanted Cal that her mind tangled with lust and confusion.

She began to work at his belt, tugging, pulling, not certain if she tightened the buckle or loosened the clasp. His hand covered hers, leaving her breast tingling. He opened his buckle. He lifted her blouse and chemise. They stood, wet mouth to wet mouth, bare chest to bare chest, breathing hard.

Her heart pounded so desperately that she thought she shook the earth with the same rhythm. Again, his hand moved between them as he undid the buttons of his trousers. Her breaths came in gasps. Her coordination left. Mindless urgency overcame her and she didn't know what to do with her hands.

His lips moved to her hair. "Shh." He soothed the nape of her neck with his confident touch. His mouth caressed her ear and lipped her lobe. His hand took hers inside his trousers.

Heat. Hardness. A momentary relief as her fingers closed around the part of him that she'd wanted to touch, bare. Her head lifted. She stared into his eyes as her palm pressed against the oiled steel of him. If anyone could look tense, desirous, and resigned at the same time, that was how he looked. And handsome with his disheveled hair falling into his eyes, a slight growth of stubble on his jaw, and his intense gaze fixed with hers.

She wanted to speak but her throat closed. He read her mind. With no difficulty at all, he lifted her skirts and bunched the fabric at her waist. His hands cupped her behind and he tilted her forward. He bent his knees slightly and wedged his part between her legs. She made a sound of surprise.

Although she wanted this, she hadn't realized how right he would feel. Involuntarily her head arched back. She adjusted him against her and pressed down on him. He left her to do as she wished but in no time she realized that losing her virginity would be more difficult than she imagined.

"I don't think we are doing this right," she said in a strangely husky voice. "I think you need to lift me."

He shook his head. His eyes closed briefly. "If I do, it will all be over in a second. I told you before. I won't take you, not without marriage."

"You can't leave us like this. I'll die."

"We'll give each other pleasure. You remember? I gave you pleasure before, in the woolshed."

"You gave me frustration and a need to have you."

He kissed her with tender control. She leaned into him, her hands on his shoulders. His male part stayed excitingly between her legs, caressing her, sliding back and forth. Never in her life had she felt anything as wondrous.

"Please," she whispered. "Please, please, please."

He scooped her up, resting her knees on his hips. Very gently, very slowly, he let his wonderful hardness part her. She moaned. She couldn't control this or guide his glide. Only he could. She wanted him deep. He gave no more than a hint of how the married act might feel, a testing barely inside her. So lost was she in the sensation that she didn't notice for some seconds that the muscles in his shoulders quivered and that he had tensed harder than the tree trunk her spine scraped against.

She wanted him to give in and take her. She'd never wanted anything more in her life. The right word or the right movement might force him, but instead she splayed her hands across his jaw and kissed him. She didn't want to force him into anything. She wanted him to want her so much that he couldn't help himself.

He straightened. His responding kiss seemed to show ownership. He kissed her as if he knew the very shape of her lips and how she would move them. She relaxed, concentrating more on how she felt about him than what she wanted. Her chest expanded with love for him. As she expressed her emotion with her mouth, his male part pushed deep inside her.

Pain shot through her pelvis. Her knees dug into his hips, she tensed, and an involuntary sound of hurt burst through her throat. Carefully he withdrew. His eyes had closed. He opened them. His hands shook as he set her back on her feet. He didn't speak. She could see reproach and a tinge of disgust on his face. Not one minute did she assume he was disgusted with her. He was annoyed with himself.

"It was my fault," she said, eyes downcast, letting her skirts drop. "Don't be cross with yourself."

"Damnation!" He turned his back.

"No harm done."

"Don't fool yourself. We did exactly the harm I didn't mean to do. But then again, maybe I did, maybe I did." He smoothed her hair back from her face and gazed into her eyes. "You shouldn't be out here with me for exactly this reason. And you know this as well as I do." He stared at her long enough to read her innermost thoughts, which unfortunately happened to be far from pure. She still hurt a little, but passion blazed within her, for him, only him.

Finally he buttoned his pants and shirt and flicked his hair back from his face. He collected his horse and led the way again. She didn't feel disdained or discarded. Perhaps she couldn't state her terms or decide on the time and place, but he would teach her something far more important than how to mend a fence.

He would teach her about his body and hers.

* * * *

Glancing to the left, Cal saw the next of Jed's signs, a twisted branch pointing ahead. For some time, he'd not needed Jed's help. The tracks he followed couldn't be more than two hours old. The last patch of horse droppings had still been warm. He kept going until the daylight left a mere gray gleam through the trees. He wanted the horses back tonight. He planned to take them and leave in the dark with Ella and without confrontation. Her safety should not be risked.

He'd felt the ache of hunger until dusk. Not for food. For Ella. He couldn't credit he'd broken through her hymen. Walking couldn't wear down his need. Thinking of their next meal couldn't wear down his need. Only she could.

However, if he had her, he wouldn't be satisfied. He would want her again and again. He wouldn't be able to go on his way—earning enough money to staff and outfit the warehouse, which must be done even more urgently now that he meant to wed this woman who could only marry a man with money.

To act on his lust now would be the act of a cad. Not to go farther and not to share with her the ultimate pleasure would be an act of waste and scorn. He groaned.

He shouldn't scorn her, not Ella, not the most splendid woman he'd ever met and was ever likely to meet. "How does this look for a campsite?"

"Appealing." She smiled. "Mind you, a bed of gravel on slime would look appealing. The only thing more appealing would be a real bed."

Although his heart skipped a beat, he ignored her accidental innuendo and glanced at Girl. The dog had a satisfied expression on her face. Along the way she'd found herself a few lizards to eat and a big-eared, small, hopping creature, a bilby, who had paused too long while watching the strangers pass. "I suppose a real meal would be appealing, too."

"I'm too tired to care. I can make more scones and if we can have a cup of tea, I'm sure I'll sleep like a baby tonight."

"We can have a quick, hot snack, and you can have a sleep. I want to go on ahead and scout out the lie of the land."

"You would leave me alone?"

"You're safe enough."

He started a small fire. With a weary sigh, she began to make the dough while he went to the river. He'd seen lilies and knew the tubers to be edible. Uprooting a handful, he washed them and took them back to her. She stared.

"They taste quite bland, and they're sustaining." He sat on the blanket she'd set out. "And with raspberries for dessert, I think we'll be satisfied."

She watched the flame of the fire in the half light. "Why would you go on without me?"

"I want to see the horse thieves without them seeing me."

"Do you think you might ask them for the horses?"

"I think I'll get the horses any way I can." He grinned. "Then I'll come back and we'll leave quickly."

"So I shouldn't be asleep. I should be awake and packed."

"Before I can answer that I want to see if it's possible to sneak up on them."

They drank their tea in silence. The night birds began to warble. The ground cover rustled, disturbed by the first foraging of the nocturnal creatures—possums, betongs, wombats, and other marsupials, most with large gleaming eyes and shy habits. A thump rattled a tall eucalypt. Jed had returned, smacking the shafts of his spears loudly against a tree trunk, a warning of his approach.

Cal watched the man emerge from the trees. He strode confidently as if he had night sight. In one hand he held a limp dead duck, his offering for the evening meal. With a smile, he dropped the carcass on Ella's lap. Jed had apparently appointed himself provider, leaving Cal to feel less than adequate.

"Thank you, Jed," Ella said politely. "I suppose I should, um, chop off its head before I cook it." She had a controlled look of martyrdom on her face.

"I'll do it." Cal took the duck, swiped off its head with the cooking knife, and threw that and the entrails to Girl, who took her spoils off to consume. He gave the feathered carcass back to Ella.

Jed sat by the fire, cross-legged, and accepted a cup of tea. "Mans rest."

"How far away?"

"Two hills."

"I can get there before...?" Cal pointed at Ella and flattened his palms together on one cheek, indicating, he hoped, sleep.

Jed nodded. "I get horses tonight."

Cal firmed his jaw. "No. I'll get the horses."

Ella grinned. "I'll get the horses."

Both men stared at her.

"We'll all get the horses," she amended, tearing the feathers out of the duck. The down drifted a little in the night breeze. "We have seven horses to collect. It's logical."

"Describe their camp," Cal said to Jed, not certain that, without any help whatsoever, he could lead seven horses quietly through the trees.

The aborigine took a stick and drew in the soil. He indicated a campfire and two men. Then he drew a circle of horses to one side. "Trees," he said, dotting behind the horses. He held up one hand, indicating the number of horses, which they already knew to be nine with the thieves' horses.

Cal leaned back on his elbows and stretched out his legs. "We'll give them a few hours, let them sleep, and I'll bring back the horses. You two can sleep if you pack first and I'll wake you when I get back."

"Cal." Ella sounded patient. "There's nothing to stop them following you here and taking back the horses."

"They won't see the tracks in the dark and we'll leave before they wake up."

"We'll be as slowed down by the extra horses as they were. That means we'll have to set a pace we might not be able to sustain. It also means they might catch us if they are so inclined. I think we should take their horses when we take ours. And their boots. That way we'll make things far more difficult for them. They deserve it. They stole the horses in the first place and put us to this trouble."

Jed nodded, grinning. "Lose 'orses," he said, placing his mug by the fire. "Lose boots."

"That's a wonderful idea. Perhaps we could mask the tracks as well." Ella said, smiling. "That would certainly give them something to think about."

"This is not a game, Miss," Cal said with a frown, despite being amused by her enthusiasm. "This is a dangerous task not only for you but for Jed. If he is spotted, he'll be taken for a savage and they'll be within their rights if they kill him."

"Dear life. We can all dress as natives and frighten the thievery out of them. We can look like a horde. In the dark, they certainly won't recognize me as a woman, should they see me."

"I would."

She gave him a mischievous glance. "I'm glad. Cal, I would feel less nervous if I could go with you. I don't want to sit here worrying. If we make plans now we'll know what to do and we'll do it efficiently. If the men are awake we'll wait. I won't be in any more danger there than I would be here alone. If something happens to you..." Her voice trailed off and her bottom lip trembled.

He could see she wasn't nervous about herself, and her certainty that she would be safe with him expanded his chest. He tapped his fingers on the side of his cup. "Promise me you'll obey my every command."

She nodded. "I promise. I don't want to be a pest. I want to be of use."

They ate the scones and the tubers as they discussed their plans. Ella left the duck to stew while they settled down for a few hours rest. Cal didn't think he would sleep, but he made a pretense so that Ella would. Jed snored like a mating possum and Girl came back and curled at Cal's feet.

Some few hours later, he awoke. The fire had died and the duck had almost melted into the bones. He served the meat on a single plate and woke the others. Ella sat up, wide-eyed. Jed yawned and stretched. After they'd eaten and cleaned up, they packed the horses, leaving them tethered to the trees.

Jed noiselessly led the way. Cal and Ella had darkened their faces and hands with mud. The wet soil dried rapidly and didn't do more than take the shine from their skin. Nevertheless, he could see Ella had confidence in her disguise. She reminded him of a child play-acting.

"It's the first adventure I've had in my life," she whispered, and he believed her. Her eyes glowed with excitement.

They took an hour to walk through the scrub to the men's campsite, a patch of bare earth closer than he had imagined. Jed's description was accurate. The horses stood tethered in an outcrop of trees. The men lay by their dead campfire. Spotting two empty rum bottles thrown aside, Cal smiled. Unless the men had harder heads than he supposed, they would pose little threat.

As discussed, he, Ella, and Jed began to pick long grasses. With Jed demonstrating, they tied the grass to their boots, covering the soles. Ella stood between two trees, marking the most direct way through to their own camp so that in the dark no one would be confused as to direction. Jed crept toward the stolen horses. Cal moved belly-flat to the fire.

One of the men emitted a porcine snort. Cal froze. The man threshed an arm; rolled over; and, after a period of not breathing, began to snore rhythmically. Cal moved on, reaching out a hand for the two pairs of boots that sat by the ashes of the fire. He tucked the footwear under his arm, warily inspecting the sleeping horse thieves. Neither looked particularly prepossessing in the moonlight. The snorer had a gray-streaked, unkempt beard and he looked rotund. The other was younger, with long, limp, greasy hair, receding at the front. Cal recognized them as the men who had asked Vianna for directions.

An open sack sat beside the sprawled and sweat-hardened saddles. Cal peered in. The men had garnered a substantial food supply. With an amused tilt of his lips, he took the sack as well, sliding backward until far enough from the sleepers to stand upright.

He moved quietly toward Jed, who held the rope halters of all nine restive and alert horses. Cal took the Clydesdales, the stock horses, and Miffy, leaving Jed to manage the men's horses with one hand and the carriage pair with the other. Without a spoken word, Jed and Cal separated. Jed went farther into the bushland riding one of his four horses and Cal led his group on foot to where Ella stood. She grabbed one pair of boots, tied the laces together, and slung the footwear around her neck. She tied the next pair and slung them around Cal's neck. Then she mounted one of the stock horses bareback, using Cal's cupped hands as a boost. Cal balanced the sack over the other stock horse before he mounted.

Then, silently, he led the Clydesdales back to their camp. Girl bounded from nowhere, following. When Cal saw the silver ribbon of the river, he laughed aloud.

"I might take up a life of crime," Ella said with a jaunty sideways glance. "It's far easier to steal horses than I expected." After whirling them around her head, she threw a pair of men's boots into the water.

Cal untangled the other pair and set them sailing high into the dark night, watching them splash into the center of the river. "Should the thieves wish to follow," he said in a satisfied voice, "they'll do it the hard way."

Chapter 14

The midday sun blared across the wilting landscape. Wiping her sweaty brow with her forearm, Ella glanced around at the site of their very first camp. "How on earth did we make such good time?"

Cal eased his saddle position. He hadn't shaved for the past two days, but having a stubbly chin didn't detract from his looks. Instead, a slight disreputability added to his clean-cut appeal. "It's always harder to leave than to return." He now rode one of the Lannock's horses and Ella the other. Jed had spirited away the stock horses and the carriage pair in an effort to confuse any would-be follower.

"That sounds profound."

He shrugged. "Don't you find it so?"

"I suppose. We mainly walked from here, but we rode back because we know the way. Should we go farther?"

"How do you feel? Do you want to rest? We've been on the go for half a night and half a day."

"I have the idea that if I get off this horse, I won't be able to get back on. Let's continue until we find a good place to cross the river. Then we can stop."

Cal glanced at Girl, who had taken the opportunity to rest. She and the stolen horses, together with a dun and a piebald belonging to the thieves, had walked without stopping for almost twelve hours. Cal kept the thieves' horses on lead reins but long since, he had removed the rope halters from Miffy and the Clydesdales. Whenever they or Miffy grew distracted by green feed, Girl nipped at their heels, keeping them up with the riders. "A good place? Do you mean a shallow place?"

"Of course. We don't need to make anything more difficult than need be."

Cal nodded and in another hour, he found a rocky riverbed where the water trickled, wide but shallow. Without looking at Ella, he crossed, the tethered horses behind him. Ella watched closely. When he reached the reed-covered bank, he dismounted and removed the saddle from his horse.

Now certain she would not be out of her depth she began to guide hers through the gleaming water. Her horse, likely sensing her apprehension, picked skittishly at each shining ripple. With a tense back and a pounding heart, she finally arrived beside Cal. She, too, dismounted, rubbing the back of her neck, conscious of his assessing gaze.

As he loaded his saddle onto the thieves' piebald, he said, "Perhaps if Girl hadn't rushed at you that day you would be swimming with us by now."

She made a rueful mouth. "The billabong was a test I failed."

"I'm sorry," he said simply.

"It doesn't matter. Swimming won't be a part of my future. I'm about to be a city girl, remember?"

He nodded. "We'll let the stock rest while we make a cup of tea. As soon as we've eaten, I'll change you over to the dun. That way, we can keep going until almost dark."

She let out a breath. "I could certainly do with a snack. What do we have?" Girl licked her hand. She glanced down and patted the tail-wagging dog. "How sweet, Girl. Thank you. I think she just congratulated me for crossing the river without a word of complaint," she said with a lightness she was far from feeling. "And she is very brave herself and probably very tired."

Cal tossed over the bundle he'd had since the foray into the thieves' camp. "Look in the bag. See if I stole anything edible."

"Oh, my," she said, peering inside. "There's something to be said for a life of crime. We have leg of ham or a good portion of one. I haven't tasted ham in a twelvemonth. There's a round of cheese and a chunk of that lovely German bread. Dried fruit, too. We can have that now and the rest tonight."

Cal chewed dried apricots while the billy boiled. She made the tea. When she rinsed out the cups, he busied himself transferring the other saddle. The dun lifted his head and nickered, watching the scrubland. Jed appeared, riding one of the stock horses and leading the other and the carriage pair.

"How does that man know when we stop?" Cal asked her in an undertone.

"He always used to find Papa wherever he was. I don't know how he does it, but it's a handy skill."

Jed slid off his horse. "Lose 'orses now?" he asked, looking regretful.

Cal scratched his dark chin. "Perhaps not. I've wondered… We have no proof that their horses were not stolen, too. I think we should take them back with us and deliver them to the police station in Noarlunga."

Ella smiled. "Now that's inventive thinking."

Jed shuffled his bare feet. "I go this way." He lifted a hand and indicated his direction with a sweeping palm. "Through bush. Too 'ard for Missy. I go homestead tonight and tell other missies we done good."

"You can get back tonight?" Cal lifted his eyebrows.

"Quick, 'ere." With a bright grin, he took his horses back into the scrub.

Ella's gaze followed Jed. "I suspect the thieves aren't close behind us. He would have said if they were. Anyway, I think we would have utterly confounded them with Jed taking his horses in one direction and us going in the other. They wouldn't have known who to follow."

"You're probably right but I think we ought to put as much distance between them and us as we can before dark. We can follow Jed, or…" Cal cupped his hands, prepared to help Ella onto her fresh horse.

"He said it's too hard for me. I don't want to test if he's right. We came this way and I'm content to go back this way. So, lead on, MacDuff."

He gave her a strange glance. For a moment, she wondered if even now he hadn't told her his true name and then she wondered at herself for doubting him. The man was truly incredible. He'd taken on a great deal of responsibility to collect seven horses, none of which belonged to him. He had trekked for days, making decisions that neither she nor Jed could. Her safety during this time had rested on his shoulders and she had relied on him, completely. He could call himself MacLangdon for all she cared.

"You said once you'd not taken on responsibility before," she said, examining his strong face.

He gave her a twisted smile. "Only for small matters. My greater test will be—"

She heard a loud crack and a crash of splintering wood. The ground shook. Birds scattered into the air, screeching. A long, low keening sound fought through her throat as she watched the fallen leaf canopy of a red gum shudder in one last rustling throe. She covered her mouth with both her palms.

Cal stared at her, surprise etched on his face. "That was some yards away. We weren't in any danger."

She noted his concerned expression and realized she was weeping. "A branch like that dropped on our property six months ago." She gasped in an effort to stifle her sobs. Using both palms, she wiped her wet face.

"Papa was beneath. Now I know he didn't have a chance. I thought... I couldn't understand why he didn't get out of the way."

"As you saw, it wouldn't have been possible." He took a step closer to her.

Taking a step back and warding him off with a shake of her head, she found her lace handkerchief in a little pocket near the waistband of her skirt and energetically blew her nose. "When I saw the debt he left I wondered if perhaps he couldn't see any other way out. But it was an accident, fate if you will." Her voice cracked. "I expect that, had he lived, he would have pulled us out of debt the same way I plan to. He clearly knew the value of the carriage horses because he made sure that if anything happened to him I would own them outright."

"That may be so. It's possible they wouldn't be counted as assets should the mortgage be called in. So, perhaps he did leave you protected."

She glanced at him, uncertain. "You don't think they could be taken now if one of our debtors wanted his money back?"

"If the debts are considered to be your father's, and the horses are considered to be yours..."

"I won't test the premise." She stiffened her spine. "As soon as we get to the city I shall sell them and buy a house for my family."

"A noble sentiment."

"You may scoff, but you don't have the same priorities I do."

He nodded, the subject evidently not important to him and rightly so. Turning, he glanced at Girl, who pattered along stoically. He gestured and, with bunched weariness, she leaped to the saddle in front of him, settling like a limp handshake. Within half an hour, she sat like queen of all she surveyed.

And so was Ella, too, now her horses had been reclaimed. When the carriage pair sold and the wool money arrived, she could have not only a house but a small income as well. Another four or five days of shearing and Cal would be gone. Ella would have no further private moments with him. Her only chance to experience passion had passed.

* * * *

Legs comfortably crossed, Edward occupied a low, comfortable armchair by the fern-filled fireplace in Irene's drawing room. "I want you to go to Noarlunga," he said to Sam.

"I ain't spyin' on him." With mutiny on his face, Sam tightened his arms across his chest. "The lad don't deserve it. Find someone else to do your dirty work."

"I don't want my grandson spied on. I simply want to know where he is and why. You can have a room in the hotel, any room, any hotel in Noarlunga, and all you have to do is gossip with the local shopkeepers, which I know you will do anyway."

"Gossip about the lad? That's spyin'."

"I don't want you to gossip about him," Edward said irritably. "Far from it. I want you to find out if there is any gossip about him and a young lady on that station. If he is planning nuptials, I want to know. If they want to stay there, I might consider giving them the place. Who knows?"

"I knows. You want him back at Farvista. You wouldn't be content to have him at a piddling little place like that when he can have the biggest in the colony."

"Who said he can?" Edward pushed his jaw forward pugnaciously.

"We both know he can. You just want to work out how you can take back your words without having to take back your words. Not never will you apologize," Sam said bitterly. "Might be he won't come back until you do."

Edward swallowed. He leaned forward in his seat, fixing his eyes with Sam's. "I want him back. Heaven knows. But not unwillingly. I want him to return of his own accord. If I know where he is," he said, trying not to sound as if he were pleading, "maybe I can help him get what he wants, be it a woman or a business. And if I can help..."

"You can still be in control," Sam said with emphasis. "I'm not spyin'."

"Just go there. Please. See if you can learn anything. He might need me and think he can't ask. There might be something you or I could do for him."

Sam's lips tightened. He stared at the window, tapped his hands on his knees, and finally blew out a breath. "Got the same sky here as at home. Guess the sky in Noarlunga ain't much different. I'll go for a week, no more. But I'm not spyin'."

Edward rose to his feet, ready to order the carriage for Sam. He needed to know what Charlton meant to do, but not because he wanted to be in control. The time had come to make amends.

* * * *

By late afternoon, Ella wilted. She barely had the energy to guide her plodding horse. "Cal," she called, trying to sound bright.

He turned in his saddle, eyebrows raised.

"You look tired," she said in a sympathetic voice. "I think we should stop."

He smiled. She doubted that he often mistook her meaning.

"Over there." He pointed to a group of tall red gums. As usual, he led the way. As usual, she and the rest of his retinue followed.

She slid off her horse. Her knees trembled. The inexhaustible Cal unsaddled the horses and rubbed them down while she unpacked the bedrolls, stretching her back to ease her cramped muscles.

Cal unfurled his blanket. "I'll make a cup of tea."

"We can have that ham now." Ella reached over for the plates, finding her appetite in an instant.

Cal stared at her for a moment but said nothing. He made up the fire and boiled the billy while she kept up inconsequential chatter designed to disguise her aches. When she'd served most of the food, she gave the ham bone to Girl, who trotted off with her treat into the scrub.

Finishing her meal, Ella gazed at the pink-tinted clouds that stretched across the horizon. "We can't be more than a couple of hours from home. Should we go on?"

Cal gave her a shaded glance. "We've earned our rest." He took off his boots and reclined on one elbow. "I think a dip in the water would refresh us."

"You dip. I'll rest."

His mouth curved enigmatically. His heavy-lidded gaze scanned her. He leaned over, straightened her legs, and began unlacing her boots.

His touch on her ankle sent a tingle up her leg. Her insides stirred. She sat, hoping the moment would extend. He pulled off her boots and stockings and stood, offering one hand.

"You don't honestly believe I want to swim?"

He took her hand and pulled her to her feet. "I believe you would like to bathe with me."

An unbidden warmth touched her cheeks. She smiled, breathless as he scooped her soap out of her pack. With his hand on her waist, he guided her to the river's edge, where she stood uncertain, wary but energized as he pulled his shirt out of his waistband and over his head. "Undress."

Her body quivering with anticipation she dropped her blouse by his shirt, knowing her chemise covered her modesty. In that moment, he stepped out of his trousers. He stood naked before her. She stilled, not certain where to look. He made the decision for her when he began to untie her skirt and so she watched his hands, large and strong, square-fingered, warm, and brushing her belly. Her pulse pounded so hard she could hear the thud.

Before a single doubt could enter her mind, she kicked off her skirt, leaving the fabric puddled beside her, and crossed her arms at the hem of her thigh-length chemise, scooping up the muslin. Finally, she stood naked with a naked man who looked so perfect that her thundering heart almost stopped.

With a tender expression on his face, he reached over and pulled the pins from her hair. Using gentle fingers, he combed her locks into a crinkled fall across her shoulders. Then, smiling, he picked up her soap and, taking her hand, led her into the water. The flow tugged at her ankles. She pulled back. At its deepest, the river was waist high, but here in the shallowest part the water-slick rocks were a test of her balance. If she slipped...she didn't want to go farther than her reach from the bank.

He stopped and toed a few stones out of the way. "We'll be safe here. We don't need to go any deeper," he said, clearing a section with his foot. His hand slid under her hair to the skin of her back, transferring his confidence to her. He sat, drawing her down with him.

The water had warmed with the day. She found herself between his knees, her back to his chest. He lifted her hair, dropping a fall forward over her breasts. His body heat added to the luxurious experience of his bare skin against hers. Not yet able to relax she tensed with sensuous enjoyment. His lathered palms began to wash her rib cage, paying no particular attention to the undersides of her breasts, which somehow got in the way. The man meant to tease her, make her forget about being in the river. He stroked down her arms and across her neck and shoulders, but her every nerve ending knew that stimulation was his priority. Giving in to pleasure, she angled back, gasping as he traced the suds over her breasts.

His fingers caressed her nipples until she couldn't breathe while, achingly aroused, she slid her hands the length of his thighs and back again. Her head rested against the junction of his shoulder and neck. She turned slightly and, with sensual testing, ran her lips across his bristled jaw.

His mouth met hers. He groaned, gripping her waist, turning her to face him, and lifting her across his thighs. His male hardness pressed against her buttocks. She curled her hands onto his shoulders, and he leaned over her, leaving her hair to float in the current. Within an instant she panicked. The sound of water rushed in her ears. She stiffened, pushing her palms into his upper chest.

He cupped her head, his lips gently persuading her to relax. Her arms relaxed a little as he lifted her head higher and began to lather her hair. His fingers were strong but gentle. None of her memories included her hair being washed by another. She kept her gaze on his face, nervous, pleased, and yet dreading her next immersion, less intimidating for he smiled. His confidence persuaded her to leave herself to his unknown mercies.

Finally, he helped her sit again and, with an expression of concentration, wrung out her hair. This small gesture touched her to her depths. Needing to express her appreciation, she took the soap from him, smiling at his reluctance. She disciplined her mouth and made foam with her fingers. Then, using massaging strokes, she rubbed over his bunched biceps, his wide shoulders, and his muscular chest, lingering over his masculine form until she had changed her luxurious reciprocation into a sensual indulgence. The man had physical qualities that heated her past endurance. She loved his size and strength, and she loved the way he set the benchmark for the perfect male body.

She threw the soap to the bank, and he grabbed her into his embrace, kissing her with passion.

His time for deliberation seemed to have passed.

Chapter 15

Ella had never been so sure about anything in her life. The water streamed off Cal's wide shoulders as he carried her to the shore. He deposited her on her feet, smiling softly as he wrapped her in her towel. His eyes stayed on her while he wiped himself down with his shirt. "Why not drop that?" He indicated her towel. "And let me see all of you."

She let her towel drop as for the first time she scanned his big, beautiful body. The sight of his arousal set her heart thudding. She couldn't fit him inside her...but she had, before. Her body heated and tingled, and she trembled. He took her into his arms and walked her backward to his blanket, sinking to his knees and carefully placing her on her back.

He kissed her and then rested his gorgeous weight on top of her.

She parted her legs, aching with need. His skin was steamy hot. She clung to him. His muscles tightened. His tongue tipped hers and entered into the heat and wetness of her mouth. His male part entered her and withdrew with tantalizing slowness. The painful anticipation built. She moved with him. She could concentrate on nothing but sensation. He thrust deeper and harder and she wanted him to continue forever. The expectation of each thrust was as pleasurable as the stretch inside her. Her hands gripped and clenched his buttocks, encouraging his rhythmical entry. And then he withdrew.

"No."

"Shh." He breathed out hard and slid down her body, taking her with his mouth.

At first, his tongue seemed too soothing, as if he wanted to lull her storm. But within seconds, she appreciated the delicacy of his touch and understood that he stimulated her where her nerve endings met. She jolted spontaneously and, without knowing how or why, she went into a spasm of sensation. She clutched at his hair, panting and apologizing.

With barely a pause, and certainly ignoring her confused entreaties, he moved to his previous position, dropping his mouth across hers. His enjoyment of what she decided could not possibly be wickedness, for she reveled in the taste of herself on his lips, added to hers.

Soon he entered her again and they moved together in a pattern so compelling that her insides exploded with pleasure. One contraction followed another while he stilled and lifted onto his palms, then he slowly withdrew. His strong face tensed and he groaned, moving downward and out of the bracket of her legs. She stared at him, glorying in his maleness.

She didn't know what to say. "Thank you" seemed inadequate. She reached out and ran her palms over his shoulders. He turned his head and kissed one of her hands. For no reason she could imagine, she wanted to cry. Instead, she smiled. "You'll have to ask me to marry you now."

She wished she'd bitten her tongue when she saw the expression on his face. She'd meant her words as a joke, but he hadn't heard them as such.

"I'm afraid so." He rolled off her, his expression unreadable. "Will you marry me, Miss Beaufort?"

"I don't accept proposals made under duress."

He sat up and leaned over his bent knees. One hand lifted to knead his forehead. "You might have no choice. I didn't give you my seed, I hope, but despite my best intentions..." He glanced at her from under his thick lashes. "If anything eventuates from this, please remember that I'm prepared to take responsibility for my...dashed...idiocy just then."

"Idiocy?" She breathed in. "I had the impression that my charms overwhelmed you."

"Let's hope they didn't overwhelm us into becoming parents."

Her throat dried. "Should I be left with your child, I'll seek you out with a shotgun."

"You'll send me word."

"Oh, dear life. A woman never gets pregnant the first time," she said, managing to inject a tone of frivolity.

She pulled her damp hair onto one shoulder and began to twist the length into a semblance of order. Not so her mind, which she couldn't untangle. From the first he'd been clear that he wasn't a marrying man. If she trapped him he would hate her. "Aside from that..." She took a deep breath. "I couldn't take my money to a husband. My sisters' security would be at risk. I can see a way ahead for us now and I can't give up."

"However, if I had some money you wouldn't have a problem."

"Few women have problems with monied men. They can live where they like and choose their lifestyle. Mine has been predetermined until Vianna is at least eighteen."

"I thought the same about my life until I changed it."

"Men! You have those opportunities. We women are stuck with what you leave us and we have to make the best of the worst. I'm darned if I want to be forced into making the best of another losing situation. I'll take a rich man or I'll take the risk of my future into my own hands." She stood and marched over to her bedroll, where she found her comb and distracted herself by roughly untangling her hair.

He stared at her face, then he nodded. "I understand. You've made that clear."

Her mind awhirl, she dragged at her hair until, mainly dry, the sections were ready to braid. She would have liked him to argue with her and tell her that he could use her portion of the money in a way that would assure her family's livelihood if she cared to be with him. However he sat, staring into the dying fire until darkness began to hide the landscape. With nothing more to be said, and with him apparently disinterested in her charms now that he'd taken the edge off his idiocy, she slid into her chemise and set her bedroll at a distance from his.

The waxing moon cast silver highlights onto his naked chest. She wished he would dress. Her attraction to him hadn't lessened, probably would never lessen while his beauty of body and strength of character only served to emphasize the contradiction of her need for autonomy and her wish to have her future assured.

When he held out his hand to her and said, "Come here," she rose and went to him. If nothing more, she could enjoy his momentary comfort.

He enfolded her in his arms and lay back with her while she gazed at a million shimmering stars. Surrounded by his calm she slept.

Sometime in the night, she felt his mouth meld with hers. He gave her body a respite she hadn't realized she needed until his thrusts built her to an intense release. Again, he spilt his seed into his own hand and again she slept. And again, he woke her, this time during the pale light of dawn, making slow and expert love to her until she wondered if he or she would ever slake the desire they had for each other. Her body seemed to belong to another person, one who had no responsibility other than for pleasure.

She dressed when he did and left the camp with few words and the painful thought that this secretive episode would one day be only a memory in a life empty of all but duty.

* * * *

Cal rode toward the woolshed, leading the herd of horses with Ella bringing up the rear. Within moments, Frank's grinning face appeared in the shed doorway.

"It's them," he yelled loudly enough to shake the rafters. He and the other shearers whooped and raced outside over to the stable paddock gate.

"Took your time," Alf said, breathless.

"Jed turned up this morning," Ned said from a position beside Cal's stirrup as Frank swung open the gate. "He brought back the chestnuts and the stock horses and disappeared after saying you and Missy would turn up later. You're earlier than we expected."

Cal dismounted while the shearers ushered the horses through the gate. One of the Clydesdales whickered a greeting to the horses as they entered. "I thought Alf said we had dallied."

"You know Alf. He don't like to pay anyone a compliment." Ned began to unsaddle Cal's horse.

Cal helped Ella dismount. Although she didn't need help he wanted to hold her one last time. She didn't linger in his arms, a deed he regretted and applauded at the same time.

"Thank you. My, but it's nice to be home." She smiled brightly at Ned. "Are we in time for lunch, or have you eaten already? I'm afraid I'm not as good at telling the time by the sun as I ought to be."

"We've eaten." Benji unsaddled her horse. "Here's Miss Rose. Reckon she'll find something for you in a trice."

With an expression of concern, Rose took both Ella's hands in hers. "You're as brown as a berry. I suspect you haven't been wearing your hat. We'll need to get some lotion on your face."

Cal scowled at her. "Your sister has been doing three men's jobs for the past four days, and now she is tired and hungry."

Rose lifted her cool face to Cal. "And so I shall feed her and you, and then she shall rest. We missed you, Ella. You must come inside and tell us about your adventure."

At that moment, Vianna came flying from the homestead. The back door banged behind her. "Miffy, Miffy," she yelled. "Oh, she's back, the darling, darling thing." She pelted into the stable paddock, where her pony had already nudged between the Clydesdales at the water trough.

"I expect she's pleased to see *you*, too," Cal said wryly to Ella.

Ella grinned. "I might grow conceited if I thought I stood before a pony in my sister's esteem. Well, Cal." She hesitated. Taking a deep breath, she moved toward him; put her hands on his shoulders; and, standing on tiptoe, kissed his cheek. "You're a hero. I don't know what any of us would have done without you."

After a quick glance at Ella, Rose kissed his cheek, too. Then Vianna, who had been acknowledged by her pony and politely ignored in favor of a long drink of water, scooted through the gateway and kissed him, too. He stood, bemused. Ella's kiss had been careful and friendly and, as her sisters had repeated her action, not inappropriate. So he nodded to the ladies and stepped aside as they made their way to the house.

"Me and Miss Vianna groomed Jed's group of horses this morning and fed and watered them," Frank said proudly. "I reckon I'll do the Clydesdales, too, if Ned will do the others."

"I'll do a couple," Benji said. "What about the borrowed horses? Want me to take them back to the neighbor when they've had a feed?"

"Tomorrow. They've traveled a fair distance. I think they should rest before their next trip."

"Likely the dairyman can take them back with him in the morning," Alf said prosaically. "Don't you do another thing. The lads'll tend the horses for you. Got nothing else to do this afternoon."

"Have you finished today's shearing?" Cal glanced over to the woolshed, where the yard stood full of cleanly shorn sheep.

"Yes. We're planning a little celebration now you're back. Got us a keg of beer on Sunday, waitin' for the right moment." Ned pushed his hair back from his face.

Alf nodded. "'Spect we'll finish shearing on Saturday. Benji's been filling the holding yard each day and whoever wants a good walk has been herding the shorn sheep back to the long paddock, like you said. We're shearing to plan."

"We're shearing to Alf's plan," Frank said. "Each day we shear an extra hundred between us for you."

"What do you mean, for me?"

"Alf wanted to pay you fifteen shillin's a day while you was away. Course, we know you would earn more than that because you shear fast, but between us we couldn't keep up."

"That's kind of you," Cal said, his mouth tight. "But I don't expect charity."

"It's not charity." Alf tapped his pipe on the fence post. "I had to pay you anyway. You got back my Clydesdales. Know how much it would have cost me to replace them? More'n ten pound each, that's how much. So if I give you five pounds as a reward, I'll come out of it ahead."

Cal rubbed his chin. The men had made a wage for him while he'd been away, and now this extra five pounds. If he'd been here shearing he would have made very little more. He had lost nary a penny. "I'm grateful to you, but I didn't get the horses back to make a profit. I got them because the ladies needed theirs."

"Don't you think we know that?" Frank dusted off his hands. He had put the saddles away and Cal had no doubt someone would clean them later. "Probably wouldn'ta helped you if you'd done it for profit. We'da lct Alf pay you the reward and left it at that."

Cal eased the kerchief around his neck. He didn't know what to say. "Well, thank you. Maybe I'll go and change my shirt."

"Reckon we'll go and sit with you and Miss Ella while you eat." Tommy, a shearer who rarely spoke even when spoken to, glanced over at the homestead's veranda. "Looks like the food is coming out now."

"What about the beer?" Frank asked in a loud whisper.

"Tonight," Alf said reprovingly. "We need to wait 'til at least supper time."

* * * *

Rose stared closely at Ella. "That kiss was nicely done," she said. "Not too friendly. Not the kiss of a woman who has been compromised by a man."

Ella knew that her sister was too busy to question her now, but she certainly would try later. Ella would certainly avoid her later. "I haven't been compromised. We had Jed with us most of the time. He found us before we'd been gone an hour and he simply left a little early because he had to go walkabout with the others."

"He arrived here before dawn. That means he wasn't with you last night."

Ella's blisters had hardened and her hands toughened. She'd also firmed her attitude. Her private life was her own. She would neither share her secrets nor admit them. Nor would she make love with Cal again. She had to live in the real world now, the world of making her family secure.

"Jed wanted to take a shortcut he thought I couldn't manage. Perhaps he meant to cross the river a number of times and you know I can't. There was no help for it." She filled her bedroom jug with warm water from the kettle. "Aside from that, who knows that I went with Cal other than my sisters and a few shearers?"

"The whole district."

"Mr. Lannock thinks that Cal and Jed went."

"Are you certain?"

"No. But there's no need to bring up the subject. We have the horses back. No one in the district will want to talk about more than the theft."

"Pray that's so, Ella. After the sale of the horses, we'll have enough money to leave. We won't be rich, but if we don't have good reputations, we will be seen as no account."

"We won't be seen as no account. We'll be seen as strong and brave women who ran a station when their father died. We'll be respected." For no discernable reason, tears welled in Ella's eyes. She brushed at them angrily. "I'm tired. I'd rather rest than eat." Her voice cracked. "Cal said we should start the dipping as soon as possible. As soon as I work out how to manage it alone, I'll begin."

She spun on her heel and left the room. She wanted Vianna to attend a good school. She wanted Rose to find a suitable husband. She wanted to live in the city.

She wanted to be held again by the man she loved.

* * * *

Cal folded his arms behind his head and stared at the chinks in the slate roof where the moonlight glinted through. He'd turned down the lamp long since, but despite being weary and even a little beery after the companionable celebration he couldn't sleep.

Mentally totaling his wages of the past three months, at fifteen shillings per hundred head of sheep shorn, less room and board, he had earned more than eighty pounds. With the wage from the Beaufort clip, he would have close to one hundred pounds. Three months ago he'd committed himself to getting together exactly that sum, for with one hundred he could match his silent partner's investment.

He had to move quickly. He'd made love to Ella more than once, and although he hadn't released inside her, he still might have impregnated her. Many a man who had taken precautions had been caught out. However, he loved her and he fully intended to wed her as soon as he could afford to support Rose and Vianna, too. As the sisters couldn't leave Beaufort Station until they had the wool money, he had at least three months to make a success of his business, or at least have the promise of success.

If not, he had another option—he could go back to Farvista a failure, his pride in the dust, and live the wealthiest of lifestyles. For Ella he could do that, but for Ella he wouldn't. She wouldn't expect him to degrade himself for her sake and she wouldn't respect him if he did, despite her insistence on marrying a rich man. In her eyes, "rich" meant "comfortable." Independently, he could promise her no more than that— and all his heart. This meant he had no time to waste.

Massaging the back of his neck, he took a deep breath. By Sunday, he would be in Adelaide, where he would have to stop off and see his mother. He hadn't let her know his plans and she didn't deserve to be left any longer in ignorance of her only son's whereabouts. However, he wouldn't stay with her. She always had so many functions organized that a man couldn't get out of her toils in a six-week period.

He'd agreed to be present for the beginning of the ball season. Two weeks maximum. Every year she used ploy after ploy to keep him for five. She accepted invitations for him and looked disappointed that he might not be there as her main support for the functions she planned. And she planned functions one after the other—tea dances, music recitals, garden parties, suppers, and dinners.

Added to that, she hauled him to every ball on the social calendar as her partner, she said, or she might not be able to attend. Naturally he didn't believe that a sophisticated woman like his mother would be at a loss without a partner, but he couldn't deny her what she obviously wanted—the presence of her son. She had no ulterior motive to keep him. She merely wanted to introduce him to as many eligible young ladies as she could. No doubt she wanted grandchildren while she was of an age to enjoy them.

In this, he had disappointed her. No lady he had met through her had shared his interests, and his mother wanted a lady for him or no one. She preferred those like herself—charmers who would enjoy impressing others with their wit and fashion sense.

A tremendous snore erupted from the far corner of the shearer's quarters. Cal sat up, ready to throw a boot at the offender. The noise wasn't repeated. He lay back down again, his train of thought interrupted.

He had the warehouse and he had wool from five stations stored already. Not enough. He needed at least another two. He had to talk to growers and he still needed to set up appointments with buyers or their agents. Using an assumed name gave him little standing, but because he refused to trade on his grandfather's reputation or imply a guarantor, he had to rely on investors trusting him, a stranger.

Although he hadn't wasted a day since he'd first mapped out his idea, his task had now grown urgent. He had a scant three months to set up the auctions and begin to earn himself a commission. After that, Ella would have her wool clip money, perhaps a house in the city, and many hopeful suitors. His head ached.

If he couldn't make a go of supporting her by himself.... The thought of being Edward's yes-man before his next haircut infuriated him. He punched his fist into his lumpy pillow.

He would pull out all stoppers to be a man worthy of the bright and beautiful woman he loved.

Chapter 16

When Ella saw the laundry that had accumulated over the past five days she shuddered, wishing Rose had kept up with the chore. But, of course her sister couldn't when she had to prepare the men's meals without Ella's help. Perhaps doing the laundry gave Ella a feasible excuse not to begin the dipping, for she certainly didn't know how she would manage that task alone.

She filled the copper, put the water on to boil, and hurried into the kitchen to find a bite to eat. Today she wouldn't join the others at breakfast. Despite Cal's excellent training, while she had laundry duties, she couldn't perform the same tasks as a man on this property. While she stirred and poled the wash, she thought of nothing but Cal, his deep voice, his strong face, and his hard, exciting body. She dreamed of being held naked in his arms again.

"I see you had toast for breakfast," Rose said, startling Ella into noticing the suds topping the copper and about to trail over. "Would you like a glass of milk?"

"Later. Why are you wearing your Sunday best?"

"It's my Thursday best. Vianna and I *always* go to Noarlunga on Thursdays and I have to see the bank manager today."

Ella glanced back to the suds, feeling quite unfairly martyred. The only time she'd been off the property in the past six months was to chase after a pair of horse thieves. "If he doesn't want to free up the money to pay the shearers, you can always tell him about the carriage pair," she said, trying not to sound put out.

"He'll give me the money. Our wool clip is surety. And this morning..." Rose gave a smile of pure satisfaction. "Alf gave me three pounds for the team's bed and board. Now I'll be able to pay for our weekly supplies."

"Oh, yes. The team will leave tomorrow." Ella's heart sank to her toes. After tomorrow she would never see Cal again. She cleared her throat.

"Could you buy more soap? And sausages? We should be able to afford a treat for the men's last day."

"I'd like to buy something better than sausages, though sausages will do until we can afford better. Don't worry about lunch. We're leaving now and I'll be back in time to prepare it. Oh, and Cal is coming with us."

Ella stared at her sister, her hands on her hips. "He should be shearing. He needs the money," she said, truly jealous. She would like to wear a pretty dress and go into Noarlunga with a handsome man, too, rather than rubbing her hands raw on other people's shirts and underwear. Cinderella lived the life of a princess compared to her. All she had to do was sweep the ashes and prepare the meals.

"He wants to deliver the robbers' horses to the police station. He thinks it could be seen as stealing if he didn't report having them right away." Rose lingered. "Mr. Lannock took his horses back this morning. You're right. He thinks Jed went with Cal."

Ella turned back to the washing

"We won't take long," Rose said cheerily.

Anyone with an ounce of kindness in her soul would have taken over the washing and let Ella be with Cal every waking moment before he left. One single tear dripped down her nose before she straightened her shoulders and told herself Rose would have done so had she known how Ella felt. Since she couldn't ever be told, Ella may as well get used to Cal's absence right now. For a full half hour she tried but thought of nothing but beautiful Rose and handsome Cal relaxing together while she huddled over steaming suds.

The laundry room lightened. "We're havin' smoke-oh." Ned peered through the chink in the door and the steam. "Thought you might make time for a break."

And so she sat limp-haired on a log outside the woolshed with the men, swilling her tea and staring into the depths of her cup.

The call of a white cockatoo seeking out food for his flock raised her head. With his wings at full stretch, he wheeled around the orchard and gave three echoing screeches. "If he thinks he has found ripe fruit to raid, he can think again," she said grumpily. "I wouldn't mind if they took a little fruit, but they spoil more than they eat."

"Them peaches have been ripe for a couple of days. I picked a few for Miss Rose yesterday," Ned said as the sulfur-crested scout flew higher than the tallest tree and turned into a speck in the sky.

"I suppose I'll have to pick more today then." Ella heaved a sigh. She expected when she'd picked a few, she would have to help Rose bottle them and she simply didn't have the energy.

"The men'll help you do that after lunch." Alf scratched his stubble. "We've almost finished the clip. We can go a bit slower now. You'll have a hundred and fifty bales o' wool after tomorrow." He swallowed the last of his tea in one big gulp. "You'll get a tidy sum for it."

A tidy sum was what she wanted—and a tidy new house in the city and a tidy laundry maid and no sheep to dip. While she imagined her better life in the city and her respite from financial woes, she hung out the third load of washing, not taking as long as she had expected. She had barely emptied the sudsy water and warmed the irons when she heard the clop and squeak of the trap wheeling toward the stables. She shaded her eyes, squinting as Rose and Vianna stepped from the vehicle. Cal dismounted from the dun. He held the piebald by a leading rein.

"Was the police station closed?" she called to Cal. She wanted to keep her distance from him, determined not to give away the fact that she would be desolate when he left.

"The constable in charge says they don't want the horses." In stripping off the dun's saddle he avoided her gaze. "They don't have an impounding area and asked if you could board them until they're claimed. They'll pay for this until their proven owners appear. It's not the hardest way to earn extra money."

"That's easy for you to say," Ella said, her hands on her hips. "You don't have to keep filling the water trough and lugging chaff."

He laughed. "Nor do you. I have found you a man who is willing to do your odd jobs until you leave. He will begin with the dipping next week. He will want meals while he's here and one live lamb a week until he leaves."

Rose peeled off her gloves. "Cal interviewed him. He thinks he is trustworthy, though how he decided that I can't say. He got into a conversation with him at the post office and that was that."

"The postmaster vouched for him." Cal unbuckled the chestnut from the trap and sent her and her twin into the paddock. Girl, ever vigilant, dogged his footsteps. "While I was there, I sent off an advertisement to put in the Adelaide newspaper about the chestnuts being for sale. I think you'll have a good offer within a week or two."

As he turned toward the shearing shed, Vianna stopped him. "I brushed Miffy down before breakfast. This morning I helped Frank with Salvation

and Prejudice, although they are very tall and very hard for me to reach."
She aimed her pitiful little girl look at him.

"Salvation and Prejudice?"

"Sally and Judy. The carriage horses," she explained, untying the pretty straw bonnet Papa had bought for her last summer. "Should I brush them every day even when we don't use them?"

He glanced down at her. "They are very valuable assets. To take care of them would be a responsible and grown-up thing to do."

Vianna turned back, looking satisfied. Anyone could see she admired Cal. Anyone could see he liked her and would advise or praise her as he did to Ella, whom he'd also taught to care for her assets.

And she had to learn to exist without this wonderful, clever, hard-working man.

* * * *

Cal couldn't concentrate on shearing today, although he should have been making up his quota. He'd had quite a shock in Noarlunga. He'd spotted Sam.

He'd quickly turned his back when he'd seen the old man, therefore he didn't know if Sam had noticed him. Likely he hadn't, for he hadn't approached and surely he would have if he'd seen Cal. Strangely, Girl hadn't raced over to Sam. She loved the ex-stable manager but instead of leaving Cal, she stuck to him like a shirt to sweat and had remained at his side ever since.

For a moment he suspected that Edward might be in Noarlunga as well, for the two old men were bosom buddies, although an unlikelier combination no one could imagine, the one well born and wealthy and the other practical but uneducated. He wondered if they had known where Cal was all along but then he decided that if an irascible old tyrant wanted to spy on his grandson, it mattered not. Nothing would change the outcome of Cal's mission, and in another two days he would be gone.

Cal had lingered in the post office until he saw Rose leave the grocery store with her flour sack. Dodging under her parasol, he used the sack on his shoulder to hide his face should Sam still be around. He hustled Rose and Vianna off as quickly as he could and he didn't spot Sam again.

"You haven't caught me up yet." Frank eyed Cal's few shorn sheep. "Your days off must've worn you to the bone."

"Somebody did." Ned angled his head with satisfaction. "The little lady acts tuckered out, too."

"Insinuate anything again and I'll break your jaw." Cal narrowed his eyes.

Ned moistened his lips. "I was joshing. I wouldn't do a thing to hurt her. Not a thing. She's a plucky little sort, and I have a good deal of time for her. A good deal."

No one smirked or nudged. Cal decided that Ella had the respect she deserved from the shearers. As long as he didn't leave her carrying his child, he could leave her with a clear conscience knowing he would return as soon as he could.

* * * *

"Good afternoon," said Mildred Cameron. "You're quite the gadabout these days, Mr. Lynton."

"Not by choice." Edward rose to his feet. A tea dance, they called this function. To him it seemed very similar to the other functions he had attended with Irene. The same group of people appeared to be invited to everything and lately he had become a weathered fixture, too. "Irene can be very persuasive."

"Oh, I know, I know. Sit, do, please." Mrs. Cameron sat beside him. She was a nice-looking woman, this godmother of the Beaufort girl, well dressed in a stiff, dark blue fabric. A slightly darker velvet choker was pinned around her neck with a brooch edged by seed pearls.

A group of pretty young ladies passed and acknowledged him. He wondered how popular he would be if he didn't have either a fortune or a tall, handsome grandson. One might think him the most attractive man in the world given the attention they paid him.

"This heat is appalling, isn't it?" Mrs. Cameron used a fan painted with a rural scene to make a breeze under her chin.

"It's a veritable winter's day compared to the days on Farvista."

"In that case, I don't know how you tolerate it."

"I love it, dear lady. It's my life."

She smiled. "Has your grandson the same opinion? If so, he'll change his mind when he marries. His wife will want a house in town every bit as gracious as Irene's."

"Irene certainly didn't want to live at Farvista." Edward didn't know Charlton's opinion of Farvista. He'd always assumed the place wouldn't be as interesting to his grandson as his exciting life in the big city.

"Daniel McLaren now, he's a city man. I don't think he could bear life out on a farm."

"Station," Edward contradicted yet again, though he didn't know why he bothered. None of these town people seemed to care that there might be a difference. "And who is Mr. McLaren?"

"The young red-haired gentleman over there." She pointed to the chap with the silly sister he'd met some days ago. "He went to school with Charlton, remember?"

"Ah, yes, the one without a current position."

"Are you sure you don't have a job for him? He has a good brain and an ability to take orders without argument. He would make an excellent employee for a man who needs an assistant with a head for figures."

"The man is under his sister's foot."

"Moved from that position, who knows how far he could rise?"

"What interest do you have in him, madam?"

"Call it altruism." She shaded her expression with her fan.

The silence lingered. Edward cleared his throat. "Your goddaughter in Noarlunga? Do you have any news of her?"

"Indeed, yes. Although she hasn't settled the date, she will be arriving back in the city soon. Two days ago she sent a letter asking if she and her two younger sisters might stay with me until they found permanent accommodation elsewhere."

"She has sold the station?"

"I don't believe so, though I know it is planned. She spoke of 'good news' and 'I would be pleased to hear,' but as for facts, none. Rose is a self-contained person rather like her mother, who was my best friend. Alice never told me a thing. I couldn't have been more astonished when she suddenly married Payn Beaufort, charming though he was. I am expecting..." she heaved a tremendous sigh, "that I will be the last to hear of Rose's marriage plans. At least I am trying to make sure of her security. That is the responsibility of a godmother, I believe."

Edward heard "marriage plans" and knew, even without word from Sam, that Charlton had made a decision. In the good old days, sons and heirs accepted ladies of their family's choosing. Given an option, Edward wouldn't choose for Charlton a young lady who would lure him away from Farvista. "Self-contained." That was all very well and good, but was the woman a fortune seeker? By the sound of it, yes. She may even have formulated the plan to get Charlton to leave Farvista without word, knowing how worried Edward would be, worried enough to let Charlton live where he pleased with the harpy. "And she is very beautiful, I hear."

"Amazingly so."

"May I get a cool drink for you?"

"So kind," she said, scanning the room, no doubt looking for some other poor old man to upset.

Edward rose before the music had a chance to set his ears ringing again. On his way to the hall where the punch bowls had been set out he saw Daniel McLaren, who greeted him with a polite smile. "Good afternoon, sir."

"A devotee of loud music, I see." Edward crammed his gloves into his top pocket, impatient with wearing the useless things indoors. "If you can spare the time, perhaps you can come and see me tomorrow morning," he said, moving the younger man to the punch bowl. "I might have an interesting proposition for you."

He filled the first glass while Daniel huffed, "I'm so very much obliged."

Edward nodded. "Take this drink to Mrs. Cameron and tell her that she convinced me to find a place for you. And could you take my leave of her? At my age, the need to relax and enjoy life is overwhelming."

Hands deep in his pockets, Edward sauntered home through the quiet, shady streets, noting the sunshine, the blue sky, the trees, and the birds. He didn't believe Charlton would be influenced by a harpy. He didn't believe Charlton had left Farvista for any other reason than he wanted to prove to Edward he had grown into a fine, upstanding citizen who could manage Edward's interests. He *did* believe he should have given Charlton promotions when he deserved them instead of holding the lad back because he was afraid of losing him.

Charlton, in love or not, planning to marry or not, would be left to his own devices, left to prove whatever he had decided to prove, although he needed to prove not a thing. Edward had always known, but refused to admit, that in Charlton resided each characteristic of a Lynton that had made the family flourish over centuries: intelligence, loyalty, courage, and most of all, determination.

Just this morning Edward had met with and questioned a Mr. John Markham, who had listened to Charlton's plan for wool auctions in the colony and had agreed to invest one hundred pounds in the project. The businessman had also found and hired a warehouse that would be outfitted for that purpose before Charlton arrived in the city. In the meantime, the warehouse was filling with bales of wool from others who also concurred with the idea.

Edward had contributed another two hundred pounds to the costs and would, as a shareholder, contribute more when needed. Not being the instigator of the plan but a mere investor had mellowed him into thinking that perhaps young McLaren had certain qualities, too, if only given a chance to show them. Without a chance, where would a man be? Where

Charlton was, that's where—lingering on a station for whatever reason but without a doubt not idle.

As Charlton wanted to establish a business, Edward had found for him a man who understood the financial ins and outs who might or might not be welcome on his grandson's payroll. Whatever Charlton's plan, McLaren would have employment. Edward, ready to hand over the reins, wanted Charlton to have the assistance he needed. The lad could choose where he wished to live and the enterprises he wished to focus on.

Charlton now had the wherewithal to follow his dreams. Edward had discovered that without his grandson he had wearied of his own.

Now was the time to sit in the sunshine.

* * * *

Cal wondered what had happened to the previous formal structure of the meals at the Beaufort Station. Between the time he and Ella had left and returned, the shearers and the Beaufort sisters had formed a more casual relationship. Young Frank, normally a lanky pest, had in five days grown into a watchful big brother to Vianna, and Ned the lecher was now a helpful supporter of Rose.

The conversations over meals previously had been careful, but now they were companionable and inclusive. The shearers helped, not with the dishes, but with serving and carrying cups and plates indoors and out. Although Ella seemed too busy to find time to spend with Cal, everyone had somehow relaxed. In fact, Cal was lulled into letting his guard down when Alf held forth about a merino ram called Orimedes. "The greatest ram in the entire colony," the gun shearer said. "He had progeny who might match him but none who could better him."

"If he had a staple twelve inches long, he couldn't walk under the weight of his fleece," Benji said, folding his arms.

"He had a staple twelve inches long," Alf repeated obstinately.

"You can say that because none of us are old enough to have seen for ourselves." Ned laughed. "Just shows your age, oldster."

"Nevertheless, he's right." Cal grinned. "They had to shear him twice a year, I've heard. And one of his sons matched him in that but not in his breeding capacity. There Orimedes was second to none."

"Who told you that?" Benji frowned. "I mean, that one of his sons had a fleece as long."

"I saw it for myself when I was younger."

"Where did you see it?" Ella gave him a suspicious, under her lashes, glance.

Cal hesitated but thought he could avoid the trap. "At Farvista. Edward Lynton owns most of Orimedes' progeny. He owned Orimedes, too."

"Did you work at Farvista?" Rose passed the vegetables to Alf.

Cal nodded, not willing to share more.

"In that case, no one would doubt your word as to the fleeces," Rose said firmly. "Did you ever meet Charlton Lynton?"

"Rarely."

"Ah, the young heir." Ella frowned at Vianna, who was feeding Girl under the table. "Did you meet him in the city, Rose? He'd be a great catch."

Rose didn't even blink. "Aunt Mildred has met him, but I haven't."

"That's Rose's Aunt Mildred," Vianna explained to Frank. She wiped her hands on her skirt. "We have to call her Mrs. Cameron."

Cal had indeed met Mrs. Mildred Cameron, a friend of his mother. The woman had tried to pair him with Daniel McLaren's pretty sister, whose name he couldn't remember.

"When he did the ball season last year, he caused quite a stir. I believe he's extremely handsome. I attended one of the same balls, but I didn't see him. I heard he was flirting desperately with Grace McLaren most of the night, but nothing came of it. Grace thought he was one of those rich, spoiled men who couldn't be pleased."

Involuntarily, Cal raised his eyebrows and noticed Alf staring at him, grinning. Cal flipped his gaze back to Rose.

"I was preoccupied, and after that Aunt Mildred thought balls rather a bore. She decided we should attend more intimate gatherings."

Ella turned to Cal, who had finished his meal. "And is the young heir a rich, spoiled man who can't be pleased?"

He leaned back in his seat. "By a woman?"

"By anything."

"He's not jaded if that's what you mean," Cal said, concentrating. "But perhaps he's a little too intent on having his own way."

"Spoiled." Rose wrinkled her nose. "Just as Grace said."

Ella began to collect the plates. "That's such a shame. I don't like to think that money can make a person horrible because I mean to be very rich myself."

"By marrying into money." Cal experienced the sudden annoyance of jealousy. The Lord only knew how long it would take him to have enough money to be considered rich. "I don't think money is a firm foundation on which to build a marriage."

"Then again," Alf said, concentrating on his empty pipe. "We think the ladies we love should have the best we can give 'em."

Cal couldn't argue with that premise. He caught Ella's gaze but, as she had for the past few days, she made herself busy, this time taking the plates into the kitchen with Vianna. He did his very best to catch her alone the next day, but she continued to surround herself with others. To indicate he wanted to talk to her alone had grown damned near impossible. Even when he signaled, she looked blank. He could hardly grab her and run off with her to talk, given the watching eyes, and so not until Saturday morning, his last day on the station did he have an opportunity.

He watched Ella approach. The Clydesdales stood patiently as he harnessed each to the shearer's wagon. Had she not appeared soon, he would have had to knock on the homestead door and ask to see her. He had barely an hour left to ask her to wait a few months for him to gather enough money to support her and her family. The time span didn't seem unreasonable—unless he had gotten her with child.

He hoped he hadn't, for then he would need to marry her within the month and leave her on the station until he had proved himself—that or send her and her sisters to his grandfather having proved absolutely nothing more than he was a dilettante like his father.

"Cal, Rose and I have discussed your wool auction idea and want to participate."

He stepped back, eying obstinate Ella, clear-thinking Ella, lovely Ella, who was the only woman he would ever want in his life. "Are you sure? I will certainly sell the wool, but I might have to find the buyers in Victoria if I can't get them to come here."

"Do you think you can get them to come here?"

"I wouldn't be suggesting the project to growers if I didn't. And of course, the more wool I have, the more likely I am to attract buyers."

"Because of the horses, money isn't as vital to us now as it was. We can wait."

"This is my last shearing job. I'm off this very day to begin my business in the city. Cobb is contracted to take your wool to Goolwa. I expect he'll arrive some time next week. I'll tell him to take your wool to Port Adelaide instead." He fumbled in his pocket. "Here. I wrote out my address for you since you've been so evasive." He tried to catch her eye, but she eluded his gaze yet again to read his carefully written business address.

Folding the paper into a tight wad she said, "Thank you." She heaved a breath. "I would like you to know...we won't be obliged to marry. I found out on Thursday when I awoke."

"Oh. You sound pleased." He sounded disgruntled and he didn't know why. Perhaps because he wanted to be sure of having her.

"I would hardly be disappointed." For the first time in days, she met his gaze. "And so that's it."

"That's what?"

She shrugged. "Now we can each make a fresh start. We have to face facts. We shared an adventure that took us from our real lives for a moment in time, but you have a career to establish and I have a family to support. And I will do so the best way I know how."

He moistened his lips. "What are you saying?"

"Good-bye."

"Good-bye?" He planted his fists on his hips.

"You don't have to marry me." She stared at her feet. "And I don't have to leave my sisters in the lurch. I do hope you make a success of yourself. We want as much money as possible for the wool. I'm used to the finer things in life."

His jaw firmed. "And you won't marry without being sure you'll have them."

"No." She turned, spine straight, and headed back to the homestead.

He stared at the Clydesdales, who patiently waited in the hot sun. He stared at Frank, who brought out his sleeping pack, and he stared at the others when they began to add their own loads. Wrapping himself in silence, he took the driver's seat and in no time the remaining shearers bundled themselves in, too.

The ladies stood by the back door of the homestead and waved, but he didn't turn to watch. After all, he'd known Ella for a scant two weeks. He might have enjoyed her optimism, her humor, and her willingness to learn, but this had been a momentary episode in his life, as she had said.

Ten miles later, having churned her words over again and again, he accepted her honesty. To her credit, she'd never let him think she loved him. Strangely, he hadn't mentioned he loved her, either, though he had certainly shown her. A man wouldn't take a woman with such aching tenderness had he not been completely besotted.

He eventually climbed down from the wagon in a town not a mile away from the team's next job. With the others, he drank too much in the local pub. As he staggered into the room he had hired for the night, he recognized that every man needed a first love so that he could settle with his last.

In the morning, hungover and morose, he hired a horse and headed for Adelaide. Even if he made a fortune from his business plan, he couldn't have Ella. Only a fool would settle for a woman he had to buy.

Chapter 17

Cal arrived in bustling Port Adelaide during the early afternoon of Monday and strode past substantial Georgian structures with plaster pillars and marble fronts. Money had been invested in the port area, farther upriver from the original mangrove dock of the colony, justly named Port Misery. The grief the mosquitoes had caused the early settlers forced the shift.

In the thirty years since, hardware shops, hotels, breweries, wheelwrights, and coachbuilders had sprung up, and the town bustled about its business, making a fortune in trade. Storehouses populated the side streets, tall, looming buildings built of the local stone. Cal had hired his warehouse on Lipson Street and as he traversed the narrow thoroughfare, the tallest of the ships' masts swayed in the swell.

Stopping at a heavy wooden door, he wiped the perspiration from his face with his sleeve. He had forgotten the heat of Adelaide, but on this day, the cobbles on the pavements radiated a shimmering haze to a height of well over three feet. He lifted the latch and swung the door aside. The odor of sanded wood dusted the air and wood shavings curled on the floor.

A burly man loomed and stopped, a wide smile spreading across his hewn face. "Wondered when you was going to get here. Took your time, Mr. Charlton, didn't you?"

Cal shook the hand of Denny Quinn, a carpenter who had worked at Farvista some years back. "I had to earn the money to pay your wages. You chippies don't come cheap."

"Nor should we. You've had your value from me. Until your accountant arrived, I built your showcases, made your partitions, and inspected and recorded every bale of wool that entered the place."

"My accountant?"

"Mr. McLaren. In the office there." Quinn pointed to the partition fashioned out of red pine that he had loosely described as an office. "Been here a week now. Mr. Markham sent him."

Cal nodded. He had agreed with Markham that when his business partner thought the job was becoming too much for Quinn alone he would hire more staff. "We've had quite a few deliveries, I believe." The aroma of wool hovered in the vast space, although the bales were not visible behind a dividing wall.

"Reckon you've made a dent in the wool market. You've had everything from Alf's shearing team in the past three months, and you've had everything Cobb's been contracted to move. Dunno how you did that."

"I've known Cobb for ten years. He wants a share of this business, too. If it succeeds I'll sell a portion to him."

"I wouldn't mind a bit of it meself. You're bound to make a packet out of this. There's more'n a tad of gossip about your plan down here. Two shipowners have already shown interest. I left them to talk to Mr. McLaren."

Pleased, Cal clapped the big man on the shoulder. A man only needed an idea and the know-how to get started and the project, if sound, would be carried across the shoulders of enthusiasts with the same vision of the colony's future. "I should talk to McLaren, too." He left Quinn, who returned to banging nails into the treads of stairs that reached to the next floor.

Cal tapped on the partition door. In a year, the name of the occupant would be stenciled in gold on a glass panel. A redhead, sitting in a straight-backed chair facing away from the door, swung around. "Cal. We've been expecting you." He rose to his feet, smiling widely.

Cal reached out and shook Daniel's hand. "So, you're the McLaren. Welcome aboard. The last I saw of you, you were working in a bank and expecting to marry an heiress. I have to assume your plans fell through."

Daniel shrugged wryly. "It seems she didn't have the money I thought. And it seems I didn't have the money she thought." He pulled at his earlobe. "Something had to change. I thought perhaps I should take my career seriously. When your grandfather offered me this job, I jumped at it."

Cal stiffened. "My grandfather?"

"Surely you remember him? A tall man, about your height with thick gray sideburns and a knobble-headed walking stick he uses to direct small boys and dogs and beat on carriage doors."

"Oh, that man." Cal compressed his lips. "He can be intimidating if you are a small boy, a dog, or a carriage driver."

"Or an out-of-work accountant needing to earn his way."

"I had no idea he had poked his nose into this venture." Cal glanced at his palm, rubbing his fingers across, thinking. "Does he have a sanction from Markham?" he asked, referring to his business partner.

"Since he is paying my wages, he certainly has sanction. But that's it. He is in no way involved in the venture...other than sending me here to spy on you. Markham has my undertaking to do no such thing."

Cal sat on McLaren's desk. "He is an investor only? And he knows I'm involved in this?" He narrowed his eyes. "Perhaps you might like to report our progress to me."

"First, you need to promise that you'll come home with me tonight for dinner. Grace insisted I ask the moment I saw you. It'll give us a chance to catch up."

"Dinner. Yes. Splendid." Cal didn't have any catching up he needed to do with Grace McLaren, but he was tired and still had a few tasks to perform. "We'll talk business tonight over dinner."

"If you don't have a place yet, you can stay with us."

Cal shook his head. "I'll go to my mother's house eventually, but in the meantime I have taken rooms close to the warehouse. Thank you. Your address is unchanged?"

McLaren nodded. "Grace will be delighted to see you. Shall we say six?"

"Six." Cal left wanting and needing a bath and a shave. Hearing of his grandfather's interference in his life, Cal decided not to visit the Adelaide town house where his grandfather apparently awaited. He would take his own good time before confronting the old man.

He might, perhaps, like to get on with his own life first.

* * * *

As she had done in the seven days since Cal had left, Ella picked fruit. As she had done constantly, she thought of him. Her every task held reminders of Cal. Only two weeks ago, the peaches were beginning to yellow. Now three trees had ripened at the same time. The fruit had been nicely plumped by the extra water delivered to the trees by Cal's laborsaving method.

Each day, Mr. Lannock delivered the Beaufort's fruit to the grocery store. With theirs being the first of the season, they had made enough money to pay off the bill at the hardware store. When luck changed, other situations changed, too, a coincidence Papa had religiously bet on, although his theory didn't seem to work every time.

The station had been put on the market. The chestnuts would be sold when Ella and her sisters were settled in their city house, and the eventual sale of the wool clip would complete their plan for the future.

Ella wished she had never met Cal. She missed him so much, she thought her heart would burst.

She lugged the full bucket of peaches into the kitchen. "We can use this lot ourselves. It's not saleable. The cockatoos had a feast last night and they've taken a bite out of each one."

Rose opened the bottom of the dresser, finding the preserving bottles. "I had hoped we wouldn't ever need to bottle fruit again."

"Wherever we live, we won't be rich."

"Oh, Lord, I feel as if I will never get away from here."

"We could reduce the price of the station. That might give us a faster sale."

"How I hate this place. I hate it, I hate it, I hate it. Anything would be better than this everlasting cooking."

"The laundry?" Ella said hopefully.

Rose pursed her lips. Ella began to wash the fruit. "I went out to see if Swampy wanted help with the dipping, but he told me to go away or ungracious words to that effect. He has a system, it seems, which the presence of a female might destroy. Nevertheless, he is managing. He dips the sheep in small groups and he works with the dogs."

"Interesting. I'll make up the sugar syrup."

"He collects about a hundred at a time and lets the dogs send them through the dip while he pulls them out at the other end. They're not very good at climbing. The sheep, not the dogs."

"Do you know, if I have to eat peaches again in this lifetime, I think I would rather starve?"

"Though it's a shame he can't teach the dogs to pull them out." Ella heard a bump-along rumbling sound. From the kitchen window, she had no view of the track alongside of the house. After putting down her cutting knife, she went onto the back veranda to watch sixteen bullocks pulling a long wagon toward the loading bay of the woolshed.

The driver sat on the flat bed of the dray and raised a hand in greeting. As he drew closer, he called, "Good day, Missus. We can turn behind the shed if I remember rightly. Hey-ya," he yelled to encourage his team to keep moving.

He passed the woolshed and made his wide circle in the billabong paddock. Wheels creaking and with clanking bullock chains, he pulled up at the loading bay door.

"Come and see this," Ella called to Rose.

"I can't," her sister said. "I have to watch for the boil."

Vianna appeared at the back door. "Is someone taking the wool now?" She stood for a moment, fidgeted, scratched her nose, and went back to her riveting studies.

Ella walked over to the woolshed. "Good morning, Mr. Cobb."

The driver was perhaps forty years old and had two teeth in the front, one top and one bottom, a face creased and wrinkled by countless hours of exposure to the sun, and arms like a blacksmith. "I'll start loading now." He swung down from the dray.

Swampy, the station hand, whose first name was Frederick but had to be called Swampy because his surname was Marsh, had heard him, too, for he arrived and opened the doors of the loading bay. Ella tried to drag over the lifting hook suspended from the roof beams, but she couldn't budge the heavy tackle an inch.

"Don't strain yourself," Swampy said to her. "We can do this without you."

She stood for a moment, but she could see she would be useless. Therefore she left, planning to return later with refreshments.

"When I was little I used to love watching the wool being loaded," she said in a rueful voice to Rose. She put the kettle on to boil. "But if I stand around watching now, they'll think I am checking up on them."

Rose had cut the peaches in half and arranged the bottom layer in her second jar. "Here. Cut the rest of these and I will pack them."

"It's wonderful seeing how they swing those great bags on top of each other and balance them on the dray. It looks impossible when it's finished, so tall and so top heavy, yet I've never heard of a load falling off."

"I'll pour the syrup if you can whip the egg white for the papers."

Vianna wandered into the room and sat at the table watching, her chin in her palms, her elbows on the table. "I could cut out the paper rounds," she said. "I did them last year, didn't I, Ella?"

"That would be a help."

"Ella, you have Cal's address, don't you?"

Ella blinked guiltily and met Vianna's gaze. "Somewhere. Why do you want it?"

Vianna gave a long sigh and listlessly picked up the scissors and put them down. "I'm in love with him. I want to write him a letter."

Ella didn't feel in the least like laughing at her sister. She couldn't count the times she had gazed at Cal's Port Adelaide address. However, she had nothing to say to him other than that she missed him and she loved him. If he was still free when Vi had grown up...but a man like him would be snatched up quickly, money or not. She had no need to prolong the agony of wanting him and being unable to have him. "He's too old for you, Vianna. Best forget him."

"I'm growing older every year. Anyway, he's the only good-looking man I've ever met. Unlike *some* people, I've never lived in a city, and I could count on these fingers," she said, holding up one hand, "the amount of boys or girls of my own age I have met. It seems to me that if we don't leave here soon, I'll end up an old maid like you two."

Rose glanced up, eyes wide, brows raised. "Do you think I have missed my chance?"

"Haven't you? You're twenty-three and you haven't had any offers that I've heard of."

"Perhaps you don't know everything, Miss," Rose replied with spirit. "Perhaps I've had offers I haven't taken up."

"Well, why wouldn't you? Surely anything would be better than living on a hot, dusty station crowded with stinky sheep."

"I like it here," Ella said in a small voice, watching her sisters confront each other, Rose annoyed and Vianna pettish. "And sheep don't stink any worse than any other animal. The horses—"

"Horses are pretty." Vianna stood, dropping the scissors onto the table. "And peaches stink, too." She flounced out of the room.

Ella stared at Rose. "We've never fought like this before."

Rose tightened her face. "We've never thought we would be stuck here when we had enough money to leave. Why can't we just go and let Swampy take care of the sheep?"

"It's too much for one man alone. And if he wants to go, too, what will happen to the sheep? We'll lose the last of our assets. You and Vianna should go. I can stay and help him."

Rose stared at her. "Neither Vianna nor I would accept that sort of sacrifice from you."

Ella sat, head bowed, then she straightened her spine. Taking a deep, determined breath, she picked up Papa's riding hat, smacked the brim on her thigh, and left for the stables.

She saddled the idling piebald and left.

* * * *

Edward frowned at Sam and crossed his arms. "Took your time coming back, didn't you?

Sam shrugged. "You wouldn't have wanted me to do half a job. I spied on Charlton for you and I stayed awhile after he left so that I could spy on Miss Beaufort."

"He left? And you didn't come straight to me?"

"Couldn't be sure he wouldn't return. They didn't know who he was at the local grocery store, but I got into conversation with a neighbor of the Beaufort's, who said Mr. Charlton was the overseer, going by the name Cal Langdon."

"Cal." Edward snorted. "Baby name. That's what his father called him. It's not an acceptable shortening of Charlton in my opinion."

"It's not such a mouthful. Be that as it may, he left Noarlunga more'n a week ago. When the shearers left, he went with 'em. I follered the wagon for a while just to see where they planned on going, but they parted ways on the next property. When I made inquiries of the team boss, he said Cal were headed for the city. Had a plan to make money."

"You should have continued following him so that you would know exactly where he went." Edward sat back down on the desk chair in the study. "Take a seat," he said, waving at the armchair by the window.

"Figured you would be able to find that out." Sam made himself comfortable. Crossing his legs, he gave a satisfied smile. "Went back to Noarlunga to see what Miss Beaufort was a-doing. Maybe they had a fight. Or maybe she were expecting him to return."

"Well?"

"Lovely couple they make. You shoulda seen them the day they did the weekly shopping, him so big and dark and her so dainty and fair. She's a well-made woman, greatly thought of by the local folk. Went back to the station to take care of a couple of younger sisters. I saw one of them, a little tacker. They own a couple of high-stepping chestnuts, too."

"Trust you to notice the horseflesh."

"We don't often see horses that good. Couldn't miss 'em." Sam scratched the back of his neck. "Seems Mr. Charlton went out with the aboriginal stockman and chased a couple of horse thieves for Miss Rose. Caught 'em, too."

"Naturally. Was there news of an engagement between him and the lady?"

"No talk. The locals don't gossip about the sisters. They seem proud to have them in the district. Can't work out why they haven't left. Maybe a couple of them want to keep the property."

"According to Mrs. Cameron, Miss Beaufort can't wait to return to her social life. So. Charlton is here somewhere. He hasn't contacted his mother. Unnatural boy," Edward said, feeling disgruntled. "She's worried to death about him."

"Strange." Sam stared at his entwined fingers. "When she saw me she asked how he was. I said he looked healthy and I was pretty sure he was in the city. She said 'good.' That's all. 'Good.' Didn't look *too* worried."

"She doesn't like to show her feelings. Do you want to come for a trip with me to the docks?"

"No." Sam shook his head. "I reckon this time you need to let the mountain come to his grandpa."

* * * *

Ella rode down Lannock's driveway. Black and white cows grazed in the far pasture. The place had a cold, cobbled smell, not a dusty sheep smell like her place. Someone clanked cans in the milking shed. She left the piebald tethered to a post and poked her head into the doorway but couldn't see Mr. Lannock. She planned on going to the front of the homestead and knocking on the door, but he sauntered around the corner from the buttery. "Miss Ella. Is there a problem?"

"How guilty you make me feel. I only visit when I need something. This time, I haven't. I want to discuss a proposition with you."

"A proposition?"

"We owe you ninety pounds, plus, of course, many, many favors."

"Don't worry about the money, Missy. You'll pay when you can."

"I was thinking of letting you invest it." She smiled when she saw his expression. No doubt he was assuming she was just like her father, always ready with a slick line when she wanted money. "We have good land and your fences abut ours. You have one side of the river and we have the other. I know you don't need our land so that you can have ready access to water, but I thought that instead of us selling our land and paying you the money, you could buy our land and have a much larger holding. You have two fine, strapping sons who one day will be thinking of marriage."

Mr. Lannock blinked. "You must be one of those second-sight women. Just last night John told us he had asked for Sara Williams, the publican's daughter. He won't be getting land with her. A keg of beer, if he's lucky."

Ella laughed. "He'll be getting a very fine wife."

"They want to get married in June. June, I said? Why so soon? You've got years. I thought they could live here with us and she thought they could move into the hotel to be with her Dadda. If John lives in the hotel I don't reckon he'll turn up early for the milking."

"It wouldn't be easy. So, if you bought the land next door, our station, you could keep him closer. You have, so to speak, paid for a good percentage of our property already. The bank holds the mortgage, and I'm sure they won't mind transferring it to you."

"Hold hard, Missy. What about the sheep?" Mr. Lannock narrowed his eyes. "Are you planning on selling them first?"

"We're hoping that whomever buys the land will want the sheep, too. Swampy Marsh will likely stay on if he's paid a reasonable wage. But John might like to be a sheep farmer. There's good money to be made by a man who knows how to work the land, which he does and which alas, my Papa didn't. And, dear life, Sara will certainly know how to run the homestead. She has run the hotel for her Dadda for years."

"You have a fine way of talking, Missy." He thrust his hands deep into his pockets and smiled warily. "Your father's daughter you certainly are. I'll think on it." He stood, considering. "How much would you want for the sheep?"

"A shilling a head is what we get for them dead. They shouldn't be worth much less alive."

Mr. Lannock put his hands to the sides of his face. "Mercy me. I'm not one of those graziers with money to burn. You've got five thousand, give or take a hundred or so. You'd want two hundred and fifty pounds."

"You can pay the money in installments, Mr. Lannock. Or you can sell the sheep, probably for more than a shilling per head, and pay us that way. At this time, all we can think of is leaving. My sisters are pining away here."

"And what about you?" he asked, drawing his eyebrows together.

She smiled. "We're a family."

He turned and stared across his land, elbows tight to his body, neck tensed. Finally, he took a breath and nodded as if he had come to a decision. "I'll speak to the bank manager. If I can get the mortgage transferred and we can come to an agreement as to the full price, we can call it a deal. You talk sense." He reached out to shake her hand. "Last night John asked if we might buy your land. Funny how things have worked out."

Chapter 18

Ella sat on the edge of a turned-wood tester bed, staring out the window of an upstairs bedroom in Mildred Cameron's compact but elegant Walkerville house, built on the embankment of the Torrens River. Tall native trees hid the river but didn't block the piercing shriek of the black cockatoos while they raided the pines.

"What should we do first?" Vianna asked from her bed, supporting herself on her elbows.

Mrs. Cameron had told them to rest after their journey. As Ella and Vianna shared a bedroom, they had time to talk. Ella would have liked Rose to be present, but Rose wanted to sort out the gowns she had not seen for six months. She had the room next door, the same one she had used for the past two years, with a wardrobe full of silk and lace gowns and shelves holding hats, reticules, and parasols. Ella's room had a similar wardrobe but holding far fewer items. "We should probably buy gowns before we start looking for a house. You'll certainly need some. That school of yours wants you to dress in navy blue with black stockings and shoes for your daily lessons. We didn't have a uniform in my day."

"That's progress for you," Vianna said airily. "Fortunately, blue is my best color. I'll be glad of the uniform."

"I hope Rose knows of a place where we can buy your clothes ready-made. That would be even more progress for you," Ella added gloomily.

"Rose said Mrs. Cameron would be taking you both to balls. So you'll need a ball gown."

"I don't even know how to waltz."

"Rose will teach you. She said she would."

As if she had been waiting for her cue, Rose entered the room and, with a billow of black skirts, settled on Vianna's bed. "I can't say I'm a dancing teacher, but I certainly know the steps. By the way, Aunt is napping. We only need to leave her in peace for an hour or so and then we can gather in the drawing room to discuss our plans."

Ella pulled her legs up, crossing them. "What are they, other than finding a house and buying a few clothes?"

"I'll be going to school as soon as I have the uniforms."

"Tomorrow we'll shop for clothes. Aunt thinks it would be nice if we used our chestnuts to pull her Brougham. She thinks they would look very smart if we want to cause a stir."

"Do we want to cause a stir?"

"Of course we do. If I want a husband, I'll need to make sure I am noticed. Tomorrow I'll be coming out of blacks."

"That's wonderful, Rose, and about time." Ella picked at the hem of her gown.

"Mrs. Irene Lynton, as you know, is an acquaintance of Aunt's. She will hold the first ball of the year in barely a month. Everyone who is anyone will be there. Aunt will obtain an invitation for you, too, Ella, though it seems I'm already invited as a prospective bride for the son and heir, Charlton."

"If he's rich, surely he can find a bride for himself?"

"Perhaps he can't find one who suits his Mama. I believe there is a rash of those who wouldn't."

"That's not nice." Vianna tilted her pert nose. "He should be allowed to marry whoever he likes."

"*Whomever.* And I'm sure he will," Rose said smoothly. "But those who don't suit his Mama would be servants and suchlike whom rich young men admire very much but are not suitable to marry."

"Oh. I thought you meant a woman with a long nose or thin hair," said the poppet, secure in the knowledge of her own prettiness.

"I don't have a ball gown." Ella studied her fingernails. "And if we buy a house of our own, I would rather have curtains."

They had brought with them the best of their parents' furniture, which had been sent for storage at a city warehouse. The curtains had been left at the station with the carpets and the kitchen dressers, being too big and heavy to move. The piano had been a nightmare. It would need tuning before Vianna could play a pretty melody again.

Rose spread her hands. "We have almost ninety pounds, Ella. You can have both. Until we sell the chestnuts or get the money for the clip, we can't buy a house anyway."

"Driving the chestnuts in the Brougham would be a good way to show them to a buyer. I'm sure we'll sell them soon." Vianna wriggled off her bed and sashayed over to the cheval mirror, where she put her hands on her hips and viewed herself sideways. "If not, we'll have to write to Cal and tell him where we are so that he can send our money here."

"He can send it to the bank in Noarlunga, as arranged."

"We're placing a huge amount of trust in him, Ella." Rose's expression grew serious. "Personally, I'd be happy to see this warehouse of his. Is he too plausible? We accepted him at his own valuation, and I'm not certain that was wise."

Ella heaved a breath. "We accepted him not only on *our own* valuation—after all, he helped me with the property and he got back our horses—but on Alf's. How long have we known Alf? A lifetime? And Mr. Cobb. He said he has taken most of the wool shorn this season to Cal's warehouse."

"In that case," Rose said chidingly, "I see no harm in letting him know we are here."

"If he wants us, he can find out easily enough where we are." Ella folded her arms and deliberately changed the subject. "I don't feel comfortable about using the thieves' horses as our hacks. It doesn't seem right."

Rose shrugged. "We're boarding them legally. Anyway, we would have to walk if we didn't use them. They were a godsend. But for them, we would not have been able to sell the stock horses to John Lannock for three pounds each and so add to our coffers." She rubbed her hands together, smiling.

"The piebald is very noticeable. If the real owner sees me riding him, he'll think I stole him."

Rose stood. "So, we'll go shopping tomorrow. Right?"

Vianna swung around with a pleased grin on her face. "The school wants me to have light shoes for dancing lessons. Not boots. Dum de dum. At last."

"I really won't want a ball gown," Ella said.

* * * *

Powdered and scented, Rose's godmother lifted her cheek to be kissed in turn by the sisters. She'd been Mama's best friend. Widowed four years ago, and childless, she seemed delighted to have Rose foisted on her and apparently didn't object to Ella's and Vianna's presence. She shifted on the velvet-covered sofa in her drawing room, patting the empty place beside her and smiling at Vianna.

"My, you've grown, Vianna." She took the child's hand. "I swear you are as tall as I now."

Vianna giggled. "Almost. I'm sure I will be by next year."

"And Rose, darling, you are as beautiful as ever. How I have missed your lovely face. As, I believe, others have. Ella, you grow more like your mother by the year. She had exactly that same shade of hair—sun-touched gold. Such a journey you must have had! The roads are too, too awful."

Rose nodded, smiling. "We rode a portion of the way. That saved us time changing coaches. Vianna was a heroine. Miffy, her pony, got very crotchety. She is used to shorter trips."

"Miffy was the heroine," Vianna said staunchly. "May I pass you a slice of cake, Mrs. Cameron?"

"Oh, please," Mrs. Cameron said, delicately reminded of a young person's appetite. "Call me Aunt, as Rose does." Turning to her side table, she lifted a tiered plate and offered frosted fruitcake to Vianna. "You, too, Ella. Mercy me, I don't know where my head is. I simply haven't been managing without Rose. I've been too, too alone. Invitations are so much less forthcoming to ladies of a certain age than are ladies of a certain age with young, beautiful companions to show off to society."

Rose shook her head fondly. "You flatter me, Aunt."

"No such thing." Mrs. Cameron leaned forward. "A certain young man missed you, too. I swear he hasn't looked at another young lady since you left. And now, of course, he has a very good position with Mr. Edward Lynton."

"Oh?" Rose busied herself arranging her skirts around her on the armless chair.

"Yes. Such a surprise! He had the job pressed upon him only a few weeks ago. Grace says he's a new man, so enthusiastic. With steady work, and such important work, too, he would no doubt be in a position to marry a certain young lady were she to indicate that she might be interested."

"You're talking about Rose." Vianna frowned. "Are you interested, Rose?"

"Certainly not. I've set my sights higher."

"What is his important work?" Vianna queried, lifting the icing off her cake.

Mrs. Cameron gave a dismissive wave of her soft white hand. "Men! Daniel has been quite mysterious about the nature of his work, but Edward Lynton is very pleased with him, I can see. You wait. You'll change your mind about that young man, I'm sure."

Rose seemed preoccupied. Ella wondered if the young man discussed was the same man who had hardened Rose on the subject of love. Perhaps if he pursued his suit, Rose would change her mind. It seemed she had an opportunity. Ella had none. The man she loved hadn't hardened her at all.

He'd simply not been the right man at the right time, and she thought she would love him until her last breath.

Had her circumstances been better, or his, or had he loved her...but he'd never mentioned love. Best he had gone out of her life. When Rose married, Ella would be too involved in Vianna's upbringing to miss a man who quite clearly didn't miss her.

*   *   *   *

Rose and Mrs. Cameron fussed about getting themselves ready for the shopping trip. Ella grew bored not long after she had positioned her only pretty hat on her head and had found herself alone in the sitting room with a view of the front garden.

"We're almost ready," Aunt called from the passage. She must have heard Ella sighing with impatience. "If you have a moment to spare, perhaps you could pop down to the mews and ask the stableman to harness the horses to the Brougham."

"I have a minute," Ella answered, rising to her feet and striding to the front door.

She hastened to the mews built at the end of the street to service those who did not keep their own stables. Normally Mrs. Cameron—Aunt—used hired bays to pull the Brougham she kept. She thought herself quite a toff now, she had informed Ella, with showy chestnuts to hitch to her equipage.

Over the road from the mews, a stout man wearing a driver's coat and creased trousers leaned against a tree, gazing at the river and chewing a stalk of grass. He turned to stare at Ella, who flashed him a smile, wondering if this was his morning smoke-oh break. She turned and entered the stable yard. "Hello-oo," she called, hearing the echo.

"Morning." A thin, short man dressed in jockey's riding boots and trousers came out of the nearest stable. "What can I do for you?"

"Would you harness up the chestnuts to Mrs. Cameron's brougham and send it and the driver to her house forthwith?"

"Quarter hour. That's the best I can do. Mrs. Neild's wantin' her horse saddled and the chestnuts need a good brushing."

"Your driver is out there idling. Would you like me to send him back to you?"

"My drivers is over yonder." He indicated a neat stone building with his head. "In that there building, sittin' with tea and pipes. They don't bestir themselves until they're needed."

Ella nodded, not about to contradict the man. She left, glancing where the driver outside had been, but he had disappeared. The view from there was lovely and she imagined he had walked down to the river's edge.

Soon after, a red-cheeked cheery man, who helped them into the carriage with a friendly grin, arrived with the Brougham.

Aunt wanted to show them the sights on the way to the city but other than the houses of the very rich, including "The Lynton's Abode" spoken in a reverential whisper by Aunt, they saw only small buildings until Government House in the city. The driver dropped them off at the corner of Rundle Street and promised to be at the very same spot in three hours to collect them.

"We'll have time for lunch in the tearooms, too," Aunt said gaily.

Ella hoped so. It was almost luncheon time. Aunt marched them off to Seymour's Emporium, a department store of three stories in which they could find everything they needed. They found Vianna's uniforms, only two, but the rest would be delivered in a week, with her stockings and a pair of dancing shoes. Rose tried to convince Ella to buy dancing shoes, too, but Ella was convinced her old shoes would do. They'd barely been used, "Be they four years old, or not," she said, adamantly.

They walked past stalks of silk flowers, hat shapes, ribbons, underwear, stockings, and gloves. Rose and Aunt stopped and fingered everything. "Ella, buy something, do," Rose said as they walked through the fabric department.

"Not materials. I won't know what I need until we settle into our own house."

"That might not be for months." Aunt smiled, as if pleased.

Ella's heart dropped. She wanted to be in control of her life. Flitting around spending money wasn't her idea of something to do. She wanted an occupation. She almost envied the gray-gowned shop assistants in Seymour's, though the bright-eyed creature in the fabric department they currently passed through, stopping with every new fabric to be fingered, looked anxious for a sale.

Ella took pity when the girl's eyes locked on Aunt's hovering fingers. "Perhaps I could buy fabric for my ball gown. This?" she said reluctantly, touching a pale blue slipper satin embroidered with white roses.

"That's beautiful," Rose said, stroking the fabric. "What a wonderful color."

Aunt beckoned to the shop girl, who didn't look a day over eighteen. "What would we need? Ten yards?"

"For this lady?" the girl asked, glancing at Rose.

"For my sister." Rose indicated Ella.

The girl began to walk away. "Over here. We have an amber silk that would look just lovely on the lady."

"We asked for this one." Rose's lips clamped.

"I wonder, though." Aunt glanced at the blue and back to Rose. "The blue would be too, too perfect for you, Rose. Let's buy it and choose another for Ella. Why did you say amber, girl? Do you have some old stock you want to be rid of?"

"Never." The girl looked aghast. "It's new, brand new. The latest thing. Miss has warm coloring. The blue would deaden her skin. See?" She held the fabric against the skin of Ella's arm.

"So it does," Ella said, trying to maintain interest. They could give her puce for all she cared. "Show me the amber."

Not only did the girl prove that amber highlighted Ella's coloring, but she also sold them twelve yards and ten of the blue for Rose. Then she sent them to the glove department to buy cream evening gloves for Ella, for white wouldn't do, she insisted.

"That girl ought to be reported for her presumption." Rose chose herself a new pair of white gloves. "Her job is to sell us what we want."

"It worked out well," Aunt said peacefully. "You have a lovely fabric for a new gown and Ella has something nice, too. Don't worry," she continued in a whisper to Ella as Rose completed her transaction. "The blue should have been yours, but we need to get Rose married off this year. Next year, I'll concentrate on you."

"I'm perfectly happy with the amber. I think the little shop girl did well for me." Ella didn't want the girl reported. No harm had been done and some good.

For the first time in her life, Ella appreciated that she and Rose were not alike, in looks, tastes, or personality. Whatever suited her sister didn't necessarily suit her. How strange that she'd never considered their differences. She's always assumed that what was best for one was best for the others and that they would stay together.

"If we can't get Rose married off to the Lynton heir, and he has proved to be quite difficult to please, we have another option," Aunt said to Ella. "Your turn will come."

"I won't marry," Ella said. "I have Vianna to consider."

"I'm sure Vianna won't mind if you marry. Will you?" Aunt gave Vianna a poke in the arm.

"Of course not. If she doesn't, I'll feel very guilty when I leave her to marry Cal."

"And is Cal one of your little playmates from home?"

"Cal is a shearer," Rose said coldly. "No matter how he jumps himself up, he can't be a match for one of Papa's daughters. Vianna is being very silly, and I don't know why. She must know better."

Vianna's eyes filled with tears. "You used to be much nicer when we lived at the station. I don't know why you are being so mean."

Ella put her arm around Vianna. "We're all tired, I expect, and fractious. We've recently made a long journey after selling the home we've lived in all our lives. After such changes, I think we can allow each other some liberties. Let's have lunch. That should perk us up."

* * * *

A week passed. Ella had two fittings for her ball gown. Whenever she could, she had the piebald saddled and she rode along the Torrens River, trying to see similarities to home. She saw few. In Adelaide, the weather seemed drier, the grass more yellow, the trees taller or shorter, the birds less visible and not as pretty, and the people less friendly. She saw the fat driver from the mews twice more, but he refused to acknowledge her. As she didn't need to be his friend, she didn't care.

She didn't care that Rose thought of nothing but her clothes. She didn't care that she rarely saw Vianna, who had formed a strong friendship with a girl from school and now repeated everything the girl said.

She only cared that she'd had to say good-bye to Cal.

Chapter 19

Edward rested his knife and fork on his plate. He and Irene had just begun dinner. Normally, an uninvited guest would be asked to wait in the hall, but footsteps followed the housekeeper to the dining room. He turned.

The doors opened with a dramatic swing. Charlton stood there, his dog at his heel. Chin raised, mouth firm, wearing faded cotton trousers and a blue shirt, he looked hard and tanned and very dear. Edward rose, but Irene practically flew out of her chair to embrace her son.

"Where have you been, you naughty boy?" She pushed him into the nearest dining chair. "Have you eaten? Of course not. Mrs. Baxter, have another place set and Mr. Charlton's room made up. And take the dog to the kitchen for a nice big bone. My goodness, Cal, your grandfather has been worrying about you. I haven't, of course, because I'm not the one who has tried to confine you for the whole of your life."

"Harumph" was the most intelligent statement Edward could make after Irene's comment.

"*Have* you been worrying?" Charlton's mouth twisted, watching Girl leave with the housekeeper.

Edward pursed his lips. "In one sense. You didn't tell me you were going and I thought I might never see you again. However, I didn't worry about your safety. I know you are perfectly capable of fending for yourself." He held his breath.

Charlton nodded. He waited while the table was set in front of him with a silver charger and cutlery. "I didn't plan to see you until I'd proved my point. You wouldn't listen when I tried to explain and so I decided to show you instead."

"So I surmised." Clearing his throat, Edward bent his head, watching his long white fingers trembling on his knee. "My journey to this revelation was longer than between Farvista and here. Along the way, I learned much about you and me. I learned that I love you as much as I loved your father." His voice became unexpectedly gruff. "I learned that I couldn't force either of you to follow in my footsteps. He was and you are your own men. Your dreams might not be mine, but you have a right to them."

"Which is why you employed McLaren to spy on me?" Charlton raised his eyebrows.

Edward had missed the stimulation of his grandson's quick mind. "Indeed. Your idea was sound. I never thought otherwise. But you are the heir to my worldly possessions, including the land I've worked most of my life. I thought you might be able to use McLaren as your manager. I don't want a small business taking priority over Farvista."

"Nor do I want that."

"I thought you wanted the wool brokerage?"

Charlton shrugged. "It's not incompatible with managing the station. In fact, I see it as an adjunct. The one thing should run with the other. If we want the best prices and conditions, we can't hope others will provide for us."

Edward considered. "That may be." He lowered his gaze. "You have a sound business sense, and I'm sometimes a hasty-tempered old fool. My name is yours and you have as much right to it as I."

"I had something to prove and I did quite well without using your name." Finally served dinner, Charlton cut off a piece of roast beef and chewed with unusual relish. "I thought I would prove myself over the business of the wool auctions, but after I did I realized that beginning a business wasn't my main concern. I needed to prove my capabilities. Prove them." He speared a potato and paused. "Not have it accepted that because I am your grandson and heir I can measure up to you. I know now I'm a survivor. With your backing or without it I will get by."

"I never doubted it."

"Nor did I," Irene interjected with a charming smile.

For the first time Charlton appeared to relax. He took a great gulp of the red wine in front of him and held the glass aloft, examining the color in the glow of the central candles. "I'm pleased to be reinstated in your affections, Grandfather, make no mistake. But I will go ahead with the auction idea. I have to for McLaren's sake. He wants to marry and he needs a steady income. By the way, he will make a good manager. Facts and figures absorb him."

"I'm glad he pleases you," Edward said simply. "For if he didn't, he'd be put off."

"That would be my responsibility." Charlton tilted his chin with arrogance.

Edward inclined his head. "Point taken."

"I've contacted those who have been at the sales in Victoria and told them that we'll hold our own sales here next week. I've already interviewed wool classers and auctioneers."

Edward nodded, pleased to hear the same Charlton he had known, the man who always had a well-thought-out plan of action. McLaren had told him nothing of this. He'd heard only that Charlton had arrived and taken over. The lad was indeed a survivor.

"What about the Beaufort girl?" Irene asked with careful deliberation. "Is the relationship serious?"

Charlton swirled the wine in his glass. "You had word of her from Sam, I imagine?"

"Did you spot him?"

"Lurking around corners and asking questions of people who know nothing about me. He's not subtle, as I'm sure you know."

"I might have known he'd have a heavy hand." Edward clamped his lips.

Irene straightened her spine. "Am I expecting a daughter-in-law?"

He shook his head, his expression unusually grim. "She wants a rich husband."

She smiled indulgently. "In you she wouldn't find a richer one."

"She knows me as plain Cal Langdon and refused me as such." Almost idly, he chased a pea around his plate with a fork.

"She refused Cal Langdon?" Irene said with indignation. "Would she refuse Charlton Lynton?"

"She would marry any man rich enough to support her sisters."

"In that case, she can't be all bad." Irene's eyes began to sparkle. Edward could see her mentally counting grandchildren.

"She isn't even slightly bad. She is the most incredible woman I have ever met," Charlton said stiffly.

Irene tapped her elegant fingers on the table. "You need to be aware that she and her sisters are in town and have been invited to our ball."

Charlton sat very still. "If she sees me at the ball, she'll see me as Charlton."

"And she ought to be impressed to see you well-dressed and not smelling of sheep." Irene wrinkled her nose. "So, you love her?"

Charlton's expression looked bleak. "Past bearing. But I won't buy her love."

For a moment, the only sound in the room was Irene's fingernail tapping on the table. "You know why she needs money. And we don't know what she thinks of Cal Langdon. What if she loves him despite his lack of money?"

"I'm at your service," Edward said, sparking up. "Together, two men should be able to discover the workings of the mind of one woman."

* * * *

Rose opened the hand-delivered letter addressed to the Misses Beaufort and shook her head. "I don't believe it. Lately we've had such amazing luck. Look, Ella. It's the wool-clip money. Cal has sold our wool."

"He said he would." Ella scanned the bank draft, hoping for a personal message or even a friendly greeting, but she found only a formal accounting.

Rose put the draft into her bedside drawer. "Seven hundred and eighty-five pounds. My. We can bank the money until we need it." Apparently losing interest, she went back to gazing at her new ball gown.

The dressmaker had delivered the ice blue and the amber just an hour ago. Anxiously awaited, the gowns were to be worn tonight to the Lynton's ball. Ella had glanced at hers and had duly admired the swish of the crisp material. "We should invest the money immediately." She stared at the drawer in which the bank draft resided. Cal had come through. His plan had worked and he now had the opportunity to make a success of himself. "I need to know if I will have to find a job."

Rose frowned. "I would be most embarrassed if you did. In our own house, with the money we have already, we'll be secure enough until we marry."

"I might not marry."

"You'll meet someone here I'm sure."

"I'm not sure I will."

"Really, Ella. This isn't the sort of thing we need to discuss right now. I don't want anything to spoil my mood. I want to look beautiful tonight and attract Mr. Charlton Lynton."

"I hope you're not putting all our eggs in one basket."

Rose gave a tight smile. "Trust me, I'm not. Now, the question is, should I wear Mama's pendant?" She held up a teardrop pearl hanging from a bow of small diamonds.

"It looks very nice with the blue."

Rose held a miniature of the pendant to each lobe and studied herself in the mirror. "I want to look untouched and untouchable."

"You'll look glorious. You always do." Ella left for her own room. Her gown lay on her bed. The elegant creation had tiny off-the-shoulder cap sleeves, a pin-tucked skirt front, and a tightly boned bodice. Her elbow-length gloves lay beside the gown and her dancing shoes on the floor beneath. Her petticoats hung on the bedpost. As she had a few hours left before she needed to dress, she ordered a bath.

She soaked, wishing she could be Rose, single-minded and certain of her charms. Tonight she would be the plain brown contrast that demonstrated Rose's divine beauty. Ella accepted her place but not with enthusiasm.

Aunt's maid planned to style Rose's hair after doing her employer's. Ella would manage her own. In the steam from the bath, she ragged ringlets in the back and, once out of the water, she began to plait the front sections, wanting to imitate the fashionable style she'd seen Rose wear occasionally.

The maid's voice echoed from Rose's room. Vianna popped her head in the doorway. "You should see Rose. She looks finer than a wedding cake. She is wearing Mama's diamond clip in her hair."

Ella stepped into her gown, which Vianna fastened. The silk fitted like an expensive kid glove. She hoped the boning wouldn't impede her breathing. "Would you help me take the rags out of my hair? I keep getting tangled."

"Your hair is very thick. It doesn't curl like Rose's. Some of these bits are...dangly rather than springy. Wait a moment." Vianna left the room.

Ella examined her reflection, agreeing that each ringlet drooped to a different level. She tried to pin the curls. Her arms began to ache.

Vianna arrived with the maid, Pender, in tow. Pender said, "I've been wanting to style your hair for weeks, Miss Ella."

Ella sat with her hands in her lap while Pender undid the plaits and brushed straight the half-formed curls. "There," she finally said with satisfaction.

Ella couldn't have been more disappointed. Her hair looked absolutely plain, pinned in a smooth knot on the top. She would never have a chance to be beautiful.

"Oh, Ella," Vianna said. "You look exquisite. Doesn't she, Pender?"

"Miss is a lovely girl. In that color and with the utter simplicity of the style of her hair and her gown, she will shine like a sunbeam tonight."

"Not a star?" Ella asked dryly.

"That would be your sister. Your appeal is more subtle."

Ella examined herself in the mirror again and again. Did she look lovely? Or very, very plain? Was subtle a synonym for nonexistent? She decided she looked unusual.

"You should wear something around your neck." Vianna narrowed her eyes critically.

Ella frowned at her. She owned no jewelry other than a gold cross. Everything Mama had owned had been left to Rose. "Pender implied that simplicity is more my style." She tried to glimpse the back of her hair in the mirror Pender held.

When the maid had been thanked and had left the room, Vianna said in a quiet voice, "I think Rose is very mean not to let you have some of Mama's jewels. Your money from your horses will be paying for our house."

"Ella offered us her money." Rose always seemed to appear when she was being discussed, a talent not shared by many people. "Whatever she does with her three hundred guineas is her decision. And as it happens, I brought this in for her to wear." Chin jutted, she offered an amber necklace made of big uneven beads clasped in gold. Not one of Mama's more exclusive pieces, the beads had rarely been worn her lifetime.

Ella held the necklace around her neck. "I like it," she said, noticing for the first time the greenish-blue of her eyes, the creaminess of her skin, and the warmth of her sun-streaked hair. "It's just the thing. Thank you, Rose." She kissed Rose. She kissed Vianna.

She didn't doubt that tonight should mark a new chapter in her life.

* * * *

Ella, in awe, trailed into the Lynton mansion behind Aunt and Rose. The hallway was the length of three large rooms and lined with huge, gold-framed paintings. Mrs. Lynton stood near a pair of white marble columns greeting guests. Aunt led the way to her.

"They've hung painted silk on the walls," Ella said under her breath to her sister.

"My charges, Miss Rose Beaufort and Miss Dorella," Aunt said to Mrs. Lynton.

"Delighted," Mrs. Lynton said, scanning Rose with her eyes. "Delightful. And Miss Dorella. Such a pretty pair." She linked her arm with Rose's and bore her off into the ballroom as if she had just met the last of her guests.

Aunt made a moue of her mouth and took Ella's arm. "I think she must be taking Rose to meet the heir. I didn't realize she was in such..." She broke off. "Ah. Mr. Lynton. I didn't expect to see you at a ball, bearing in mind what you think of *supper dances*." She spoke to a tall, elderly man with white hair, thick sideburns, and a dashing moustache.

He inclined his head. "I wouldn't want to miss this one. This would be the younger Miss Beaufort, I presume?"

Ella curtsied to him. She didn't know why, other than that his tall, imposing presence seemed to expect it. "Dorella Beaufort." She smiled at the man who had Aunt's attention. "You would be the heir's grandfather?"

"The heir?" He looked startled. "You mean Charlton?"

"None other."

He gave a courteous inclination of his head. "He is my grandson, yes. Mrs. Cameron says you lived on a sheep station. Before you are overwhelmed by dance partners, may I have the honor of your company?"

Aunt stood, momentarily at a loss. "Perhaps I should go and chaperone Rose?"

Mr. Lynton, with natural courtesy, offered his arm. "I meant you—plural."

Aunt smiled uncertainly. Ella took his other arm and he escorted them into the ballroom, where he found a row of velvet chairs as yet unoccupied. Without any visible indications of his need, he summoned up three glasses of champagne, brought over by a green-coated manservant. Ella sipped the surprisingly tart bubbly liquid, not sure if she liked it. After the second sip, she did. "This is the life."

"Not like life on the station?" the old man asked. "I want to ask your opinion, my dear. Recently I met a young man named Cal Langdon. He seems a steady chap with a good head on his shoulders and he referred to your sheep station as his last place of employment." He waited.

"He was there." Ella's heart bumped erratically. "He came with the shearing team."

"Would you recommend him for a position with me?"

Ella wet her lips. "He's absolutely reliable and utterly trustworthy. I would recommend him to anyone for anything. He helped us get our station back on its feet, if stations have feet. He also helped get our stolen horses back. Because of him and his knowledge of land management, we have sold our property for a very good price and will soon be able to set up ourselves in the city." Her eyes prickled.

"What do you think of him as a man?"

"He's..." Ella cleared her throat. "He's a very good man. I have to tell you that my sister says she is in love with him. She swears she'll marry him."

A sudden smile lit Mr. Lynton's face. "That is very, very good news."

"I must explain, though, that my sister is eleven years old. She might change her mind by the time she is of marriageable age."

"Oh, your youngest sister." He looked away, rubbing a forefinger along his moustache. "And what about Miss Rose? Does she like him, too?"

"You might ask her, for here she is."

"Ask me what?"

"Let me introduce you to Mr. Lynton, Rose. My sister, Rose, Mr. Lynton."

The man stood and took Rose's hand in his, bending over her wrist with gallantry. "Delighted to finally meet you."

"He wants to know what you think of Cal."

Rose smiled placidly. "I assume he is a very good shearer. The other men thought well of him." She glanced under her lashes at Mr. Lynton. "And he did us a personal service."

Mr. Lynton bowed. "Perhaps he has very good prospects. Would that make a difference to you?"

"I would be glad that he had good prospects," Rose said. "But on the whole, shearers don't interest me. They're rough and poorly spoken, as a rule, and I would hardly call their work stimulating. I prefer gentlemen who are prepared to dance the night away."

"In that case, do not let me detain you," Mr. Lynton said. He bowed in Ella's direction and left the ballroom.

* * * *

Cal rose slowly to his feet, frowning at Edward. "She seriously said that shearers don't interest her? Every one of us thought the world of her."

"Her sister spoke more highly of you."

"Her sister doesn't have more than two thoughts in her head and both of them are about herself."

Edward frowned and recrossed his legs in his comfortable leather armchair. "I had another opinion of each lady entirely."

Cal could focus on nothing other than Ella's words. He paced across the thick Chinese carpet to the doorway and back. "Though she repeated time after time she wanted a rich husband. I knew she was determined. Why am I surprised she has barely given me a thought?" He pressed his forehead with his fingertips trying to clear his head. The ache in his chest almost brought him to a halt. "Glad for me! Perhaps I will make her even gladder by showing her how easily a rich man can evade the grasp of the best play actress in the colony."

He flung open the door and strode to the huge mirror in the hall, where he straightened his white tie, flicked the shoulders of his black jacket with his gloves, and tugged them on. Beneath a fresh haircut, a face pale with determination gazed back at him. He couldn't say he cared. Shooting his cuffs, he paced to the ballroom doors.

As he neared the area, the orchestra struck up from the balcony. For a moment, he hesitated in the doorway, trying to spot Ella. The room was too crowded to pick her out.

"Charlton," he heard, and he spotted his mother hurrying toward him. "I'm afraid you've lost—"

"Not now," he said. "Do I know anyone here who might accept me for the first waltz?"

Without a change of expression, she turned and presented him to a pretty young hopeful. He merely indicated the floor and, with studied grace, Miss Paterson partnered him. During their first two full turns of the room, while she commented on the size of the ballroom and the number of people present, he was conscious of being recognized and pointed out. He hoped Ella noticed. He wouldn't acknowledge her, of course, until she had seen him ignoring her. Then he would introduce himself as Charlton Lynton, the rich man she had irrevocably lost.

With a hidden anger, he deposited Miss Paterson with her mother. Then he spotted Grace McLaren among a group of young ladies. Because she and her brother had been so hospitable to him over the past few weeks, he asked if she might honor him with the next dance. Before he finished his sentence, she glided into his arms. She talked about her family's connections as they circled the floor.

At the other side of the room, he spotted her brother, Daniel, dancing with a blonde dressed in ice blue. He waltzed Grace toward them, wondering if McLaren was with the woman he was hoping to make his wife. When he got close enough he realized McLaren looked grim, which was so exactly Cal's mood that he smiled bitterly.

"McLaren," he said in acknowledgment.

"Ha," said McLaren, swinging his partner off the floor. "Lynton, just the man I want to see."

Cal followed, assuming his friend expected to talk to him. His glance froze on McLaren's partner. "Miss Beaufort," he said with the barest movement of his lips. Rose looked much younger not wearing black and probably beautiful. Her blue eyes widened and she stared at him as if stunned.

"You know each other?" McLaren asked. "Miss Beaufort has been insisting that I introduce you to her, but I now see it is a waste of time."

Miss Rose swallowed. "*You* are Charlton Lynton?"

"At your service," replied Cal, who didn't intend to be at her or her sister's service for a single minute throughout the duration of his life.

"And you've always been Charlton Lynton?"

"My full name is Charlton Alfred Langdon Lynton. My close friends and family call me Cal, for obvious reasons."

"I think I'm going to faint. And if you let me make such a fool of myself here, Daniel McLaren, I won't marry you."

"I thought you wanted to marry Charlton?"

"Daniel," she said, not looking any more pallid than her usual colorless self. "No woman with pride would accept being told she didn't have enough money to be an acceptable bride and then being taken up again when she had more money. I intended to teach you a lesson. I certainly won't be marrying C—Mr. Lynton. I don't happen to be in love with him."

Grace clung to Cal's arm. "Perhaps we ought to leave these two," she said in an arch whisper.

"Indeed. I'll take you back to your group. McLaren, let me know when you have sorted this out, and I'll dance at your wedding."

Cal now knew the truth of his identity would be told to Ella and that he only had to wait to wreak his vengeance. The time came sooner than expected. Before he'd returned Grace, having been stopped twice by acquaintances, Ella approached him.

"Cal," she said, her face stiff. "You are the heir."

"I am the heir," Cal stated, narrowing his eyes. She looked the perfect amber statue, slim and elegant, dangerously controlled, and with not a flyaway hair in sight.

"You lied to me."

"I didn't once lie to you," he said tersely. "I simply didn't tell you my business. And why would I?" He glanced at Grace, who gave him a sympathetic nod.

Grace took his arm in a proprietary hold and expressed disdain with the jut of her chin. "Indeed, for ladies don't discuss business as a rule."

Following her lead and glad of time to think, Cal said, "Not ladies of your class, at least."

Grace gave him a pleased smile, and he recalled the conversation at the Beaufort's outdoor table when Rose told some cobbled story about him flirting with Grace. From somewhere he dredged up an answering smile that he hoped looked complicit with Daniel's tiresome sister.

"May I introduce Miss Ella Beaufort to you, Grace? Miss Grace McLaren."

Ella nodded briskly at Grace. Never one to stop until she had finished, she said in a voice rigid with outrage, "You know you should have told me because I gave my wool clip to you. I trusted you with my family's *future*, you, a man who didn't even have the courtesy to tell me who he really was."

"Why should my name make a difference?"

Ella's eyes widened. "I just told you why."

Grace shook her head reprovingly. "Poor Rose would be shocked to hear her sister—" She didn't continue because Ella swished her skirts and flurried off.

"Thank you," Cal said distractedly to Grace, then he left to follow Ella. After three hasty steps, he grabbed her elbow and swung her around to face him. "If you had known I was rich, you would have thrown yourself at me," he said through his teeth.

She flattened her expression. "Didn't I? When I didn't know who you were?"

She had indeed. He dropped his hold on her, blinking.

"I'm going home now," she said in a deadly whisper. "And I hope I never see you again." She marched out into the hall, leaving him with a view of her erect head, her beautiful curves, and the bouncing bell of her skirt.

He stood for a moment, disoriented. He was the one who'd been discarded, not she, yet she had somehow reversed the situation. Tearing his concentration from the doorway, he noticed that the closer guests watched him. As he frowned at each in turn, they began new conversations. He stood alone for a lifetime.

A light touch on his arm swiveled his gaze.

"That was badly done," his mother said. "Miss Beaufort won't like you quarrelling with her sister."

"Why should I care what Rose might like?" he said in a growl.

"That's hardly the attitude to take with the woman you love."

"Love Rose? I barely know her. And aside from that, I can't love anyone while Ella has a complete...stranglehold on my heart."

"Ella?" Irene wet her lips. "Miss Dorella? Well! We made a mistake, Edward and I. We thought you wanted Rose."

"Ella was the sister who said Cal was a good man," Edward said from behind him. "She had nothing but praise of him."

Cal felt his heart solidify into a lump of lead in his chest. "Ella? You confused Ella with Rose. My God. What have I done?"

"Nothing irredeemable, I hope. I sent her home in my carriage. She told me she would probably kick the upholstery, but I assume she will be calmer tomorrow. We can try again then."

"*We* won't try again. She is my woman and my problem."

Chapter 20

Fortunately Vianna was fast asleep when Ella returned. She undressed and slipped quickly into bed.

Lying motionless and keeping her tears to a silent gush over her cheeks, Ella tried to forget tall, dark, handsome Cal. Rich Cal. Lying Cal. The man who had pleasured her, apparently craving diversion with a woman not of his class. Doubtless, he'd chosen the easier mark of the sisters, the plain one who had never had an admirer in her life.

Deliberately, she turned her mind to Daniel, very ordinary looking, of average height and with reddish hair and eyelashes, certainly a wise choice for her sister, a steady man, not one born to great privilege, not spoiled nor deliberately cruel, not one who would lie to a woman for his own gain.

Tired and headachy, in the vast silence of dawn she arose from bed. Not wanting to face Vianna's inquisition about the night before, for some time she lingered in the drawing room. When she heard the servants clattering in the kitchen across the courtyard she, who disliked cooking, offered to make a fruit medley. Even then, she didn't escape the servants' questioning about the ball. She declared the occasion "very fine" and kept a smile pinned to her face. Finally, when Mrs. Cameron rang for breakfast, Ella went back over to the main house, preparing to face the storm.

"You made a hit with Mr. Edward Lynton," Aunt said placidly. "He told me he sent you home in his carriage. Is your headache better?"

Ella had heard Aunt and Rose arrive home very late. She nodded. Mr. Lynton must have passed on the excuse she gave him for searching outside in the dark for a carriage to take her home. "Did you have a nice time?"

"The best. My darling Rose is engaged to Daniel McLaren. I had higher hopes for her, but her happiness is paramount. Oh, Vianna, sweet, have you heard the news?"

Vianna had dressed, but Ella would have bet she hadn't washed. Her hair had been combed at the front and was tangled at the back. "That's why I'm at breakfast so early, to hear everything. Did Rose meet the heir?"

Ella moistened her lips. "We both met him, but we already knew him." She took a deep breath. "Cal is Charlton Lynton."

Vianna sat on a dining chair with a surprised thump. "That's awful. Now every woman will want him."

"Not every woman." With no appetite, Ella took a boiled egg from the dish.

Aunt said, "I heard you spent some time with him."

"Not much time."

"I suppose he looked very dashing in a tail coat. I think he's the handsomest man in the world." Vianna reached for the toast.

"He was a shearer on your property, I hear. I don't suppose you had much contact with him."

"No meaningful contact. He lied about who he was."

"His grandfather is most distressed about that. It seems he told Charlton that he had to get by without using his family name, assuming that would force him to rethink leaving Farvista and going out on his own. But Charlton left anyway and didn't need to use the Lynton name or his grandfather's money. Mr. Lynton is very proud of him, but he's quite disturbed about forcing the lad to use an alias. He takes full responsibility for that. You must forgive Charlton, my dear. He didn't set out to deceive."

"However, he was quite satisfied that he had. I imagine he hoped he would never meet one of us again." Ella took a bite of her toast, which tasted like cardboard.

"He told me he would visit this afternoon to make his apologies to you."

"Oh, I don't care if he is sorry or not. I told him I don't want to see him again and I mean it. I'll be out."

"I hope you will stay. Daniel will come by, too. He wants to meet his new sisters-to-be."

"And is Daniel the man Rose is to marry?" Vianna asked, soaking a soldier of toast in the yolk of her second egg.

"They've been in love for two years, fancy that, and only now have their circumstances allowed them to make a commitment to each other."

Rose, dressed prettily in a soft pink floral gown, came in the room and sat beside Ella.

"How do you do that?" Ella asked irritably. "Every time we start talking about you, you appear."

"Luck. Like having you sell the chestnuts for a small fortune. If you hadn't been able to afford a house for you and Vianna, I wouldn't have been able to marry Daniel. We would have had to leave the wool-clip money whole, and then I wouldn't have had a penny for my dowry. Have you eaten all the toast, Vi?"

"Ring for more."

"That explains why you are so mean about Mama's jewelry, Rose." Vianna licked her fingers. "You weren't going to be sharing Ella's house and so you didn't think you should share your inheritance. I don't know how I'm supposed to share the portrait of Mama, other than to let you both look at her whenever you like."

"You don't have to share," Ella said, annoyed. "Nor does Rose. I don't suppose it ever occurred to either of you that I love you and would willingly contribute whatever I have to our security."

"I hope you will still say that when you are married to the richest man in the colony," Rose said in an ironic voice.

"I'm not going to marry him. I can't bear him." Ella stood so suddenly that she almost toppled her chair. "Aside from that, he despises me. To him I'm just a silly little country girl who amused him for a week or two. And I won't let any man patronize me." After flouncing out of the room, she discovered she had nowhere private to give in to her despair.

If she didn't find a house this week and move out, she would lose her mind.

* * * *

Not knowing the time Cal would arrive in his attempt to rebreak her heart, Ella hid in the tiny garden for two hours. Finally she decided she could ride along the river to the city, where she might spy a suitable house for sale. Thus far, Rose's choosiness had prevented the purchase of three acceptable houses and only this morning Ella had discovered why. Rose had no intention of leaving Mrs. Cameron until she married.

Ella changed into her riding dress and strode to the mews. Behind her she heard a patter of light racing feet. Turning, she saw a dog resembling Girl run toward her. The collie couldn't be Girl. Ella saw no sign of Cal or any other rider. She began to walk again. The dog skidded to a halt and began to walk beside her, panting.

"Girl? Is it you?"

The dog stared ahead, tongue lolling.

"If it is, you'd best go away. I'm not talking to you, and I'm not talking to your master. I don't want your company, and I don't want his. You never bothered with me before. I don't know why you're here now."

The dog sashayed in front of her and almost tripped her. Ella stopped and pointed in the other direction. "Go. Leave me. Shoo. Scatter the sheep. Round up the ants. I don't want a dog with me."

The dog sat and stared at her, head to the side, eyes wide and innocent.

"Do what you will. I'm going to take a ride." She marched to the mews' courtyard. "Hello. Anyone here?" The paved space echoed with silence. "I've come to get the piebald."

She heard a high-pitched, derisive yell and in the explosion of noise, her dun erupted out of the open stable door. Atop sat the stout man, swinging a rope like a lariat and urging the horse toward her. He dragged the reluctant piebald on a leading rope. Ella stepped back to the wall.

"What on earth do you think you are doing?" She flattened herself against the cool stones. "Stop. Those are my horses." The man clattered by. She reached for the piebald's rope, but the man angled the horses out onto the clay road.

The man swiveled in his saddle. He gave a fat grin. "They're not yours, you low-down horse thief. They're mine. You took 'em."

Ella shot a quick glance at the dog, who stared right back at her. Ella was sure the dog was Girl. The border collie widened her mouth, narrowed her eyes, and flattened her ears. Certain the dog had indicated her sympathy, Ella gave her the signal to round up—a circle with her hand—and pointed to the man and her horses.

Like a released arrow, Girl gave chase. Ella started running after them. Her hat slipped to one ear and the feather tickled her cheek.

The rider entered the scrub by the river, disappearing from view. Girl bounded over the undergrowth. For a moment, Ella paused, straightening her hat and trying to see the direction the fat man had taken—the fat man, the man she had seen only last week outside the mews. The horse thief who had come all the way to Adelaide to take his darned horses back.

"*You* are the thief," she yelled as, skirts held high, she left in hot pursuit. "Help, someone. Help me stop him."

* * * *

Cal rode up the narrow street by the river where he had been told Mrs. Cameron lived. Girl had gone on ahead, perhaps on the trail of a smell in which to roll. He had every confidence she would rejoin him, although she'd never been in this area before. She always found him after she had completed her personal business.

At the far end of the street, he heard a yell and saw a woman jump over a fallen tree by the embankment of the river. She wore a brown riding skirt and a tiny, feathered hat dangling from her neck by its ribbon.

Almost instantly, the scrub hid her from view. He turned his horse into the driveway of the Cameron house.

Vianna strolled out of the front door. She put up her hand to shade her eyes. "You look rich," she said, a saintly smile on her face. "A suit, no less, and a white shirt. And what a lovely horse."

"He was bred by my grandfather." Cal dismounted. "You've heard the story, I assume."

"I'm shocked," Vianna said piously. "I never thought you would tell a lie."

"Yours is a family of pedants. I made an omission and didn't, strictly, lie."

"Omissions are the worst kinds of lies, Ella says. She isn't here. Do you want to apologize to me and Rose?"

"I apologize. Where is Ella?"

"She went down to the mews. She planned on taking a ride to the city."

Cal's head lifted. The woman he had seen was Ella. He should have recognized that silly little feathered hat of hers. She must have been unseated by her horse and was even now trying to catch it. Making a quick decision, he swung up into his saddle again. "I'll find her and apologize to her."

"Don't worry. She won't forgive you," Vianna called after him.

Perhaps Ella wouldn't, but he'd never been faint of heart and he had a fair maid to win. At least he could help catch her mount, even if they couldn't have a productive conversation. He made a determined mouth, urging his horse into a canter. Following the trail of the flattened grass, he let his horse beat his way to the river.

High in the trees, a family of magpies gave warning trills. He heard an almighty splash, a male shout of triumph, and the thud of retreating hoofbeats. Not able to guess by the sound what had happened, Cal increased his horse's pace. He reached the river's edge to see some sort of turmoil in the water farther along. A head made a vee of the water flowing past. Ella's head. Reminded of the time he had fished her out of the billabong, his heart leaped into his throat.

She flailed. He saw her submerge. His chest thudding like a drum, he dashed his horse through the water. The riverbed receded. He directed his horse diagonally toward Ella. As he neared, her splashing ceased. She changed direction, turning toward the bank, bobbing, then dragging something black and sodden. Her hat floated downstream.

"Ella. Paddle. Don't stop moving," he called, hoping she could stay afloat until he reached her.

She gave a spluttery gasp and gurgled something like "Kung."

Iced with fear, he urged at his horse, getting no perceptible response. He thought to dismount and swim to Ella but realized he could almost reach her. Leaving one leg balanced across his saddle, he held his reins and stretched out to her. He grabbed her skirts, trying to give her floatation. This submerged her. His horse turned toward the bank, pulling on the reins. Fighting the horse and catching hold of Ella seemed near to impossible.

She reappeared, gasping, floating on the water, but going nowhere. Although it was unlikely, she appeared to be doing a form of swimming, a push forward while she pulled the bundle. With an extra kick of his legs he reached out, catching her collar. He tugged and the waterlogged weight of her inched toward him.

"Careful. Careful," she spluttered, not using her arms to help herself.

"Hold onto me, Ella."

"Can't." Finally she swiveled around enough for him to see the wet bundle of black hair in her arms.

The bundle hung limply. Girl. "Leave her go, Ella. She can swim better than you or me."

"She's tied," Ella wheezed. "She'll drown."

"So will you if you don't let her go."

Ella's mouth shut and the expression on her face tightened. He could see she meant to try and strike out for the bank, carrying the dog. With no other option he fought for possession of Girl, finding the dog wrapped in rope, legs caught up and useless. He shoved the dog on the saddle and then hauled the woman into a firm grip. "Hold onto the saddle. We're going ashore."

With the horse's panicked cooperation, they reached the water's edge in no time. Ella arose in the shallower water. Streams ran from her face and hair. She lifted the dog into her arms as she tried to catch her breath.

Cal took Girl from her, leaving his horse to stumble up the bank. "I think you were swimming. But for the dog, you probably would have made it back safely."

She covered her chest with her palm, breathing hard and coughing. "But for you, I would have made it back safely. Swimming is easy. All you have to do is try."

He sat on the bank of the river, hauling her down beside him. The limp dog lay across his lap, the rope tangled tightly. Cal began untying knots, noting the rise and fall of the exhausted dog's chest.

Ella stretched a hand out to the dog and cupped Girl's chin. "He lassoed her like a calf and slung her into the water." She gave another watery cough. "I can't believe that anyone would do anything so cruel. She might have drowned."

Girl wriggled. She lifted her head and tried to lick Ella's fingers.

Cal stared, nonplussed. His dog had never before shown a trace of affection to a person other than him. "I have no idea what happened here, but you obviously saved my dog's life. I don't know why. You're not a swimmer and you should have shouted for help."

"Help from whom? I was the only one here."

"Who threw her in the water and why?"

"Give me a moment to catch my breath." She leaned forward, head in her hands and breathing deeply. Finally, she said, "It was that fat horse thief. He stole his darned horses from the mews. Girl caught up to him and annoyed him into stopping. So he roped her and tossed her into the river."

"The horse thief?"

"He said *I* was a thief to have the horses and so I suspect they were his all along. I told Rose we shouldn't keep them and I was right."

"I should have taken those men into custody when I had the chance. I thought it was enough to get the horses back."

"We could never have handled all those horses with the thieves as well."

"You're shivering."

"I think it's shock. Imagine that." She stared at the river. "I went into the water and I tried to swim. I didn't think I ever would."

Cal struggled out of his suit jacket. "I would give you this but it's wetter than you."

"Oh, don't worry about me. As you know, I'm quite tough."

"Yes. Tough and strong and witty and clever. I came today to ask you to marry me."

"You're the heir. You can have anyone."

"But could I if I weren't the heir?"

Ella wrung the water from her hair. "You would be left with someone like me—the wrong sister. Oh, I know your family and Mrs. Cameron wanted Rose for you. I'd have to be deaf and blind not to. Unfortunately for you, Rose fell in love with Mr. McLaren two years ago."

"It's not unfortunate for me and it's very fortunate for McLaren. He will have a beautiful bride and live happily ever after."

As if she hadn't heard a word he said, Ella stood. "As will I. I shall buy a house and live very comfortably with Vi until she leaves me. She is as beautiful as Rose and shouldn't have any difficulty finding a suitable husband. So you don't need to feel sorry for me."

"I don't feel sorry for you." He stood, too, leaving Girl to rise to her feet and shake herself groggily. "You're not the wrong sister."

"I've been the wrong sister all my life." She gave a faint smile. "My Papa never thought I was worth much. He wouldn't let me help run the station and he sent Rose to the city to catch a rich husband. He didn't imagine I could do either of those things. He kept me at home to care for Vi."

"You've done a wonderful job with her. Rose wouldn't have had the patience."

"Papa knew that. He also knew that if he left the chestnuts to me, I would sell them to take care of my sisters. That's why he didn't leave me the portrait of Mama or her jewelry. The beauty was left the jewelry. The baby was left a remembrance of her Mama. I was left the means to take care of them both."

"Your father knew you well."

"He knew no man would want me other than as a diversion on his journey through life."

"And a greater role you could not play," he said, grinning widely. Too late he realized he had hurt her—in too many ways. A woman whose father was an irresponsible gambler would need great faith before trusting another man. He put his hands on her upper arms and tried to draw her close. "No one has ever diverted me quite as much as you," he said with heartfelt tenderness.

"I'm glad I was of use." She pushed him away. "To thank me, instead of an offer of marriage that would suit neither of us, you could catch the thieves and get rid of them for all time. I'll grow old very quickly if I have to chase horses every few months."

He frowned. "How does it happen that Girl saw the thief take the horses?"

"She was trying to round me up and take me back to Mrs. Cameron's house," Ella said with a frown. "Bossy dog. I don't like her any more than I like you."

"You do," Cal said, patting Girl, who was gazing at Ella. "You love her and you love me. I'm not going to chase your thief again unless you say you will marry me."

She stared at the ground. "I believed every word you said and you lied to me. My father lied to me, too. I loved him, but he didn't once say he cared for me. I won't love anyone I can't trust."

"I'm not your father," he said in a quiet voice. "I don't expect you to look after your sisters. I will take full responsibility for Vianna as long as necessary. I'll buy you a new silly little feathered hat, too."

She put her hand up to her head, possibly noticing for the first time that her hat had been lost. "I don't want hats. I don't want to lose responsibility for Vi. I'm not a virgin and I can't marry you. I made love with a shearer whose name I didn't know."

"You don't know when to stop, do you?" He lifted her chin. "No matter what you say, you can't stop me wanting you."

"Ah, *wanting* me," she said, raising both palms to his chest. "That's a whole other subject."

"You brought up making love because you're burning for me. You can't think of anything but this." He swept her into his arms and his mouth descended on hers.

He enjoyed her unplanned response. She let him meld them into one, lifting her arms around his neck and clinging to him. His need for her stunned him. He didn't know how he'd found the strength to leave her for one week, let alone five. The kiss grew in intensity, deeper, harder. He bit at her lips and nipped at her throat, licking the taste of the river from her skin.

Suddenly she broke free of him. "I won't let you do this to me ever again." She lifted her sodden gown from her legs and walked backward.

"I hope you don't mean that." He read the obstinacy in her face and sighed. Collecting his horse, he took the reins and swung on. Girl, smelling of damp fur, leaped to the saddle in front of him. "I'm off to capture Mr. Fatman. I'm going to tie him into a tighter parcel than he tied Girl, and then I'm going to find his friend and deliver them both to the police. I let them go once. I gave them a second chance. I made a mistake. I won't give them a third."

He left at a gallop with no time to waste. The sooner he completed his tasks, the sooner he could work out what she needed from him.

* * * *

Ella trudged back to Mrs. Cameron's house, achingly sad, desperately lonely, and utterly humiliated. She didn't know how she'd faced Cal today. She'd told him she wanted a rich husband. Then he turned out to be rich. She couldn't have sounded shallower.

After entering through the courtyard at the back of the house, she squelched up the stairs to her bedroom, which was fortunately unoccupied. She removed her clothes, took a towel from the rack, dried herself, and bundled up her hair. Outside, she heard the hoofbeats of an approaching rider. Daniel McLaren, most likely. Heaving a deep sigh, she took a yellow-striped day gown and dressed for the third time that day. At the ball, one of the few times she'd looked nice, she'd not been in Cal's presence long enough for him to notice. Then again, as he didn't love her, he wouldn't have cared.

She took some time drying her hair and brushing the length into the same smooth swirl she'd worn last night, thinking she may as well try for elegance since beauty eluded her. Then she wasted her whole effort by lying on top of her bed and crying about the times when she hadn't been brave enough, strong enough, or beautiful enough to help Papa.

Tears flooded her cheeks.

Cal had said Papa must have known her very well—he had expected her to support her sisters after he died if they hadn't married. That implied trust in her. She sat up and blew her nose. Perhaps he didn't think she was as inadequate as she had assumed. Perhaps she was just being maudlin because Cal, given the opportunity, hadn't said he loved her.

She'd known from the start he was a responsible citizen. When she'd been unable to manage the station, he had taken time to teach and help her. He'd not set out to make love to her. That had only happened at her insistence. And he'd offered to marry her if he'd left her with a child. She'd been the one to refuse to marry a shearer. Only an hour ago she'd refused to marry the heir to the greatest fortune in the colony—because he didn't love her. How perverse could she be? She dried her face. The least she could do was go downstairs and meet the man who loved her sister.

After an hour in the company of the lovebirds, she saw that Rose had chosen her husband cleverly. She would be able to control Daniel without too much trouble. The man would give her whatever she wanted within his means, and she would repay him by being the serene and beautiful wife he craved.

For herself, Ella wanted so much more—a husband who loved and adored her and didn't think that her face was the whole sum of her.

As she began undressing for bed that night, Rose came into her room. "Here," she said, holding out a velvet box. "I want you to keep this."

Ella opened the box and saw the amber necklace she had worn to the ball. "Are you sure?"

"It's something of Mama's to remember her by," Rose said airily. "Besides that, the beads are too clumsy for me." She left the room looking pleased with herself.

Smiling, Ella got into bed. She'd been told she could have something too clumsy for her sister. She would take that as a compliment. Either that or begin crying again.

Cal hadn't returned.

Chapter 21

"You should see this, Ella," Vianna called from the sitting room. "The most elegant carriage I've ever seen, pulled by two beautiful grays, has stopped outside. The horses would compare well to those chestnuts you sold."

Ella, about to stroll upstairs with a book, stopped and reversed into the sitting room. Although just before midday and during the time of receiving morning calls, she knew no one who might call on her. Nevertheless, she wanted to see who might own smart carriage horses. She remembered Cal telling her he knew someone with grays.

"It looks like a king and queen arriving," Vianna continued. She sat with her nose poking into the lace covering the front windows. "A gray-haired man with a tall top hat and a woman in a green gown decorated with tiny green silk leaves on the bodice. She ought to be crowned with a tiara, but she has a hat of big silk leaves instead. And behind them is a handsome prince. Wearing princely cream trousers. By all that's wonderful. It's Cal." She shut the curtains and pushed past Ella to get to the front door.

Ella grasped her shoulder as she passed. "Leave the maid to do her job," she said in a strangled voice. "It must be the whole of the Lynton family. How embarrassing. I'll get Aunt."

While Vianna scurried back into the sitting room, Ella hastened up the passage to the tiny library at the back of the house where Aunt sat reading. "The Lyntons have arrived."

"My." Mrs. Cameron put her hands to her carefully coiffed hair. "All of them?"

"All that I know about."

Mrs. Cameron took Ella's hand and walked with her to the sitting room, where they saw a polished shoe disappearing through the doorway. "Tea, instantly," she whispered to the maid who had stopped in the hall.

"And that pink-iced cake. How delightful that you have come," she said moving like a ship in full sail into the room. "I see you've met Vianna. And here is my dear Ella."

Taking a breath, Ella offered her hand to Mrs. Irene Lynton. Cal's mother wore long pearl earrings and a lustrous three-stranded pearl necklace. Ella turned to Edward Lynton, who smiled courteously. "Miss Dorella. Do you mind if we call you Ella?"

"Please do."

"Or Cinderella? I seem to recall you telling me the night of our ball that your carriage appeared to have turned into a pumpkin."

"Had it disappeared, Ella?" Vianna asked, taken from her contemplation of Mrs. Lynton's delicate flower-painted fan.

"The clock had struck twelve. My clothes had turned into rags, and instead of being Cinderella at her first ball, I was just Dorella."

"A very charming young lady." Mr. Lynton seated Mrs. Lynton on the armless velvet chair by the window. He sat on the sofa, patting the seat and indicating Vianna should sit beside him. Mrs. Cameron took the other single chair opposite Mrs. Lynton.

"Your sister is more interesting than Cinderella," Mrs. Lynton told Vianna.

"Ella?" The child glanced at her in amazement. "She understands the paddock rotation system, if that's what you mean."

"Exactly," said Mr. Lynton. "Exactly." He smiled at Rose, who stood prettily framed in the doorway, no doubt apprised by the maid of the guests. "Miss Rose, please sit here." He stood, offering his seat to Rose, then he squashed himself between Rose and Vianna.

Ella finally glanced at Cal, who had a half-smile on his face. The only seat left was the other two-seater sofa by the fireplace. Cal gave a confident sweep of his hand, indicating that Ella should sit there. For one cowardly moment she considered leaving the room, but judging by the determination he expressed, he would have dragged her back. And so, with no choice she sat beside him.

"I caught your horse thieves," he murmured over the weather conversation that had begun between Mrs. Cameron and Mrs. Lynton. "Both are currently in custody, wanted, I believe, for other offences as well."

"I won't accept those horses back," Ella said, firming her mouth. She wondered if Cal had ever looked more handsome. His shave was close, his sideburns precise, his nails perfectly manicured, and his beautifully cut trousers hinted at the long hard muscles of his thighs. "I'll buy a riding horse of my own now that I have some money."

"No need." Cal straightened the crease in his trousers. "You can have whatever you want from our stud. My grandfather would be honored. It seems he bought your chestnuts and so you haven't lost them after all."

"What's that?" Mr. Lynton asked. "It's settled, then, is it?"

Vianna twirled a ringlet around her forefinger. "What's settled?"

"My son is to marry your sister." Mrs. Lynton resettled her skirts.

"Please." Cal rose to his feet and rested one elbow on the mantelpiece. He looked magnificent. "It's for Ella to say."

"I'm not going to marry you," Ella said, springing to her feet. "And I'm not going to accept your horses. I plan to buy a little house for myself and I've planned that all along. I will live with Vi and spend my hours embroidering cushions."

Rose laughed. "That's a plumper. You hate sewing. And what would you do with thousands of embroidered cushions? Marry Cal and you'll never have to sew again."

"That should tempt you," Cal said, his voice thick with irony.

Ella's eyes filled with unexpected tears. "You don't have to marry me because I saved your dog. I would have saved anyone's dog. I wouldn't let anything drown if I could help it."

"I'm not accusing you of lying," Cal said, turning toward her. "Unlike Rose. But you can't swim. Nor do you like swimming. I recall having to ride about five miles out of my way so that you wouldn't have to cross the river until you reached a point where your horse would do no more than wet his hooves. You saved my dog and you can't swim. You risked your life to save my dog. She is a very nice dog, but she isn't your dog and you don't like her, you told me. Therefore, you saved my dog because you like me."

Ella shrugged. "And why shouldn't I like you? You saved my family from financial ruin."

"You did. You worked and plotted and planned and you were given your just reward. I did no more than add a little backup."

"You were wonderful," Vianna said. "Ella couldn't have got our horses back by herself."

"That's exactly what she intended to do." Cal firmed his mouth and pushed his hands into his pockets. "And I don't doubt she would have managed, too. But I couldn't let her leave on her own. I didn't want my future wife put into a dangerous situation."

"Your future wife?" Ella echoed. "You had no intention of offering marriage to me and you know it."

"You had no intention of accepting me and you know it."

Ella glanced at the five pairs of interested eyes aimed at her. "And this is not a subject we should be discussing in front of others."

"I agree," said Cal, taking her arm. "Let's walk in the garden."

Ella, guided by Cal's determined hold, managed to make her way outside without stumbling or glancing back at her sisters for help. This was like the Cal she had first met, a bossy man who brooked no argument and offered no explanation, not that she needed one. "It was my idea to talk with you alone," she muttered.

"Very likely. And I read your mind. Now. Would you like to explain to me why you are refusing my constant offers of marriage? You certainly didn't refuse to make love with me and if that isn't a reason for marriage I don't know what is."

"The reason shouldn't be a reward for good service." Ella folded her arms and rested her back against a tall pink gum that shaded the side of the house.

Cal laughed. "Crudely put. I didn't know you had it in you. No, Ella, my darling Ella, my very own Cinderella. I came today to see if the shoe fits, but I already knew it did. You are the only woman for me and you didn't have to make love to me or save my dog to prove it. You proved it with your every deed, your every word, and..."

"And what?" she asked warily, her hands dropping to her sides.

"I don't know." He moved closer to her. "I can't think. There's no logic to a man loving a woman. He just does. He loves the curls that escape the knot in her hair and the lovely neck beneath." He leaned forward and placed a soft kiss on the junction between her neck and shoulder.

She took a quick breath.

"He loves this particular curve." His hand followed the line of her cheek. "He loves her hands, their capability and their softness, the contrast." He held her fingers. "He loves every part of her." His eyes met hers. "Including her obstinacy."

She moistened her suddenly dry lips. "Love," she said in a voice she didn't recognize. "You haven't mentioned love before."

"It was most remiss of me. But now reminded, how many times shall I mention it?"

"Forever." She eased into his arms. "Forever. If you love me, I'll marry you. I wouldn't marry for anything other than love."

"But," he said, smiling tenderly. "You can't marry me if you don't love me. Do you love me, Miss Dorella?"

"You told me I do. I must."

"Do you know if you do?"

"Of course I do. I could tell myself a million times that I made love with you because I wanted to, because I would never have a chance to experience anything of that nature again, because I had an urge, or because of any reason. But the reason was that I loved you. Love you. Didn't know. Oh. I'm sure I wouldn't have unless I loved you. Nor would I have saved your pesky dog." She said the last as Girl's long wet tongue licked at her hand. "Did you leave her outside?"

"I left her in the carriage. She must have jumped through the window when she heard you say you would marry me."

"She can't hear."

Cal smiled. "She's a female. She hears what she wants to hear. Now, shall we go somewhere quiet and make love? Or return to the sitting room and make our announcement?"

"The sitting room." Ella felt a blush warm her entire body. "I'm not lost to all propriety. I have no intention of shocking your relatives or mine." She moved in his embrace so that she tucked her arm under his, prepared to walk inside with him. At that moment, she noticed five interested faces at the window. "What will Vi say? She intended to have you for herself."

"I think she has come to terms with my desertion." He indicated Vianna's face as he strolled with Ella toward the front door. "She doesn't look ready to cut your heart out."

Vianna opened the front door. "Ella, Ella," she said in a breathy excited voice. "I'm going to be Cal's sister-in-law. I expect I will meet all sorts of important people now. But where will I live?"

"With us," Mr. Lynton said. "Wherever you like. Now," he said, taking Ella's hands in his and kissing her cheek. "What can you tell me about the paddock rotation system?"

"It's Cal's system," she answered. "Shouldn't he tell you?"

Mr. and Mrs. Lynton looked at each other. "She is perfect," they said together.

"Yes." Cal put his arm around Ella's waist. His eyes softened and his mouth curved. "And I never would have found her if I hadn't decided to go out on my own."

"Or if your silly dog hadn't tried to drown me."

"Or if the fence hadn't been falling down," Vianna said over her shoulder.

"Or if you hadn't wanted to mend our fortunes." Rose picked up her teacup.

Ella smiled with happiness, overwhelmed by all the good wishes. She was kissed and hugged by all and head-butted by Girl. Thoughts she'd never expressed and never hoped to dream had been realized.

Cal took her into his arms. "Or if you hadn't been my very own Cinderella."

Meet the Author

From art student to stylist, to nurse and midwife, **Virginia Taylor**'s life has been one illogical step to the next, each one leading to the final goal of being an author. When she can tear herself away from the computer and the waiting blank page, she immerses herself in arts and crafts, gardening, or, of course, cooking. You can visit her website at www.virginia-taylor. com, and tweet her @authorvtaylor.

Learn more about Virginia http://www.kensingtonbooks.com/author. aspx/31648

Be sure not to miss Virginia Taylor first book of the *South Landers* series

Starling

An aspiring dressmaker, orphaned Starling Smith is accustomed to fighting for her own survival. But when she's offered a year's wages to temporarily pose as a wealthy man's bride, she suspects ulterior motives. She can't lose the chance to open her own shop, but she won't be any man's lover, not even handsome, infuriating Alisdair Seymour's...

To prevent his visiting sister from parading potential brides in front of him, Alisdair has decided to present a fake wife. He lost his heart once, and had it broken—he doesn't intend to do it again. But stubborn, spirited Starling is more alluring than he bargained for, and Alisdair will risk everything he has to prove his love is true...

Set against the sweeping backdrop of 1866 South Australia, *Starling* is a novel of cherished dreams and powerful desires, and the young woman bold enough to claim them both...

Starling on sale now!

http://www.kensingtonbooks.com/book.aspx/31133

Chapter 1

Adelaide, South Australia, 1866

"Straighten your collar, girl," said the sharp-faced clerk guarding the office door. His olive jacket faded into the green-papered walls of the anteroom. "Mr. Seymour don't like to see his employees looking scruffy."

Starling Smith fingered the starched white cotton around her throat. She didn't look scruffy in the Seymour's Emporium uniform she had worn with pride for the past two weeks. She looked neat and anonymous in the plain gray. Any female lucky enough to be employed selling fabrics should be nothing less than tidy—and diligent, too.

Yesterday, when the owner, Mr. Alasdair Seymour, had toured the emporium he stopped to inspect the materials she had ranked using the rainbow color scale, a new idea of her own. He had taken her name from the department manager, and now he possibly meant to commend her.

His office door opened. "Miss Smith?"

Remembering her place, she leapt to her feet.

He glanced at his clerk. "I'm not to be disturbed. Come into my office, Miss Smith." Broad shouldered and tall, he looked younger than he had the day before, under thirty and handsome enough to deserve those sighs from the shopgirls.

Starling's knees wobbled as she hastened past him through the doorway.

"Take a seat," he said, taking his own. He wore his dark hair fashionably collar-length.

She perched on a carved chair upholstered in dark green brocade. The hovering red of sunset shone through the tall windows dressed with swags of yellow-striped silk. Sparkling motes floated to his desk where he sat, picked up a pen, and tapped the end on his blotter. His forehead was smooth, his nose precisely chiseled, and his jaw firm.

"Do you enjoy your job?" He looked straight at her. His eyes, an assessing luminous gray, sent a shimmer of panic through her.

She quickly lowered her gaze, trying to regain her breath. "I do." Her voice sounded embarrassingly husky. "I like working with fabrics."

"You worked in a hotel before you came here." He scrutinized a page lying on his desk. "They gave you no reference."

She had thrown away the crumpled piece of paper that described her as "a good worker," hoping she could gloss over the six weeks she had been employed at the Star Inn, mentioned in the South Australian police records as a site of gambling and prostitution. "I didn't think a temporary job would matter when I was waiting on the Seymour's list for more than a year."

He glanced up, his gaze again causing a strange jumble inside her. "You've had a small amount of education? That is, you can read and write?"

"Yes, sir. Or I wouldn't have applied here."

"Unfortunately, you've been annoying my customers." He set down his pen.

She drew a surprised breath. "I sell them what they want, sir."

"You sell them what you think they should have."

Shaking her head, she stared at her fingers knotted in her lap. "I sell them what they need. It wouldn't be right to sell fabrics not strong enough for their purpose or too heavy or the wrong color."

"And it seems you have decided on the colors they should have."

"I advise them on what might...suit."

"I don't pay you to advise my customers to buy cheaper fabrics than those they choose or less material. I pay you to make money for me."

"I do, sir." She leaned forward. "Just the other day, a young lady came back to buy more fabric. She said I'd given her just the right material for her ball gown, and she wanted me to help her again."

"Mr. Porter thinks the fabric department can cope without female staff."

"Female staff?" she queried, shaken. "But he told me I'm a quick learner."

He shrugged. "I'm sorry but I am not going to keep you at the emporium."

"You're going to get rid of me? Oh, no, you don't mean that. I get twice as many sales as Mr. Porter."

He shook his head, placing his pen in the holder. "I can, however, offer you a different position." He aligned his blotter with the edge of the desk. "In my home."

A quick shake of her head dealt with his offer of a maid's job. "I won't advise your customers about colors. I was wrong, and I'm sorry." Her voice rose with hope. "I would accept a position in any other of your departments."

"I don't have a position in any other department. I *do* have a list a mile long of women wanting to work in the emporium, as you know." He evaded her gaze.

Focusing on her weary black shoes, she exhaled her last hope. She'd loved measuring the soft fabrics, feeling the quality, and sliding the sharp scissors across the width. She'd loved working out the profits. She stood, not caring that her shoulders drooped.

He pushed out his chair and stood, facing her. "You could earn quite a bit of money if you accept my alternative. I'm much in need of a woman like you."

She straightened. *A woman like her?* "If you don't want me, I will get a job at Harris's."

"Unlikely, given that they don't employ females *with* or with*out* references. I won't beat around the bush." Pausing, he eased his black cravat with a forefinger. "You look respectable. I need a woman to pose as my wife for a couple of weeks."

Aghast, she took a step back. He didn't want a maid. He wanted to tup her. "I don't know what gave you the impression that I might do that, but—"

"Money." His lips tilted cynically. "Now, what would you say to five pounds for the two weeks?"

"No." Her jaw tense, she backed to the door. "I worked as a laundress at the inn. Not a prostitute."

He raised his eyebrows. "You only have to *pretend* to be my wife."

"I'm not good at pretending. I never have been." She opened the door and walked out.

Cheeks hot with humiliation, she strode past the clerk and down to the fabric department where, with shaking hands, she grabbed the cloth bag holding an apple, a clean pair of cuffs, a handkerchief, and a few pennies. Tying her shawl across her shoulders, she took the staff exit leading to a narrow alley off Rundle Street. She didn't have time to weep.

First, she would need to retrieve her belongings from the emporium's boardinghouse and next find accommodation for the night. The Star Inn might let her use the laundry room. If not, her friend Meg would find her a safe place.

Starling's chest hurt and her eyes prickled. As she pulled the heavy door, she noticed the purple haze hovering over the sunset. She stood staring, her dreams shattered and her life in pieces. Gathering her bag under her arm, she hurried down the cobbled alley, chased by the aroma of fresh horse manure and settling smoke. A hot wind whipped her hair across her face, forcing her to pause. Blinking hard, she tucked the strands behind her ears.

Dashing the back of her wrist over her eyes, she cornered into Rundle Street. Mr. Seymour stepped in front of her. His high-crowned hat cast a shadow across his features.

"This way." He seized her elbow.

She wrenched her arm out of his grip. "Let me be. I don't want your money or you."

"I have to have you tonight." He drew a deep breath. "I'll give you six pounds."

She backed away, disgusted. "I know at least three women who would accept your proposition. Go to the Star Inn and see which you would prefer."

He shook his head. "I wouldn't be standing here with you if I hadn't already tried that. None could pass as a lady."

"So, now you want a lady? I thought you said a wife."

"My wife would, of course, be a lady. I spent the last two weeks interviewing whores and actresses. Then I looked at my staff yesterday, and there you were with your careful speech, your background at the Star Inn, and your neat and plain appearance."

"Neat and plain." She firmed her lips.

"Good Lord, girl." His voice softened. "I'm offering you real money, far more than the fourteen shillings a week you earned here, to live a life of luxury for two weeks. You don't need to look at me as if I'm Satan. I'm giving you the greatest opportunity of your life."

"I had the greatest opportunity of my life—a job as a shopgirl." She blinked hard. "And for reasons of your own, you've taken my best chance from me."

His brow creased. "I'm offering you a better one."

"I have plans that don't include being anyone's wife, real or not."

"Two weeks, that's all I ask," he said in a long-suffering tone. With a sweep of his hand, he indicated she could move in the direction he wanted her to go.

She folded her arms.

He gave her a sideways glint. "I'll pay you *twenty* pounds."

"No." She wet her mouth.

"Perhaps you *won't* suit," he said, shrugging. "Mr. Porter said you were intelligent, but you are acting like a simpleton. I have offered you more than half a year's wages, and all you can do is persist in your belief that I want to bed you."

"Mr. Porter said I was intelligent?" Her voice rose with hope.

He raised his eyebrows.

"So, why can't you put me back in the fabric department?" She brushed down her sleeves, stalling while she thought. "I'm good at selling materials because I like selling materials."

He didn't want her as a maid, and he didn't want to tup her? She didn't understand what he wanted.

He heaved a monumental sigh. "And I'm sure you'll like pretending to be my wife because if you make a convincing job of it, I'll give you *forty pounds*."

Her mouth dried. Forty pounds! That was double twenty. For twenty pounds she could hire a little shop of her own. For forty pounds, she could not only buy stock, but also employ at least two other *Birds* from the orphanage. Robin and Nightingale would be her first choice.

Her breath fluttered. "You don't want to bed me?"

He looked her up and down. "Do you think you're my type?"

She put her hand to her hair and, blushing, quickly brought her arm down again. A gentleman who owned a number of emporiums, proving a head for business, wouldn't invest more than a few shillings in an untried, drab bed partner. He could take his pick of women.

"Well, what would the job entail *exactly*?"

"Just doing whatever wives do. Having breakfast with me in the morning, arranging flowers, eating cakes, drinking tea, sitting in the drawing room doing whatever you please until I tell you otherwise."

"What might 'otherwise' be?" She eyed him narrowly.

"Standing by my side and agreeing with every word I say while smiling pleasantly at my guests. You can smile, I suppose?"

"I'm not sure."

He gave her a suspicious glance.

"The job can't be as easy as you say." For forty pounds, there had to be a catch.

"It's as easy as you want to make it. I have a household that runs perfectly already."

"Then why do you want a wife? Other than to idle away the day."

Pushing aside his unbuttoned jacket, he slid his hands into the pockets of his biscuit-colored trousers. How he maintained a fit, broad-shouldered physique while sitting behind a desk all day was a mystery to Starling. Although she'd met no other rich men, she had assumed they were those with barrel bellies. "Last week my sister notified me she is bringing a lady with her, a lady she is sure I would like to see. She arrives from Victoria tomorrow."

"I don't understand."

"I don't like my sister's plan. She has tried this matchmaking before." His mouth tightened. "I told her I wouldn't marry any of her hopefuls."

"You don't need to marry the lady simply because your sister knows her."

"Nor do I need to have prospective brides presented to me so often that I give in out of sheer self-defense."

"Life is hard for rich men," she said sweetly.

"Exactly." He nodded for emphasis. "If I present you as a *fait accompli,* I will stop my sister in her tracks. So, are we agreed?"

She caught her bottom lip between her teeth.

"My deadline is today. I need to present a wife to my household by tonight. And, since I doubt you own suitable clothing," he said, averting his gaze, "we'll pick out a couple of gowns and, er, the trimmings before the emporium closes."

She deliberated. "I only have to smile, idle the day away, and agree with you?"

He nodded. "I want you to be as meek, quiet, and respectful as a good wife should be."

"And I will be a wife in name only?"

"That is our agreement."

Growing hope straightened her shoulders. Perhaps her dream was not lost.

He began to herd her along North Terrace. "I expect it will be worth forty pounds to prove my point," he muttered.

"That you won't ever marry? Are you a lady-man?"

His eyes widened momentarily. "A lady-man? Do you mean...? You do. Don't use gutter terms around my guests, or you'll be out of the house without a penny before you can sneeze. Of course I'm not bent. I simply want only one woman."

She could but wish. If she'd thought he only liked men, she could relax. "But isn't that a reason to marry?"

"I'm not sure intelligent and smart are the same thing. Enough. You have agreed to our bargain. The lady I want is already married, and it's time you became the sort of wife I require."

Starling nodded. He had specified a wife with a neat, plain appearance. She was neat and plain. Ordinary. Her body was slender, her skin was sallow, and she had brown hair and eyes. No male had ever glanced at her twice. At the inn, her plainness had been her best protection. Meg had told her she could be pretty if she tried, but she had no need to be pretty. She didn't want or need a man. In fact, her plan depended on her remaining single. No husband would let her follow through with her business idea. Married, she would blight more lives than her own.

She had nothing to lose by doing as he asked and had gained instead an opportunity to earn a great deal of money. She would obey Mr. Seymour's every edict. Opportunity had knocked, and Starling Smith only had to widen the door to reach her goal.

Half a pace behind Mr. Seymour, she passed the lawyer's offices, the pastry shop, the tailor, and a saddlery. The main commercial thoroughfare of Adelaide was familiar to her: the old wooden sheds, the new Georgian buildings, the constant grind of carriage wheels, the thump-thump of hooves, the bustle of people, and the push of their presence. Not only had she worked in the city, she'd lived nearby her whole nineteen years, watching the adornment of the newest constructions with ornate pillars and pretty plastered curlicues. She couldn't imagine living elsewhere.

Mr. Seymour pushed open the front door of his emporium. Dimly lit, the shop was preparing to close. He led the way to the ready-mades area upstairs and stood waiting for attention. The floor manager bowed from the waist.

"Miss Smith needs assistance," Mr. Seymour said.

The manager clicked his fingers for a shopgirl, who hastened forward. Starling knew Jinny, the red-haired assistant, from the boardinghouse.

"Three new gowns. Nothing gaudy. Help Miss Smith choose. I'll be back in half an hour." With that, Mr. Seymour strode away.

Jinny widened her eyes at Starling, who smiled and shrugged. Jinny moistened her lips and bustled about finding ready-made gowns while Starling stood by her left shoulder, pointing out those she wanted. Brown, being the cheapest dye, had been the color for the foundlings. She had worn brown her whole life until two weeks ago, when she'd exchanged that color for the gray of the Seymour uniform. Knowing neither flattered her, she decided that because this handsome man had chosen a plain woman for his bride, she should not try to change her appearance.

She kept on the last gown she tried. Patterned in a jaundiced green and brown, the high-buttoned fit was as unflattering as the other two she'd chosen. Continuing her disapproving silence, Jinny parceled them and Starling's uniform. When Mr. Seymour returned, he took the purchases, cramming them with a few other parcels into a new holdall. Next, he let Starling choose a plain brown hat. She wore that, too, certain she looked even more thin faced wearing a flat-brimmed poke with a long ribbon tie.

Finally, he took her to the jeweler's shop and bought her a plain gold ring. Keeping her face expressionless, she slid on the circlet. How she would pass as the wife of a gentleman, she didn't know. Nor did she know why he thought she might. She could only hope that the colors she had chosen to wear would merge her into the background, as she didn't plan to lose the forty pounds before she'd seen a single penny.

When he marched her outside the shop again, she totaled his purchases: one pound for the ring and more good money for a hat and gowns. He had shelled out a tidy sum to deceive a sister who merely wanted to see him happily married. Starling hoped she could play her unworthy role.

She kept pace with him, her bonnet ribbons fluttering as she moved closer to her goal. Eagles might soar. Starlings took chances when they saw them.

www.ingramcontent.com/pod-product-compliance
Lightning Source LLC
Chambersburg PA
CBHW031406250626
47155CB00004B/1431